METANOIA

MICHAEL HARBRON

WARNING

This novel includes depictions of abuse and violence.

Contents

THE OTHER MAN

A dull red bludgeon in the darkness followed by the acrid breaking of pain all over his body. *Stop, please. M—*

That had been how Damien had woken up on Monday. It was Friday now, and every time he woke up, vestigial pain haunted him behind his closed eyes.

Until, that is, he opened them and bore witness to the dread of the world.

———

"Lucy! Lucy! Wake up," Damien whimpered, tugging at his elder sister's sleeve. He knew better than to touch her face to wake her up. That would earn him a prompt swat on his hand, and pain was an old friend, one that Damien avoided, even if it was just a harmless swat from his sister.

"Whatchuwant—" Lucy groaned, blonde hair all over her face, and what wasn't covered by hair was covered by the comforter. Truly lost in the continent of slumber, the ten-year-old with her heavy snores and her eyes squeezed shut.

Between trying to wake Lucy up and the creeping reality of his waking nightmare, Damien shot a glance at the bedroom window, not liking the way the moonlight made mist tendrils look like the tentacles of some night-demon who had enveloped all of Pinebrook. These snakelike wisps wove around the dimmed streetlamps, coiled around parked cars, and suffused through the street, the lawns, the porches.

Damien knew it was his own fault for peeking through the window at four in the morning. His own fault for seeing him standing there, dressed like a deranged nomad, holding some kind of cane with a lamp hanging from it.

And was that a skull of some kind on top of his head, like a helmet?

This wasn't the first time he'd seen the Other Man, though this was the first time the Other Man had stepped in front of their home, standing right there on the street, a lone spectacle in a world of gray and darkness.

"He's here again," Damien said, standing close to her, the faculties of reason hijacked by fear and terror, making it seem that this second-floor bedroom had no walls at all. That they were exposed to the mist and to the menacing gaze of the Other Man.

Lucy shifted, uncovering her face, then sat up in bed, stretching her arms, her face puffy and sulking. The purple streak running across her right cheek was neither the sign of deep sleep nor the cold intruding upon her pallor. It hurt when she touched her face. If she pressed hard, it felt like the cheekbone shifted in a way it shouldn't. It hurt to speak. It hurt to laugh. But the pain had subsided since a few days ago.

She kicked the comforter off. It was a soft, plush thing with the density of a thick cloud and the comfort of all the hugs in the world. She hadn't wanted to leave it. Tomorrow being Saturday, she had intended to sleep till late. She ran her hand across the coarse cotton sheets that, if they were any coarser, would have felt like sandpaper.

Lucy liked her bedsheets rough enough that they'd give her traction in bed. The white silk ones her mother had gotten her were the worst. They felt like a layer of slick oil was smeared across them. No matter how she tried to lie still, they'd slip and threaten to throw her off the bed. After one night, Lucy demanded her mother take them away.

"These cost a fortune, Lucy. In the old days, queens used to sleep in sheets like this," her mother had said as she'd pulled the sheet off the bed.

"Let the queens have their silk. I'm a warrior," Lucy had said, grinning, quite proud of her for upturning her mother's decision. "A warrior needs the comfort of cotton."

"Suit yourself," her mother had said. She had a hand in raising that warrior, and fighting her on this front would be futile, especially since there were so many fronts to fight her on.

Lucy brushed away the thoughts of her mother—

who had been absent for five days now—and brought the room into focus. Damien stood in front of her, a cowering little boy, terrified of being alone in the house, his skin pale gray, deep circles around his eyes.

"Where is he?" she asked, reaching out and holding Damien's hand. That first touch made Damien break into silent ears, his eyes spilling each fat drop individually on his cheeks. He shook his head and just pointed at the window.

She tried to peer, as if her head was a periscope, but from this side of the room, the world that lay beyond the window was hidden. She rolled up the sleeves of her pajamas, implying she meant serious business now that she was awake. A distracted glance at the unicorn, rainbow, and dessert sprinkle pattern on her pajamas made her realize that no amount of sleeve-pulling would take away from the childishness of her clothes, which brought another thought to the forefront of her mind.

I am a child. How is this fair?

She walked on her tiptoes—a habit from sensory issues she'd developed in her childhood—and went to the window, the bitter stings of cold making her aware that the room, and by extension the house, was too cold. What had happened to the thermostat?

There was no one standing on the street, but that wasn't saying much given that the street was obscured by the fog. She squinted and focused her eyes to make out an outline, any outline, to confirm her brother's sighting.

But there was no one.

"He's not here," she said tiredly, but that did nothing to sway her brother's terror.

She went over to him, tugged his arm, and brought him to the window, opening it. Cold wind and a bitter smell greeted their faces, but this had to be done. She had him look around the street.

"He was here before," Damien whispered, eyes on the street, but the color now returning to his face.

"He's not here anymore. The Other Man has better things to do, I think," Lucy said, shutting the window. It was a terrible trade-off. Bear punishing cold or bear the stuffiness of the house. The house had been stuffy for several days now.

Ever since Lucy and Damien woke up with no parents and no people on the street.

It was the fifth day, which had confirmed Lucy's suspicion that something was dreadfully wrong with Pinebrook, the small town that was home to their second abode when their father was not entertaining contracts and big-time clients in Chicago at his law firm.

"Sun's gonna come out in a few," Lucy said, feeling resigned in a way every elder sibling does when the brunt of parenthood falls upon their shoulders. "How about I make you some breakfast? PB&J, a bowl of Frosted Flakes. You'd like that, wouldn't you?"

A grumble emanated from Damien's face. He wiped his tears and managed to give his sister a weak smile, then a nod.

"Come on then," Lucy said, closing the curtains to the bedroom they were both sharing for the past five days after Damien had started to panic from *the event*. At least that's what Lucy called it.

Because what else could you call it when you woke up to dense fog as Pinebrook had never seen before, the people of the street mysteriously disappeared, and no sign of her parents?

It was *the event*, and the real harrowing thing about it was that neither Lucy nor Damien remembered anything of the events that led up to it.

And then, suddenly, before they'd even made sense of what misery they were thrown into, the Other Man showed up. At first Lucy hadn't believed Damien when he'd described the skeleton-adorned walking nomad-man with the lantern-stick.

And then she'd seen him.

———

The house had been in disarray from the first day. The stench coming from the kitchen, Lucy had surmised, was coming from the plastic trash can. It had a black garbage bag in it overflowing with empty cans, rotting vegetables, and a pool of black liquid at the bottom. There were other things in there too. Slices of meat with flies clinging to them. Expired sauce bottles.

The trash can had been heavy. She'd called for Damien, but Damien had been in another room, rummaging around things now that he could rummage around without getting a firm slap on the back from their dad.

She'd checked on him, making a tower from DVD cases in their father's study. She'd winced at the thought that if their father were to walk in the house just now and see what had become of his DVDs, the hell he'd put Damien through.

But it had been the second day since *the event*, and her parents hadn't appeared in a full forty-eight hours, and the house smelled horrible.

She pulled the trash can and yanked it out of the kitchen door, bringing it out the back. It leaked black goo from the bottom where it was cracked. The goo squirmed on the floor, reminding Lucy of the fungus videos their science teacher had shown them.

What was it Mr. Haytham had said? Humans and fungi shared 50% of their DNA. Lucy had been too afraid to lift her hand and inquire about this mysterious thing called DNA. I wasn't Mr. Haytham she was worried about. He was a safe person, she had assessed, his voice never above a normal decibel, and his tone always friendly, taking the time to explain the hardest of concepts to every child, no matter how hard they struggled.

It was Sady Perkins and Rhea Thomas that she was afraid of. They'd sat behind her in the class. And while they were not full-blown bullies, they were terrible enough to make Lucy regret coming to school. They'd snicker behind her back, and laugh every time she'd open her mouth.

Better to be ignored by these two than draw their attention. She decided that if her mother's laptop was lying around unattended, she'd google *DNA* herself later on.

But the rest of the class had been fun. Mr. Haytham had shown them so many types of fungi, like rhizomes, sporangia, mushrooms, yeasts, mildews, and molds, telling them that we didn't have to fear aliens and monsters and viruses as much as we should be wary of fungi and what they could do to us if we rubbed them the wrong way long enough.

Lucy had wondered what that was all about, but later that day she'd watched half an episode of *The Last of Us* behind her mother, and that had been enough. Her entire week had been filled with mushroom-festered corpses walking around eating people.

Lucy had finally brought the trash can to the front of the house and was considering leaving it there for the garbage truck. In fact, that was exactly what she was going to do. But the problem with this was, every house around her had overflowing garbage cans, mounds of trash leaking out of them, and it looked like the garbage truck hadn't come in some days.

Still. Better that this filth was outside the house than inside.

She'd only turned to leave when a hand draped in some kind of bone-glove had fallen upon her shoulder and pulled at her.

She had screamed, her shrill sound carrying through the heavy fog, and the only thing she'd seen before her fight or flight instincts kicked in was the nomad-man with the moldy bedroll on his shoulder, a dirty cloak that looked like he'd ripped the forest floor and put it on, and the bone-helmet.

He'd reached out, meaning to say something, but she had screamed harder, and kicked off in the opposite direction. The man had stood there by her upturned trash can, cane in hand, the unforgiving yellow light from his lamp tearing a line of sight in the otherwise impenetrable fog.

Lucy had shut the kitchen door, then proceeded to bolt every window and door.

And that's how every door and window had been since then.

No one knocked or rang the bell, and since there was food in the kitchen and the adjacent pantry, there was no reason to go out. There was power in the house. Some warmth in here despite the stuffiness.

And, of course, her brother.

She could not just leave her brother.

———

They'd tried everything. They called their parents from the landline, from the family iPhone, but their numbers hadn't responded. Lucy had even tried calling her aunt, but no response. When they'd spent another day without any human contact, the two of them had plastered their faces to the living room window so that they could catch sight of someone, anyone, walking through their street.

No one did. Not even a lonesome car came driving through the fog.

"What if we're alone?" Damien had asked, tugging at her sleeve.

"Don't be stupid," Lucy had said. "No one ever leaves children alone."

"But what if the whole town decided to play a prank on us and leave us alone? What if this is like one of those Mr. Beast videos where we're gonna get a reward for the prank?" Damien had asked, his eyes growing wide.

The YouTube Industrial Complex that comprised Mr. Beast, Logan Paul, Minecraft videos, and those brain-rot compilations had truly gotten to her younger brother. At any given moment when he was free and unsupervised, he could be found with his face buried in his tablet, watching twenty-minute-long thinly veiled commercials for whatever new product some YouTuber was peddling through their challenge videos.

"Do you see cameras anywhere, dum-dum?" Lucy had asked, giggling.

That conversation had been three days ago, and now, looking at the fridge, Lucy could see that this was the last bit of milk and bread. Somehow, they'd have to do the unthinkable—go out into town and get groceries.

But that would come later. With what she had in the kitchen, she made Damien and herself some PB&J sandwiches, a bowl of Frosted Flakes, and a cup each of orange juice.

In the dim lamplight that looked more like an interrogation chamber fixture than something that should hang over a dining table, the two ate breakfast half-heartedly. All the curtains were drawn, giving no view of the world outside. The TV was on mute, PBS playing an old episode of *Mr. Rogers* for whoever the hell was awake and watching PBS at four-thirty in the morning.

She finally said the thing that she was afraid to say.

"We have to go out today."

Damien put down his spoon in the bowl in a way that made him look much older than he was. He gulped and then wiped his face clean of the chocolate milk on his chin. "Why?"

"Because we're all out of supplies, dumbo," Lucy said, pointing to the kitchen. "I can open cans, I can make cereal, toast, and I can pour juice into glasses. That's it. We're all out of that. I can't cook meat, and besides, it's in the fridge at the top. I can't reach it."

"But we don't have any money," Damien said.

Lucy was hoping he'd say that. Her eyes lit up and a smile scythed across her face. "We do. We have a lot of it."

Ten minutes later, the breakfast done, they were standing in their father's study beside the computer table. Here, right at eye-level, there was a painting of a woman in red standing at the edge of a cliff, looking at the torrential sea. Underneath the painting, it said, *Tempest.*

"He was drunk when he was opening it one night. He didn't even see me," Lucy said, pulling the painting off the wall, revealing a wall-safe. "Do you remember that jingle Dad keeps singing?"

"The one for Jerry McGrath, Tax Attorney?" Damien laughed, looking intently at the safe. The only reason he knew the name and the occupation of this

Jerry McGrath guy was because he'd gone viral across social media for the jingle, *"Two-One-One-Two-Nine, Jerry on the line's gonna save you money and time."* The commercial itself was hilarious, featuring a plus-sized man in a very loose suit cooking books on a barbeque grill while cop cars blared behind him on a suburban street. It was a strange commercial for a Pinebrook tax lawyer, but it was what remained on the tips of every-one's tongues for the duration the ad lasted on TV, on the internet, and on the bus-benches in town.

A year ago, the ad campaign stopped when Jerry McGrath was found beaten to near-death in his home. He'd been in a coma, from what the news had said, but Damien didn't know what a coma was, and why someone would beat Jerry McGrath, beloved meme icon of this small Midwestern town.

"Yep, that's the one," Lucy said, punching in 2-1-1-2-9. The safe beeped once, its LED light turning green. She pried the door open, revealing stacks of bills. Damien gasped.

"We're rich," Damien whispered.

"Until our parents come back, yes," Lucy said, taking a stack out and pulling two hundred-dollar bills from it, then promptly placing the rest back. She closed the safe, put the painting back on top of it, and then walked out of the room with her brother close behind. The long tower of DVDs he'd made was still standing in one corner of the room, resembling a Christmas tree.

Lucy dressed herself up in warm clothes, and then did the same for Damien. There was a spare set of keys hanging by the door. She jumped up and reached for it, yanking it off the wall.

They stood behind the door, all lights of the house closed, holding each other's hand.

"I'm scared, Luce," Damien said, his gloved hand shivering. "We don't know the way."

"We can find the way. Just like we're going to find our parents and everyone who's gone missing," Lucy said with shaky resolve in her voice, and then pulled the door open, stepping into the thick mist.

PINEBROOK

Two silhouettes shifted in the ephemeral street. Around them, all was still. The mist was a thick, constrictive blanket. In it, they could see no lights in the windows of all the houses they had crossed. Ahead there was a crossing. Four roads going off in their own direction, never to interest again.

The road had crisscross paint on it at the center. Four signals hung opposite each other, all their lights fixed at red. The signs of each street were barely visible against the darkness and the fog.

Lucy checked her phone. It was seven a.m. If they made it downtown in another fifteen minutes, then the shop would be open. She knew it because on the few occasions when their mother had driven them to Pinebrook Elementary instead of the bus, they'd stop at the store, and it would be open at seven in the morning with its many aisles and its vegetable and fruits section.

Zyn's Grocers. A strange name for a strange store

with a parking lot as big as the store itself. Pinebrook, Lucy's mother had said, was not short on space. It was short on just about everything else. Her mother wouldn't be exactly sober on those few and far between drives, and would ramble without being concerned if she was saying something explicit or if her children could understand.

A haggard, blonde-haired woman with a sunken face bearing acne marks and deep aging lines that shouldn't be on the face of someone in their late thirties, Valerie Bessemer looked the part of the strict innkeeper who foretold evil at the start of an indie horror movie. She had all her teeth, but they were yellowed, a symptom of her ill-kept oral hygiene. Her mouth smelled, when not of liquor then of other, ranker things. In her words, she was a part-time parent. The rest of the time, it was God, the government, and whatever good shit was playing on TV or YouTube.

Amongst such banal inanities, once she'd said that Pinebrook was where dreams came to die because the real estate was cheap and misery loved nothing more than company and low prices.

"Why'd you go quiet?" Damien asked as the two of them stood at the crossing. Lucy had also let go of her brother's hand. "What are you thinking? Where's the sun?"

"Would you zip it?" Lucy scoffed, then realized quickly that she had no business being curt to her younger brother. "Sorry. I'm just...I'm just trying to think. Is It Elburg Ave or Jonathon?"

"Are we going to Zyn's? It's on neither. It's straight ahead, on Durham."

She turned to look at him, frowning. "Now how would you know that?"

"I once looked at a map of the town online," Damien said nonchalantly. "I kind of memorized the entire thing."

"Bull."

"Nu-unh. Not bull. Ask me a question," Damien said, grinning at her. She wanted to throw water on his face, but resisted the urge.

"How far is Zyn's from here?"

"Uh..."

"Go ahead."

"I..."

"That's what I thought," Lucy said, rolling her eyes. It might have been a clever lie, but it gave her an idea. She pulled the phone out, hoping there was cellular signal on it. She opened the maps app.

The app was frozen. She waited till it unfroze, then zoomed in on their location.

On the map, they were standing in the middle of nowhere. There were no roads, no buildings, no markers of any kind. She zoomed in. There was nothing on the map.

"Darn thing don't work," Lucy said.

"I'm not lying, you know," Damien said. "Mr. Haytham said it's eye-eye-eide—it's something!"

"Eidetic memory?" Lucy said, still fidgeting with the phone.

"Yeah, that's the one."

"Funny, because if you had eidetic memory, you'd remember how it was pronounced."

Damien stared at her blankly, then blinked. Finally, he said, "You're being mean."

"That's because I'm scared, dumbass," Lucy said, shooting a 360-degree glance around her. She'd just now felt something moving. She stowed the phone in her pocket. The mist all around was illuminated by a sun that they couldn't see, its wisps now thickening into one impenetrable cloud. "And I don't think we're alone."

That shut Damien up for good. He huddled close and clutched his sister. "I saw it too."

"Come on," Lucy said, crossing over to Durham, holding Damien's hand.

When the dark figure shifted behind him, the two didn't see. When it started pursuing them from behind cover, they didn't hear. The sound of their feet on asphalt was loud and echoey enough that it masked the sound of the lurker.

———

It turned out that Zyn's was indeed on Durham, right next to a little strip mall with a massage parlor, a manicurist, a drug store, and a tattoo shop. The parking lot of Zyn's was empty except for one car and a few stray shopping carts just standing there.

The two could see the wide window panel of the shopfront lit by fluorescents across the parking lot. It wasn't that far. They'd walked for a total of fifteen minutes, and as the time had passed, the fog had turned lighter, though never disappearing.

"Maybe it's like that virus. When everyone was indoors," Lucy said.

"What are you talking about?"

"You were two years old, you wouldn't remember, despite all your claims of eidetic memory."

"There was a virus? Did the world end?"

"It sure seemed like that. I don't remember a lot. I was just five. Everyone was avoiding everyone. It was some kind of flu. We'd see people coughing in the streets. Once, I saw a man throw up blood on the sidewalk. I remember *that*."

"Shut up. You're pulling my leg," Damien said as the two crossed the parking lot.

Lucy grinned, brushing aside her blonde hair, tucking it under her hoodie. "Gotcha!"

"That's not funny!" Damien squealed.

She didn't press him further. They pushed the door open and stepped inside the warm store. Mr. Vikram Singh, the turban-wearing, long-bearded shopkeeper, wasn't sitting behind the counter. In his place, a young, scrawny man barely in his twenties sat and read a paperback.

"Mr...Vikram?" Lucy called out.

"Oy, Mr. Vikram's not here," the man said in a strange accent, not looking up from his paperback. "I'm Nigel."

It was such a relief to see another living, breathing

human being, one not wearing bones and cloaks, that Lucy wanted to cry. The man had dirty brown hair falling on his forehead, and a pimple-infested face. He looked at her as she walked up to the counter and gave her a brief smile.

"Not lost are you, little lady? Is that your brother with you?"

"Where's Mr. Vikram?" Lucy asked as Damien busied himself with filling contents from the aisles in his little basket. "He's always here." Mr. Vikram Singh was an old man with a small portable radio always playing Indian songs on a low volume. He'd always greet Lucy with a warm grin and ask her how school was going. The fact that he wasn't here rubbed her wrong.

"Oh, don't you worry about him. He's visiting his homeland, from what I heard, and how about that? Strange innit? Almost in a providential way. Here I was, Nigel Clive, fresh off the ferry from across the pond. Took a truck to this town in the middle of nowhere. Though, if I'd known, quite frankly, that this'd be the weather round here, I'd have stayed at Redbrook. Ha!" He laughed, clapping his hand on the countertop. "You know, it's the funniest thing, innit? Redbrook? Pine-brook? I bet that's why my mind made me come here. Though, I'll be honest, I don't really remember when I came here."

"We're just here to get some stuff for the house."

"Alone, are you?" Nigel said, leaning over and inspecting Lucy with a little concern in his eyes. "Where's your parents?"

She wanted to cry. But she held herself together and simply said, "I don't know."

"That's proper dangerous. Kids out in the fog without their parents. Do they do this often?" Nigel asked, putting down his paperback.

Lucy shook her head, a single tear leaking down her cheek.

"Oh, no, sweetheart. Don't you cry. Tell me what you need and Uncle Nigel's going to help ya. I'd call the police and tell 'em that you're lost, but the phones aren't working. Something about the cell towers down."

"That's okay," Lucy said, wiping her tear and standing tall. "I can find my way home. We just need some things. We'll be on our way."

Lucy did as she'd said. She took a cart and filled it with necessary things—cereal boxes, canned food, bread, peanut butter, jams of different kind besides just the grape one, different fruits, drinks and juices from the fridges, some cookies, a couple bags of chips, some jellies, rolls of toilet paper—and when she was done, and Damien had finished filling up his little basket, the two went to the counter and stood patiently as kindly Mr. Nigel bagged up their things and presented them with a bill.

"That'd be eighty dollars, forty cents," he said, placing the paper bags back in the cart.

Lucy paid him, took the change, and then stood there a little confused.

"Tell you what, you sweet kid. You don't have a car. If your house's not that far, you can take the cart and return it next time you're here. And if you're ever in trouble, you can come to Uncle Nige, okay?"

Lucy nodded, not looking at the man's face.

But Damien was. He couldn't help himself as he said, "What's that on your head?"

Nigel traced his finger to where Damien was pointing. It was on top of his forehead, above his temple, hidden by his dirty hair. He pressed in the hole, blood and pus oozing out and dripping down his face.

"Oh, dear me. Oh, that's not good," Nigel said, studying the blood on his finger. He rubbed the hole on his head some more, more ichor and sickly goo coming out. "Ow... I...I seem to have hit my head something terrible."

Damien dug his fingers in Lucy's arm. The pain unfroze her. She pulled the cart back and directed it toward the door.

Nigel was still touching his forehead, a little dazed. He saw the two making for the door.

"Oh, don't go off and run like that now! It's nothing! I just banged my head or summat. I'll get it looked at."

They didn't hear what else he said. By then, the two, panting at the top of their lungs, were already out of the store.

"Come back anytime!" Nigel called out. This much they heard.

They didn't talk to each other until they had cleared the parking lot and were back on the sidewalk.

Before they had a chance to catch their breath, a big

black bird swooped low toward them, cawing, its eyes red, its beak open. It was not alone.

Lucy pulled Damien and ducked behind the cart. The flock streaked through the mist, weaving it away with their wings, and then broke the dive. They rose and went back into the sky.

The mist grew just a little thin, and now Lucy could see leafless skeletons of trees with their branches hanging against the fog's dense backdrop, twigs snarling like fingers, dark figures moving behind the trees.

A pair of yellow eyes boring upon them from behind the bare poplar, the hunched weeping willows, the dead oaks.

"Run!" Lucy yelled as the birds broke into a dive again.

Damien was already ahead of her, unburdened by the weight of the cart.

She pushed and ran until she'd gone and lost herself in the thicker part of the fog. She didn't know where she was going. She just knew that the dark things were pursuing her. She could hear their snarls as they closed in on her.

"Damien!" she cried out, wondering what kind of help her little brother would be. He'd disappeared in the blindness ahead.

A lone figure stood ahead, right in the middle of the street, the lantern on his stick glowing an unsettling shade of yellow.

Terror thrusting itself up her esophagus, her heart a malfunctioning machine that pained as she rain, squelched with each laborious beat, she didn't care what happened to her anymore. She ran straight ahead, because even if she were to try to stop herself, the inertia of the cart wouldn't let her.

The Other Man took a step to the side, allowing her to run past him. She shot a look back, watching him stand there, faceless, bone-covered, his mossy cloak dragging on the road, the light from his lamp keeping the demons at bay.

Her house popped out of nowhere on the right. She dug her heels in the asphalt and braked the cart. She turned around again. The dreadful Other Man who had seemingly saved her life wasn't standing there any longer; or he could be, but there was no way of telling because of the gray.

"Damien!" she cried.

Behind her, in the distance, long, black shapes tore through the sky, flying in the opposite direction, and then disappearing from sight.

"Damien! Where are you?!"

Despite how much she'd ran, and the many clothes she'd layered upon herself, the cold that seeped through her skin was bitter and sharp like a thousand knives.

And the Other Man stepped in through the mist, this time his lantern's glow focused on Lucy. It wasn't warm light. It felt like the strange chemicals she'd seen in the school's lab, chemicals she knew would burn her skin if she'd touch them. And now her skin, besides being cold, was also burning.

She left the cart right there on the road, dismissing it

as lost cause, and ran toward the house, fishing for the spare keys in her pocket. She was sure she'd put them in there.

"Damien!"

Now why did he have to run off like that—

He lay there on the sidewalk beside the plastic trash can. He was lying on his stomach, blood dripping out of his head. Lucy screamed. The slick liquid that had leaked out of the trash can had pooled there on the sidewalk, and now her brother had slipped on it.

She turned him over. His closed eyes shifted. There was a gash on his forehead. She squirmed looking at it, but she kept looking at it. It was shallow. She could do something. She felt his heartbeat. It was elevated, but thank God he was alive.

She pulled him up and ran for the door as fast as she could while bearing the weight of another human.

She yanked out her keys and touched the doorknob.

For that brief second, everything came back, lifting the fog in her mind, making her remember what she had done.

And then she pushed the door open and brought her unconscious brother to the living room sofa, and fell next to him, her head spinning, her vision vignetting into black.

I have to close the door, she thought as she looked at the ajar door and the tentacles of mist pouring into the house.

The Other Man stood in the doorway.

Whether it was because of sheer fright or sheer

exhaustion, it did not matter—but Lucy passed out, unable to do a damned thing about her predicament.

And remembered the red bludgeons of pain, the fireworks of agony cracking in her mind like bones fracturing, the screams of a man, the yells of a man, and a final, big bang that was *the event.*

When she woke up, trying hard to remember it all, her mind reflected the town, drowned in thick murk.

The door to the house was shut.

The shopping cart was inside the house, all its contents there. When Lucy, unable to believe what had happened, unable to understand why she'd been spared, got up, she saw that Damien's forehead wasn't bleeding. The gash was there, and it would need cleaning, and this wasn't the first time she had cleaned a wound, but thankfully it was not bleeding anymore. Blood had crusted atop the wound, and dried, preventing more spillage.

She went to the door to lock it from the inside.

It boggled her as to how it was possible that the door was already locked from the inside. Was someone else in the house with them?

Before she could think more on that, her eyes fell upon the lamp by the door. It was there, on the ground, with a note underneath it.

She plucked the note out from under the lamp.

Use this the next time you go out. And whatever you do, don't ever lose it.

LAMPLIGHT

When Damien woke up, it was to the sensation of pain, but it was different pain than the one that haunted him in his waking moments. This pain was real and localized to just his forehead. He touched there, but it was covered with a bandage.

He opened his eyes. All the lights of the house were lit. A delicious aroma was wafting from the kitchen. He wondered what that meant. Was Mom back? Is that why the house was looking so tidy?

He heaved himself off the sofa, this action requiring deliberate effort and much strength, strength that he wasn't sure he had in him. But oh, that smell. What was it? Spaghetti and meatballs?

No way Lucy knew how to make that. Mom was back.

This made him afraid. What did it mean that Mom was finally back? Was Dad here too?

Oh shit. Damien felt his insides constricting. Had he already gone in his study? Had he seen the DVD tower? *Shit.* That meant that Damien was due a beating of a lifetime.

"Damien, you awake?" a voice called from the kitchen. It was not his mother. Damien breathed easier and walked into the kitchen to a strange sight.

His sister was standing there over the stove with a ladle in her hand, her sleeves pulled back, her hair all over the place, intense concentration on her face, her tongue out.

"What are you doing?"

"What does it look like I'm doing? I'm making spaghetti and meatballs."

"How?"

"What do you mean how? I looked up the recipe. The easiest one on YouTube."

"Does that mean the internet is back?"

"Yeah. It seems to be working fine."

Damien reached for the phone on the shelf. Lucy swatted his hand, giving him a frown. "*Occupado.* I gotta finish the recipe."

"You're *really* making spaghetti and meatballs?"

"That's pre-cooked canned meatballs and easy-to-make spaghetti to you, mister. Mom would throw a fit if I tried to do something in the kitchen," Lucy said, turning her attention to the stove. "Mom's not here, is she?"

"How...did we get inside? Why does my head hurt?"

"Over dinner. Go make the table. Those are the plates. Those are the glasses."

Confused, Damien went over to where the utensils were and took them out, placing them on the dining table.

He helped himself to a glass of water, driving away the dryness and pain in his throat. He waited in the living room, turning the TV on, finding Cartoon Network, and leaving it on. Damien went to the bathroom and cleaned his face, his hands, and the layer of grime he'd accumulated on his neck from the walk outside today.

When he came out, there was a steaming pot waiting for him on the dining table.

"Come on!" Lucy said, her face bright and covered in sweat. She smiled from ear to ear as she poured spaghetti, spaghetti sauce, and meatballs in a deep plate for Damien. Then she helped herself to it. There was a can of grape soda for each of them on the table.

Damien took a bite out of what his sister had made, afraid that—

Holy moly! he thought, his face stretching into astonishment, as delicious, hot food found its way into his mouth. He could cry.

"This is so good!" he squealed in a high pitch.

"You can eat as much as you want to. I've made loads," Lucy said proudly, digging her fork into a big meatball.

"How did you make it? I didn't even know you could," Damien said, opening his soda and drinking a deep gulp from it, chasing away the spice of the sauce down his throat.

"I didn't either. But then you were asleep for such a long time, and I couldn't really go out, could I? So I fixed up your forehead, yeah-unh, that was me, and then cleaned the house a bit. I still had time to kill. So I put all the stuff we'd bought into shelves, cabinets, all that boring grownup shit."

"You just said shit," Damien giggled, even though he'd thought the word a few minutes ago.

Lucy blushed, then looked around. She turned to Damien, saying, "I guess I did. Shit. Here I go, saying it again."

"Can I say it?"

She frowned at him, then her face eased into a small smile. "Just once."

"*SHIIIT!*"

Lucy laughed, closing her eyes. It felt good to laugh. She imagined if their parents were here and Damien had said shit like that, her father would have snapped a wrist or broken her brother's clavicle.

There was that one time when the neighbor called CPS. Lucy could remember that clearly. Her mother was asleep upstairs, dosed on Ambien. Her father was drunk. Damien had fallen off the sofa and had broken a glass. He was five years old. Five-year-olds were prone to doing that kind of thing.

But their forty-five-year-old father had let loose on him without mercy, twisting his arm, slapping him across the face, punching his ribs. Lucy had tried to stop him, but she'd gotten a fast backhand slap on her face that had thrown her off.

Damien had been yelling and screaming and crying so loud. Lucy remembered someone peeking in through the window.

Five minutes later, the cops had shown up with CPS, and their father was at the door trying to tell them that he was sober, that Damien had fallen off the sofa and that's why he was crying, and that all was good. The CPS officer had barged inside the house and asked Damien and Lucy if their father had beaten them.

They'd both shaken their heads.

She wondered what would have happened if they'd told the truth that day.

Would they still be here?

"I love you," Damien said, bringing her to the present, his eyes welled up. "You...you made me my favorite thing."

"Hey, cut it out," she said, giving his head a good old ruffle. "Stop being cringe."

"Sowwy," Damien said, digging into his spaghetti.

They talked as they ate, helping themselves to second and third servings. They talked about the horrors they had endured in town. The yellow-eyed monster lurking behind the trees. The red-eyed crow-things. The—

"I thought I saw dogs. A whole pack of them. Were there really dogs chasing us?" Damien said, his voice going low.

"I didn't look back all that many times. I was just... trying to get home alive. I was worried for you. Now why'd you have to run off like that in the fog all by your-self, you idiot?"

"I was scared!" Damien said defensively.

"Did you see the Other Man standing there on the street?" Lucy asked.

"No. Did you?"

"He lit his lamp and that somehow made the monsters keep away," Lucy said, nodding at something by the door. The same lamp that she was talking about was there, on the floor. She hadn't touched it.

"I don't think he wants to kill us, Damien," Lucy said. "When I brought you inside, I passed out. The door was open. He was standing there. I think he brought the cart inside. I think he closed the door. Somehow he also locked the door. He left a note telling us that we should use the lamp when we go outside of the house."

"He's not a bad guy?" Damien asked, his plate empty a third time. The pot was also empty now. They'd finished all the spaghetti and meatballs that Lucy had made. "He looks like one."

"Looks can be deceiving. Like Mr. Nigel in the store today. What the heck was coming out of his forehead?"

"Beats me. I'm not leaving the house again," Damien said, drinking the last of his grape soda. "I'll just watch TV and play videogames and wait for Mom and Dad to come back."

"What if they don't come back?" Lucy asked in a low voice. "It's been five days."

"So? What are you trying to say?"

"I'm just saying that this place is not...normal. Where

are all the people? And the people that we've seen, the Other Man and Nigel, they were so freaking weird. Have you ever seen creepy stuff like that in our town before?"

"Shadow curse," Damien said, his eyes narrowing, focusing on the lamp.

"What?"

"Shadow curse. You know, like in the videogames. There's this shadow curse that falls upon a place and covers it in fog. I was playing a game..." He didn't mention the part that he was playing a game he wasn't supposed to be playing on the PlayStation, a game with an ESRB 18+ rating. Perhaps it had belonged to his mother. Or maybe his father. It was his father who sometimes played the PS5 on the weekends. "The characters go into a place where there's darkness and fog everywhere. The shadow-cursed lands. Do you think we're in the shadow-cursed version of Pinebrook?"

Lucy shook her head. "I think it's just bad weather and strange—"

"Then why did the Other Man give us the pixie lamp?"

"The what lamp now?" Lucy scoffed.

"The pixie lamp. You know, pixies have magic light. Like Tinker Bell. Their light repels the shadow curse. Maybe there's a pixie in that lamp. Maybe we need to break it open and let her out."

"And then be trapped in the house forever?" Lucy asked, hating herself for falling for the trap. The argument Damien had created had forced her to acknowledge the existence of some kind of magic in that lamp. Then again, she had seen the Other Man use it quite effectively.

She didn't know what to think.

"Do you think the Other Man is safe? What if that was the only lamp he had and he gave it to us?" Damien asked.

Lucy didn't say anything. She was concentrating hard, trying to remember what she'd forgotten. For a second, the memories had surged, reminding her of unpleasant things. The next second, they were gone.

"I can't remember anything, Damien. Like, what was happening in our lives five days ago?"

"I can't either," Damien said, being a good boy and taking all the empty plates off the table and taking them to the kitchen. "I don't want to."

"Why?"

"My mind says it was nothing good. *This* is good. Sure, it sucks outside. But you made spaghetti and the house is warm and we're alone. We can just..."

"Chill out?" Lucy said, giggling.

"Yeah. Let's watch a movie. One that's not on cable. You know what we can do? We can watch one of those grown-up movies from dad's DVDs."

"Nice idea, but I kinda wanna do something else," Lucy said. "I wanna take that lamp out for a spin."

A shadow crossed over Damien's face. "Right now?" he asked. "But it's nighttime."

"Someday, when you're my age," Lucy said, her face breaking into a wry smile, "you'll understand that we have to do unpleasant things, things that we'd rather not to do. Mom and Dad haven't been home for five days. We have to go out and find a grownup. We need to tell them."

"Did you try to call someone?" Damien asked, nodding to the phone.

"The Wi-Fi works, but when I try to make a call, I get nothing," Lucy said, sliding the phone over to him. He tried to make calls, but got the same thing. "I downloaded the map of our town so we can use it next time we go out. The police station is just two streets away. Ten-minute walk. Do you wanna go and tell the cops that our parents are missing?"

"What if the lamp doesn't work?" Damien asked, walking over and picking it up. "How do you even turn it on?"

He looked around and found a switch. This cast disappointment over his face. Not a pixie. Just an assortment of tightly coiled filaments. He turned it on. Pale yellow light shone in the room, dominating all other light sources.

Outside the house, somewhere far away, he heard a shrill scream. He almost let go of the lamp. Its walls were all glass, its body made of polished wood. The hair on the back of his neck raised as he held it.

He looked at Lucy, who was staring mesmerized at the lamp.

"There could be a pixie in there," Lucy said softly, her skepticism ebbing away, such was the lamp's glow.

"Do we really have to go to the cops tonight?"

Damien asked, turning the lamp off and placing it on the table beside the entrance. "Can't...can't we..."

"Do it tomorrow in the morning?" Lucy completed for him.

"Yeah. Like, one more day off," Damien said. "And besides, it's nighttime. Everyone knows not to go outside at nighttime."

She didn't argue further. Instead, she disappeared into the kitchen for one final flourish. She emerged with two frothing mugs of hot chocolate.

"What?!" Damien gasped. "What did you *not* buy at the store today?"

"You were so busy buying junk food. Someone had to be sensible," Lucy said. She'd put marshmallows in their hot chocolate.

The two sat down on the sofa, sipping their steaming drinks, watching *Toy Story 3* on Disney Channel. Buzz Lightyear was getting up to his shenanigans.

Tonight, even though it was mercilessly cold outside —as cold as it could be without rain and snow—the inside of the house felt warm. And while the gravity of their dilemma wasn't lost on the two kids, tonight, just for these few hours, they felt like they could act their age.

Tomorrow would come with its fresh share of hell. But tonight was as warm as they could make it, with the heat from the kitchen warming up the whole house, and the rooms—at least the ones they were inhabiting—all tidy.

It hurt to admit that she missed her parents.

It hurt even more to admit that she wished they wouldn't come back.

DOWNTOWN

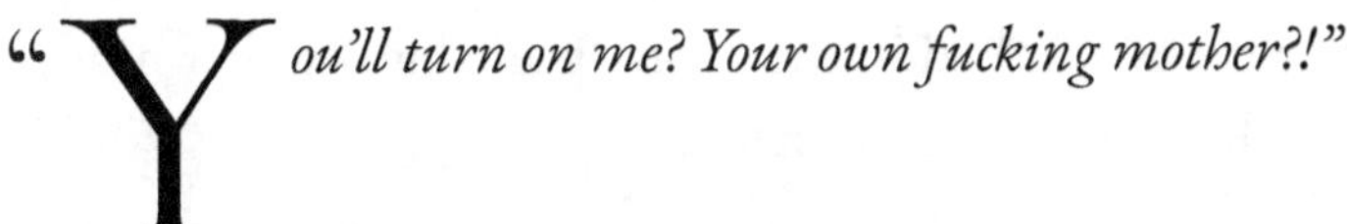

Lucy woke with a start. Somewhere between *Toy Story 3* and *Lilo and Stitch*, they'd fallen asleep right there on the couch. The clock on the wall said ten o'clock. Damien was shivering, tucked in a fetal ball.

Lucy couldn't feel her fingers nor her extremities. Still, she struggled to get out of the sofa and head to her parents' bedroom. There was a duvet there she could put on Damien lest he freeze to death.

Her parents' room was quite immaculate, everything in its place, the bed made, the bedside tables affixed with an ashtray (her father smoked), a couple of cheap paperbacks, and a lamp each. Makeup, accessories, perfumes in neat rows stood sentinel-esque on the dressing tabletop. A few campy frames with quotes hung on one wall.

Live. Laugh. Louvre. In the background of this highbrow quote was a picture of Paris's Louvre.

There was another one with a cat hanging from a tree branch saying, *I'm just a cat in a pickle.*

Lucy grimaced at the poor taste of interior décor and pulled the duvet off the bed. Heavy, black, and quite warm, this was perfect. She took it out to the living room and spread it over Damien's shivering body. He immediately stopped shivering.

The sofa seemed so tempting, she couldn't help herself. She climbed in the duvet, pulled it over her head, and fell asleep almost immediately.

She did not even notice the figure peering in from the window.

———

When they got ready after a quick breakfast, it was one in the afternoon. The fog outside was thick as ever, but Lucy wasn't as afraid anymore. They had the lamp, and regardless of if it was magic or not, it did something that they'd desperately needed.

Its light tore through the fog, allowing them to make out the fronts of houses, the parked cars, and—

"Tracy and Megan wouldn't be caught dead without their bikes," Lucy said, noticing the two bikes lying on the neighbor's front yard.

"Megan's the big one. She gave me a noogie last

month because she said I was staring at her funny. My head hurt for a whole week. She had fingers of iron," Damien said.

"Do you know what a theory is?" Lucy asked, standing with the lamp in her hand, its light shedding upon the two bicycles, one pink, the other a ghastly green.

"No. But I have heard that word before."

"A theory is like a thing you say is true. Then you test it. Repeatedly. When it turns out that thing is indeed true, it becomes a law."

"And what makes a theory?" Damien asked, walking on the lawn and picking up a bicycle, then turning his head to see if anyone would come out of the house and scold him. No one did.

"A hypothesis," Lucy said, nodding at the house. "My hypothesis is that most of the people are gone. Which means that if we take these bicycles, Megan and Tracy or their parents won't come out. You wanna test the hypothesis?"

"I'm already there," Damien said, putting his leg over the bicycle and driving it off the lawn and onto the street. "See? No one's coming."

When she was certain that no one was, Lucy got on the other bike and kicked the pedals. She hung the lamp on the front. The lamp's light seemingly eradicated the fog, the mist, everything. It showed things like they were, but only in a certain area of effect. All around them was still the wall of mist, impenetrable. But they needed to go straight ahead. That's it.

As they cycled, Lucy in the front, Damien behind her, they saw a man walking on the sidewalk, disheveled, talking to himself.

"Isn't that Fred?"

"Neighbor's son?" Lucy asked.

"Yeah. You know, Fred the Freaky Tweaker."

"Shut up. That's not nice. You shouldn't call someone that."

"That's what Brady said Fred was. Brady's Fred's younger brother. Brady says Fred's always in his room and it always smells terrible. What's he doing out in the mist?"

They passed him by. He looked at them and continued to talk to himself.

As they neared downtown, they saw a few more people. A woman was walking her dog; she looked like she was drenched in water, as if she'd just come out of Pinebrook Lake. A man sat with a cardboard sign asking for money because he'd served in Vietnam. He had so many holes in his socks, they looked like Swiss cheese. When they cycled past him, he smelled like Swiss cheese.

This was Main Ave, the road that ran through downtown and, crisscrossing with Pinebrook St, divided the downtown into four equal parts. Lucy remembered that she had to turn left on Pinebrook St. Here, there were two boys in overlarge hoodies talking to each other beside the police station. They paid the two children no heed.

Lucy got off her cycle and waited for Damien to get off his. She took the lamp off, and then stood at the entrance of the police station, her mouth dry. She looked left and right, and when she was certain there weren't any lurkers or dangerous things in the shadows, she stepped inside.

There was a police officer in the booth behind the glass, looking sleepy and bored. She walked up to him, noticing just how empty the rest of the police station was. The officer had a name tag that said *Cody*.

"Umm...sir..."

He peeked over the counter, and when he saw Lucy, he smirked.

Lucy, on the other hand, was frozen stiff.

The cop had a gray face. Not white or brown or any other shade of skin she knew. It was gray like the fog outside. His facial hair was peppered black and white, and he did not seem all there.

"Whatchu want, kid? Why are you out all by yourself? Ain't you seen how bad it is out there?" he said, filing his nails, looking thoroughly uninterested.

Damien tugged at his sister's sleeve, then whispered, "I smell blood."

"Ain't you too young to know what blood smells like, you twerp?" the cop said, now standing up and leaning over the counter, his forehead against the glass, his breath fogging up the surface.

Damien realized that the smell was coming from the police officer. More specifically, his mouth.

"Turn that damn lamp off. It's all up in my face, you stupid little shit," the cop said, glaring at her. Lucy's shaky fingers found the switch and turned it off.

The cop's face didn't look gray anymore. Though,

the smell of blood still hung in the air. The station had turned extremely dim.

"We can't find our parents," Damien said, his voice breaking.

"What are their names?" the cop said, taking a register from the shelf and holding it up.

"Valerie and Andrew Bessemer," Lucy said.

"Hmm."

The cop looked through the register for a full minute, then walked out of the booth. He was stout, and his pants were all the way up to his potbelly. Now that there wasn't any glass between the two of them, the stench coming from him was even worse. Sickly sweet, like poison.

He leered at them, studying them from head to toe, then toe to head.

"Tell you what. I've got two people in the drunk tank. How long did you say your parents was missin'?"

"Five days."

"Ain't no one ever been drunk for five days, unless they be drinking every night. I dunno," he said. "It is a man and a woman. Mid-forties. Maybe they're them."

"Can you take us to them, please?" Damien asked, looking up at the tall and strange cop.

"Oh, ain't that just cute. Grease my palm, kid, and not with your spit. And maybe I'll take you to 'em," the cop said, biting his nails.

"Whaa?"

"He's asking for a bribe," Lucy whispered in Damien's ear.

"Do you want money?" Damien asked.

"Keep your voice low, you little shit. No, I don't want your money. I make seven thousand dollars a month. You think your pocket money's gonna cut it?" He scowled, then looked greedily at Lucy, and then at the lamp she held.

"I'll show you your parents for that lamp."

The words on the note raced through Lucy's mind.

Whatever you do, don't ever lose it.

"Are you sure they are there? In the drunk tank?" Lucy asked, imagining a room filled with alcohol, and two humans swimming in it like pickles.

"I don't know. Gimme the lamp and find out for yourself. Besides, what else are you gonna do?"

"I..." Lucy stuttered, remembering a line from a show she'd watched from behind her father. "I'll talk to your supervisor."

The cop gave a cruel laugh, holding his stomach with both hands. "The supervisor's gone! Along with most other people in this town. Don't you idiots watch the news? Of course you don't. This place ain't clean no more. People have left in droves, or ain't you noticed that neither?"

Damien's heart sank. What was this cop saying? Was any of it true? Was it possible that their parents had left them here, in Pinebrook, on purpose? No.

Yes, an alien voice spoke in Damien's head. *They have been known to be cruel. What is this, if not the latest flavor of their cruelty? Some people drown their kids in the bathtub, some parents microwave their newborns alive so that they're rid of 'em. Yours just left you for dead in a diseased town.*

He clutched Lucy's arm and pressed tight. Lucy winced, then said, "What happened?"

"I'll talk, but you gotta gimme that lamp."

"Is this a test?" Lucy asked, holding the lamp tighter.

"I ain't no one's goddamn schoolteacher. They make thirty-two-hundred dollars a month. Broke-ass educators. If this keeps up, I'll be sheriff. I'll make ten thousand a month. That'll show 'em all. Now, you giving me that lamp or what?"

Lucy lifted her hands up, and no sooner had she done that, the cop snatched the lamp from her hands. He lit it, squinting against its light, all his body gray now, a deep gray that resembled ashes.

"Come on," he said, holding the lamp up and walking toward the staircase leading into the basement. They followed him quietly while he spoke. "If they ain't here, they might be at the hospital. That's always how it is. People either get sick or they get arrested. If none of that, then they run off, and if they don't run off, they die. That's policework 101. And remember, it's always the ex-wife. That's another rule they teach you at the academy."

The basement was cold, damp, and dark, lit only by the lamp in the cop's hand. Lucy regretted giving him the lamp. How was she going to go home? Maybe she could beg, and he'd return it. Maybe it *was* a test.

They followed him as he talked on and on about the mist and the disappearing people and the surprising vanishing of the population and how the hospital was over capacity until they finally reached the drunk tank.

He unlocked the door, and led them inside.

They didn't hear him as he locked the door behind them.

"There. Those two."

The room was long, with cells on the right side. All of these cells were empty except for the last one, where, indeed, two people lay on their sides on the cold benches. Lucy could see her breath fogging up in front of her face. She didn't want to walk farther, but the cop roughly pushed her and her brother.

"Go ahead. Say hi to maw and paw."

The cop stayed put where he stood. Lucy held Damien's hand and walked to the end of the room.

The two people who lay there in the cell had ashen hair and crumpled bodies.

They did not move.

When Lucy reached the cell, they didn't even turn their heads to look at her.

Behind her, Damien whimpered.

"Mom?" Lucy whispered.

The woman didn't register her.

She poked her finger through the cell and touched the man's back.

"Dad?"

The man rolled over the bench and fell on the ground, turned over.

He was dead.

So was the woman.

The lamp light turned off.

The cop stood wreathed in shadows in front of the door. Only his yellow eyes were visible.

"Now," he growled. "Let this be a lesson for you to not go snooping where you ain't got no business."

He started walking toward them with slow, deliberate steps, his fingers banging against the metal rails of the cells.

Damien screamed, but he wasn't looking at the cop. A hand had reached out from within the cell and grabbed his arm, pulling him. It was the woman, her eyes sunken, her face distorted with death, her fingers digging into Damien's skin.

"It's dark in the basement," the cop snarled, closing the distance between them. "No sound escapes the basement. The things I could do to you two in the basement."

PIXIE

V alerie Bessemer had wanted to be a model in her mid-twenties, this inspiration occurring to her after she scrolled the newly popular Instagram and found that modeling, which had once been this highly exclusive thing reserved for the most beautiful and youngest of women, was now somewhat accessible with the advent of social media. Twenty-somethings were becoming influencers with hundreds of thousands of followers, and all they needed was their phone camera and a bunch of dresses.

Of course she could do it. After all, just about anyone and everyone was getting famous. And this was not rocket science, as her own mother had made sure to remind her at every turn of life.

"You can't do this, Valerie. For you, it might as well be rocket science," her mother, Elizabeth, would say when Valerie would attempt a new endeavor. Elizabeth had no faith in her daughter, and begrudged her the fact that she was born. Elizabeth had plans, and those plans hadn't included an untimely pregnancy. So, everything that Elizabeth hadn't been able to do, she didn't let Valerie do. Tit for tat for ruining her life.

This pattern repeated in Valerie's own life, when, in her twenties, she met a man who promised her the world, and only after they were married did she learn that most of those promises were lies. The promise of wealth—there was no wealth. He hadn't passed the bar back then, and was still earning a paralegal's salary. Later, when he did pass the bar and became an up-and-coming lawyer, money did come their way, but it was a little too late. Some aspirations and dreams have an expiry date, and Valerie Bessemer, pregnant in her mid-twenties, wife to newly hired associate lawyer Andrew Bessemer, bore great malice in her heart for the child that was in her belly.

Once the child was born and was of some age, Valerie made sure to let the child named Lucy—because that was the name of the nurse who had helped deliver her—know that her presence was a burden upon the mother, and that if she wasn't a successful influencer, it wasn't because she lacked the tech savvy or the "it" factor necessary to become online-famous; it was because of Lucy.

As a result, Lucy had learned at a rather young age how to escape the clutches of her mother and hide in places where her mother wouldn't be able to get her during one of her high-blood-pressure beating sessions. Lucy would hide in the closet, under the sink in the kitchen, behind the maze of machinery and unopened boxes in the garage, and sometimes even on the roof if it was an especially aggressive session.

Most of the time, if it was just a series of slaps on the face, Lucy took it like a good girl. But sometimes, her mother would be drunk, or worse yet, she'd have taken some of her medicine. Those times, she'd kick Lucy to see just how far the kid would be thrown. Or, if in a bruising mood, she'd punch Lucy across the face or in the ribs just to see how much the child could take.

The justification that she had for inflicting such violence upon her child was that why should she be spared? If her own mother had beaten the living shit out of her, then she was owed beating the living shit out of her own child.

But the child had learned her mother's patterns. If at any time her mother had a drink in hand or was fidgeting with an orange bottle, Lucy would take Damien and disappear in one of the many nooks and crannies of the house.

Once, they'd even hid under the house, amidst all the dust and the skeletons of racoons and rats.

Lucy's brain recalled all these instances in the dim jail as the police officer approached them. And without thinking, she pushed the cell door, pushing Damien in and then herself. Before she could think about the horror of what she was doing, she pulled the corpse of the woman off the berth and shoved her against the cell door. Then she did the same with the man's dead body.

Luck was in her favor, given that the cell doors swung inward as opposed to outward.

The cop—Cody—banged his hands against the bars.

"You fucking wiseass. Open the door!" he growled, his rancid breath carrying through the bars.

Damien ducked behind his sister, noticing that this man was not entirely a man. He wore the skin of a man, talked like a man, but what kind of man was he that shadows flocked to him? That despite there being no light in the basement, his eyes seemed to emit an unsettling reddish-gray light? Or that when he spoke, there was an undertone of an animal's growl in his voice.

He grabbed the bars and pushed, but the combined weight of the two corpses against the cell door prevented it from nudging.

"You fucking shit. You think you're clever? What do I fucking care? Stay in the cell with the dead. That's what you deserve. Maybe next time when I come down here, *you'll* be dead!" He backed away from the cell and walked back to the entrance, picking up the lamp along the way. As he stood in the doorway, he looked back at them and scoffed, "Dipshits."

Once they were alone, Lucy collapsed and burst into tears, with Damien kneeling beside her, doing the same. Their wails filled the basement jail, and whenever they lifted their heads, it was to the sight of the gray, decaying dead bodies piled against the cell door, and this would bring forth a fresh burst of tears and terror.

"S-t-stop. We gotta stop," Lucy said, wiping her eyes. "If we keep crying... If...if we keep crying then we won't ever get out. Don't you know what happens when kids keep crying?"

"Do they die?!" Damien wailed, then buried his face in his sister's armpit, sobbing vehemently. "Can you die from crying too much?"

"Yes," Lucy wept, hugging her brother. "We can get dehydrated, and I don't think there's any water in here. There's no bathroom either. I gotta...I gotta pee bad. I'm so— If they're dead, why doesn't the cop do anything?"

"He's a crooked cop. Like on the TV shows. He's a bad man. He might have killed them," Damien said. "And he's going to kill us next. We should have never come here."

Lucy ceased her sobbing, which was not to say that she was not terrified. The spectacle of death before her eyes had her terrified still, but there was also clarity. These two dead people were not her parents. Yes, they were dead. Yes, they were stuck in a cell in a police station with dead bodies in a city that had suddenly changed to the point that magical lamps were needed to move through the fog and to keep the demonic beasts at bay. But at least their parents were not in this police station.

"What about your pixie, idiot?" Lucy giggled, knowing that the onus of distracting her brother was upon her and no one else.

"What pixie?" Damien asked. It wasn't that he was trying to actively look at the two corpses. It was that they smelled so rank, and not just from their decaying bodies —their clothes smelled of piss and shit and dried vomit. Their wet pants had a fungal stench that made the kids' eyes water.

"The pixie in the lamp," Lucy said, giving Damien a

playful pat on the head. "If there was a pixie, she should have saved us."

"Why? We didn't release the pixie from the lamp. They are really selfish creatures, just like the fae. They do something for you only if you do something for them," Damien said, his eyes focusing in the distance.

"You know what that's called?"

"Huh?"

"Quid pro quo," Lucy said, puffing her chest. Her English teacher had been really proud of her for knowing what it meant. And to think that she'd picked it up from watching *Jeopardy* late one night on TV.

"You wanna know what else it's called?" Damien asked, grinning. "I scratch your back, you scratch mine. And we didn't scratch the pixie's back. Come to think of it, we didn't scratch the Other Man's back. Why is he helping us?"

"Because we look like two miserable little kids stuck in this place. Maybe he pities us," Lucy said. "Come on. It's been long enough. That cop isn't coming. It's time we get out of here."

Damien and Lucy, with much disgust and fear, dragged the two bodies away from the cell doors. It took them all their might to do it, and even then, they weren't able to fully drag them away. Just a little so that the door would inch open and let them out. They leaped above the bodies and escaped through the door.

Lucy was afraid that the cop might have locked the main door, but it was unlocked. The two of them crept up the stairs and then stepped in through the door in the police station's hallway. It was dim as ever, dimmer now that the light from the sky was growing hazy. They'd been in there long enough. It was evening now. There was no way they were going to go home without the lamp.

Lucy held Damien's hand and walked up to the counter where they'd first encountered the crooked cop. He was still there, staring dead ahead.

Lucy's heart sank. Damien nearly yelped.

But the man did not move his head. His eyes had glossed over. It was as if he'd been blinded. His mouth hung open, rattling, foggy breath coming out of it. He did not appear to see the two children standing right in front of him.

Lucy stood unmoving, her hand over her face.

The cop groaned, staring straight ahead. Lucy followed his gaze. The door to the police station was open. A thick fog hung in the night air, defusing the light of the yellow streetlamps.

There was nothing there that the cop should have been staring at.

"I think he's asleep with his eyes open," Damien whispered in her ear so suddenly that Lucy jumped with a squeal. And still, the cop did not turn to look at her.

Lucy put a finger to her lips, glaring at Damien. "Stay here," she mouthed. Then, on furtive feet that had learned to stay clear of a mother who hated her for ruining what would have been a glitz-and-glamour-filled online modeling career, she walked through the ajar door and into the booth where the cop sat. His arms hung limp by his side, his legs splayed. The confiscated lamp was beside his feet. Lucy got on her knees and went under the table, reaching for the lamp.

Just as she grabbed onto the lamp, there was a loud explosion outside. The explosion shook the windows, sent a shockwave through the floor. The cop snapped awake, the gray of his eyes disappearing as he looked at his feet and found Lucy there, holding the lamp.

"You little shit!" he yelled, kicking her in the ribs.

But Lucy already had what she wanted. A kick to the ribs, though painful, was not debilitating enough to paralyze her. She skittered with the lamp and ran out of the door.

"Get back here, bitch!" The cop was not as quick to get out of the booth.

Lucy grabbed Damien's hand and pulled him out of the police station. They ran panting into the bleak night.

No sooner than they'd stepped out, something black and winged swooped at them, throwing them off their feet. It screeched like a huge bird, but was hidden by the immense fog.

"The lamp! The pixie!" Damien yelled.

Lucy's shivering hand found the switch. She turned the lamp on. The concentrated yellow light shone from it, splitting the fog.

The bird was no bird, but a big, black, winged, half-decomposed creature with its bones and meat showing underneath the missing feathers. It was the size of a car, its beak open in a snarl, sawtooth edges lining both beaks. It screeched again, putting its wings above its face to protect itself from the glow of the lamp.

Lucy couldn't believe her eyes. It was as if the lamp was slowly tearing away at the bird's flesh. It backed off, its enormous talons skidding against the tarmac.

Lucy got to her feet, pulling Damien up. Behind them, the cop had come out of the police station, wielding a service revolver. He aimed the gun at Lucy and pulled the trigger.

Lucy turned the lamp off and disappeared in the darkness before the cop had a good shot. The gun roared in the night.

"I hope you're dead!" the cop yelled as he came out into the street, waving his firearm around, finding no sign of the girl or her dipshit brother. "I hope the fog eats you alive!"

With one hand on the lamp and the other pulling Damien, Lucy ran in the cover of the fog, aware of the scampering sounds coming from the bird. Another bang echoed through the night.

"Did he get you?" Damien asked. "Were you hit?"

"No," Lucy panted. They ran until she was sure that the cop wasn't immediately behind them, and then she turned on the lamp once more.

The behemoth bird stood right in front of them, its wings stretched from one end of the street to the other. Its half-rotten beak opened and it shrieked as Lucy held the lamp up to its face. It clawed at her with its talon, but Lucy was far too little to be hit by its swing.

The lamp boiled the putrescent red flesh on the

bird's battered body, scorching it, making blood and pus ooze out.

From behind them, the cop reappeared, his voice no longer angry or agitated, but afraid. He whimpered, "Please don't leave me in the darkness. Please. I hate it when these things appear."

Lucy had no pity for the man who had kicked her in the ribs, trapped her in a cell with two dead bodies, and taken her lamp from her.

She tugged at Damien's arm and ran toward a rusty brown Nissan SUV. They ducked behind the car. Here, Lucy turned the lamp off once more. Through the fog, they watched as the cop, wielding an ordinary LED flashlight and his revolver, came up to the bird.

"Oh shit," the cop yelped. He lifted the gun to aim it at the bird's head, but the bird, far more agitated and larger in size, was quicker. It dove beak-first and separated the cop's head from his body.

Damien clasped both hands on his face to hold back his scream as he watched the bird swallow the cop's head. His headless body stood there for a second, pouring blood everywhere, then fell to his knees, and then, finally, fell torso-first on the ground.

The bird crunched the man's head in its beak, then swallowed it whole. Lucy watched with tears of fear in her eye as the bird dug its talons into the cop's corpse and then took to the sky, the dead body in its claws spilling blood everywhere.

It hadn't been a full minute when a deep snarl came

from behind them. Lucy turned the lamp on to the sight of three dogs, similar in appearance to the bird, standing there, wreathed in blood, melting flesh, and bones jutting out of their disheveled bodies.

"Back!" Lucy shrieked, waving the lamp in their faces. They barked, growled, their spit lacing the ground. The lamp seared them, making sure they wouldn't step farther. The dogs growled, backing off one step at a time.

To Damien, they did not look like dogs at all, but the hyenas he'd spend hours watching on the National Geographic channel that'd be on in the background in the living room. Their backs were more angular, their fur coarse and yellow, their mouths shorter yet possessing longer teeth. Amidst all the fear-wrought thoughts that raced through his mind, there was one eccentric thought that struck him as odd.

What if I could tame one of them? he thought, but the next instant, when one of the dogs leaped and tried to bite his feet, Damien put all such thoughts to bed.

Above them, the dark bird flew in circles, not coming close. The dogs, unable to stand the intensity of the light, disappeared into the bushes by the road, their yellow eyes glaring from behind the underbrush.

Lucy picked herself up yet another time, her psyche and body battered by all the physical and mental violence inflicted upon her. Tired, she handed the lamp to Damien, then walked with her brother, keeping an eye on their surroundings, making sure nothing else would come close.

They did not turn the lamp off until they reached home. And not even when they were inside and all the doors were locked.

GAMEPLAN

The impact this dread-filled and eventful outing had upon their minds was so brutal that both kids did not speak a word for several hours, both of them just huddling with each other under a blanket in Lucy's bedroom. The curtains were drawn, the lights on in the room, the tablet in the charging dock playing Toy Story on Disney.

They weren't watching the movies. The background sound from the show made them feel less alone, and it blocked out the howls and screams coming from outside.

Damien fell asleep in his sister's embrace.

When he woke up, it was to the smell of grilled cheese sandwiches. His sister was on the floor, biting down on a sandwich hands-free, hunched over a large grid paper that she'd taken from Dad's study. She had a marker in her hand and was writing something in big block letters. In one section of the page, there was a rough map of Pinebrook. All around it were rambling notes.

"You're up," she said without looking at him. "I made sandwiches." She pointed to the bedside table. There were indeed two sandwiches and a glass of juice.

Damien's stomach grumbled. He helped himself to the food while still in bed, the exhaustion and emotional whiplash giving him vertigo. His eyes drooped, his face too sunken and sulky for a mere eight-year-old. And yet, the things that he had seen out there in the dark...

"What are you doing down there?" he asked, rubbing his eyes once much needed nutrition had gone into his body. He found that he could swing his legs over the bed and stand on his feet without the weight of the horrors he'd witnessed weighing him down.

"I'm coming up with a gameplan. Come here," Lucy said, deep in flow state, writing away on the paper. It was immaculate what she had done with it. There were little multicolored notes stuck all over. Some places, the paper folded in upon itself, and when unfolded revealed more information about specific things, such as how the dogs looked, what manner of bird it was that had attacked them and killed the cop.

This was an exhaustive inventory of all the things that they had done, experienced, or witnessed in the past few days. An entire section of the notes was on the Other Man and who he might be. Another section divined upon the mysteries of the lamp with one word written with a question mark next to it.

PIXIE?

"This is all we know so far," Lucy said, pointing at the map of the city. "Something terrible has happened to Pinebrook, causing the people to disappear, including our parents. There's a strange fog outside, and in it, weird creatures lurk around. There's a man stalking us who doesn't appear to mean us harm. He gave us a lantern. The usual shopkeeper's not there at Zyn's. At the police station, there was a mad cop who nearly killed us or was about to do something terrible had we not saved ourselves by going in the cell with the two dead bodies. Who were those dead bodies? Our neighbors aren't here, but somehow Fred is. The internet and the phone are on the fritz and have a mind of their own. We don't know when our parents will come back, or if they'll come back at all. We don't know where they are. Those are all the facts. Have I missed anything?"

"Yes," Damien whispered. "I've been having difficulty remembering it, but the more I sleep, the more I dream of it. Do you remember what happened before... the town got all fudged up?"

Lucy's eyes went out of focus as she stared in the distance, trying to recall a memory that kept slipping from her mind.

"Do you hear it when you're waking up from sleep?" Damien asked, sitting beside his sister. "That awful sound?"

"I don't remember—"

"I think you do. I think I remember too. But I think we're trying so hard to forget it," Damien said, taking his sister's hand in his own.

It came back to Lucy, at least in some parts, and when it did, she could not help the tears as they rolled down her eyes and wetted her cheeks. She sobbed silently, remembering her mother and father ganging up in some kind of drunken or drug-induced stupor, both adults cornering both children in the garage... Or was it the attic? Or was it the living room?

She did not remember the exact details, but she remembered the important part.

The part where she and Damien were being beaten to within an inch of their lives. Belt lashes, coat hangers on their backs, blunt punches, and harsh slaps.

It had been a fight of some kind. A fight that had brewed between her parents, and when they had exhausted all avenues of fighting with one another, they turned to their children, who had, up until that point, been playing with their toys.

She tried to recall the exact details. Just who had beat who and how much. But all she got were these flashes of dull, red pain, and the sounds of punches and slaps meeting flesh. The sound of Damien crying, begging for them to stop.

The sound of a snap of something loud, hard and unbendable.

"Our parents had lost it," Lucy said, her voice carrying grief in every syllable. "They wanted to kill us."

"Yeah. It came to me while I was sleeping. Was I dreaming? I don't know," Damien said. "It was like I was watching a replay. But Dad was standing over me. I remember that. He had a coat hanger in his hand. He'd beaten me with it enough times already. Then he hit me here," he said, pointing to his forearm. "And it snapped in two. It was made of wood. I raised my hands at him, trying to protect myself. Or maybe I was trying to beg him to stop hitting me. I remember his face, Luce."

Damien stared at his sister, and now he was crying.

"He was Dad, but I don't think he was Dad. Do you know what I mean? I think some kind of demon had possessed him, or maybe some Skinwalker sort of thing had worn his skin, because the way he had been looking at me, I'd never seen him look like that. I don't remember anything afterward. Maybe he hit me so hard I got knocked out. Maybe you don't remember because you got knocked out earlier."

"No," Lucy said. "I wasn't knocked out." Damien's mention of the coat hanger brought back a fresh wave of memory. "Mom had grabbed me like they do in wrestling. I remember seeing Dad beat you with the hanger. I heard the hanger break. I saw blood all over your face and your arms. Mom was choking me. She said, 'Die already, whore.' That was strange. I've never known boys."

"What's a whore?" Damien asked.

"It's a really bad word for a really bad woman," Lucy said, looking away, not wanting to tell Damien that Megan, their neighbor, the one whose bike they had stolen, had cornered Lucy one day in school, index finger jutting against her chest, spitting, "Your mother's a whore, did you know that? Do you know what she does?"

Then, Megan had explained the concept of "whore" to nine-year-old Lucy, who, prior to that, hadn't even considered something like that in her entire life. And to think that her mother was out there doing that with many men.

"I remember one last thing," Lucy said, rubbing the back of her head. "I remember Mom slamming my head into the wall. And then I passed out. Whatever happened afterward, I don't know."

"Maybe they felt super guilty for beating us like that and they ran off."

"Yeah," Lucy said, shrugging. "But why aren't we injured? Where are the bruises?"

"Maybe it happened a long time ago. Bruises heal. Bones fix themselves."

"Maybe the Other Man saw our parents beating us, and he took them somewhere," Lucy continued. "Maybe our next order of business is to find him and ask him about our parents."

"And then what?" Damien asked unsurely.

"I don't know, kid. I haven't thought of that yet. That was as far in the gameplan as I'd written."

"Do you really wanna find our parents?" Damien asked. "I mean, remembering what they did."

"Do you know the other option?" Lucy asked, tears in her eyes again. "The Child Protection Services come and take us. And when they do, we'll be put in foster care. Or worse. We could be separated. You'd have to live with someone else, and I'd have to live with someone else. We won't see each other. And do you know what happens if we land a shit family? They could be worse than Mom and Dad."

Damien gulped, then looked at the intricate game-plan, focusing on the part that talked about the Other Man.

"Then let's focus on finding the Other Man."

"We don't have to," Lucy said. She nodded at the window. "He's already there, standing in the street. He's been standing there for some time now, as he does every night."

"Rock, paper, scissor," Damien said, throwing up his fist.

"Best of three," Lucy agreed.

Damien drew rock first. Lucy drew scissors. Damien drew scissors. Lucy drew paper. They had the third round anyway. Damien drew rock. Lucy drew rock.

"Fine," Lucy said. "You be a wuss. I'll go."

The two of them went to the window, looking out at the street. Eerie as usual, the street was quiet. Nothing moved in the shadows. Only the hermit-like Other Man stood at the center of the street, a long staff with a lantern at the end of it in one hand, a big bag in another. On his back he bore several bags. He was covered in layers of unmatching clothes.

He looked up at them and dropped his bag. He raised his hand and waved at them.

Lucy waved back, then Damien did too.

The Other Man pointed to their house's door. Lucy gave a nod, and then went down the stairs.

REVELATIONS

When Lucy opened the door, the Other Man was already standing on the porch. He put a finger to his lips. Lucy nodded in understanding. She stepped aside to let the man in. Damien watched from behind the staircase's bars as the man walked in, tracking dirt and grime in the house.

He was unbelievably tall. To Lucy, he looked like he took up the entire space in the living room. He first put his bag down on the floor, then unhooked his lamp from the long staff he held. It turned out, it was not a staff, but a long rifle. He fiddled with it till the scope, the barrel, and the butt were all in place, then checked the bullets. When he was sure that his firearm was in order, he looked at Lucy with his piercing blue eyes.

They were the only part of him that were visible underneath the mask and scarves he wore. He had goggles on, and now that Lucy could look at him up close, he had a cowboy hat that had been weathered to the point that it no longer looked like a cowboy hat. His long white hair fell down to his shoulders, drenched and silver.

"Do you know that you two are not alone in this house?" he asked in his deep voice, pointing a tattered glove at the basement door.

Lucy's heart quickened. She shook her head.

"And you, little boy. Did you know that there's one of them in the house with you?" the Other Man asked.

Damien shook his head behind the staircase bars.

"It's a wonder how the two of you have remained alive so far," he groaned. He picked up his lamp in one hand, aimed the rifle ahead of him, and then walked toward the basement with careful steps. "I saw it getting in through the basement window. It's about the size of a dog, but don't let them things fool you. They're not dogs."

Lucy sped up the stairs so she was with Damien. She didn't know what the man was talking about. The two kids watched him open the basement door and disappear. There was absolute silence for a minute, and then the sounds of snarls and howls came from below.

Lucy froze, her fingers digging into Damien. The thought that one of these creatures was lurking in their house without them knowing made her head spin from terror. She was down there just an hour ago, making sandwiches, pouring juice in glasses, and rummaging about for supplies. How had she not known?

The question that petrified her was this: What would she have done if she had known? How would she have held her own against one of those demonic things?

There came a loud bang from within the basement, followed by a loud whine. Then the sound of a body dropping. The two kids stared affixed at the ajar door until the Other Man's shadow appeared. He pulled the door, and stepped into the living room with the corpse of one of those hyena-dogs they had encountered in the street earlier. The dead creature was leaking blood all over the floor. The Other Man walked out of the house and ditched the body by the trash cans.

He came back inside and locked the door, then finally took off his hat, goggles, scarves, and mask. The last thing to go were his gloves, which revealed heavily burned hands. He looked at the children on the stairs and said, "You can come on down now. It's all right. They must have picked up your scent from earlier. I killed the other two out in the street. This one must have slipped by me. Let this be a lesson to you to lock all the windows, including the ones in the basement. You, girl!" he said, snapping his scarred fingers at Lucy. "Get a mop or something and clean this blood before it sets into the floor."

Lucy did not question the man. She did as he said, fetching a mop from the kitchen, and began wiping away the blood and dirt on the living room floor.

In the meantime, the Other Man took off the backpack and rucksack and set them down on the sofa. Then he slumped in the sofa and sat there staring dead ahead, rubbing his palms as if remembering the terrible thing that had happened to them, making them scarred and withered.

"Boy! Are you going to stay up there on the stairs or lend your sister a hand? I do not like boys who leave everything to their big sisters. Get on down here and lend her a hand!"

While she did not appreciate the curt way in which he addressed Damien, Lucy couldn't help but be grateful for what he'd said. Many times she felt distressfully alone, even though Damien was around. They had a two-year age gap, but for some reason she had never expected Damien to lend her a hand.

"What do I do?" Damien stood beside her, dumbstruck, his face bearing a *Am I expected to do something?* expression that deeply vexed Lucy.

"Stop bothering her! Come here!" the Other Man said.

Lucy stuck out her tongue at Damien as she finished mopping the floor. Damien stuck out his tongue at her too.

"Children!" the Other Man boomed, then looked at them, saying, "Long ago, a god bargained for infinite knowledge, and for that knowledge he hung himself from a tree with a spear in his side. He plucked his eye out and threw it in a well. He learned the name of things. He learned how the world would end. Do you know what he learned?"

Lucy shook her head. This wasn't one of the stories her grandmother used to tell her at bedtime. Damien nodded. Lucy shot him a quizzical look.

"*Assassins Creed*? *God of War*?" Damien said, looking at her impatiently. "Odin."

"You're right, boy. Maybe I was wrong about you. You know of Odin?"

"Yeah, he's a huge dick," Damien blurted.

The Other Man chuckled. "I suppose he is. But he saw Fimbulwinter. Endless fog and frost covering the world. He saw the gods rise out of cinder and battle each other. He saw the heat death of the universe and called it Ragnarok."

"Uh-huh." Damien nodded in agreement. He walked up to the man and tugged at his sleeve. "Do you need something? Coffee? Tea? Anything cold?"

"I'll have a can of Coke if you've got that," the man said. Damien, feeling safe in the presence of the man, immediately fetched him a Coke from the fridge.

Lucy watched warily as the man popped the can open and drank from it.

"Despite the world going to shit in a handbasket, Coke still tastes good. It's the little things," he said, smacking his lips. Then he looked at Lucy and said, "You may know this. Two thousand years ago, a man in the Middle East warned people about the end of times. Fire and brimstone, he said. End of days. A catastrophic event that will end with all the righteous beamed up like *Star Trek* characters and all the bad seeds left on earth. Be meek, be mild, enter ye the kingdom of heaven. Know who I'm talking about?"

"Jesus," Lucy said.

"You know Jesus isn't his name? Jesus comes from

Yeshua, which means 'God saves.' Yeshua in English would be Joshua. So Jesus ain't even Jesus. He's Josh. Looking around you, sweetheart, do you see yourself being saved? So I don't think Josh saves, despite what his name says." The Other Man chuckled and drained his Coke can in one long gulp.

"Do you think you're a bad seed, girl?" he asked, looking at Lucy. "If it's all real, and if we're screwed seven ways to Sunday, do you think you're left behind because you did something horrible?"

"I didn't!" Lucy retorted, her eyes beginning to sting.

"Calm down," the Other Man said, raising a hand. "I was just messing with your head. I get bored out there by myself. I was always a trickster in my old life. Always playing pranks on the wifey. I don't know where she is. I haven't been able to find her ever since this whole thing started."

"You had a wife?" Damien asked.

"Most men my age have 'em," the Other Man said. "I suppose that's what makes the world go round. Know what I'm saying?"

Damien shook his head, and then brought to his lips what he had been wanting to say ever since the Other Man had sat down. "We cannot find our parents."

The Other Man set down his empty can of Coke and looked at the two of them standing beside him. He had pity in his eyes. His moustache was long and covered his entire lips. He had white facial hair, with just a few black hairs remaining. The same was true for the hair on his head. He gave Damien a weak smile, then ruffled the boy's hair.

"I suppose you can't," he said. "I suppose there's many kids out there like you who can't find their parents. And I suppose that's a sad affair. You might be wondering where they went. You might think they're dead. But before you lose heart, or worse yet, lose an eye like All-Father Odin in search of knowledge, know this. There's a good enough chance that your parents didn't ditch Dodge. It may very well be likely that the same curse that took this town rendered them diseased like so many people here. I mean, come on, child, have you not noticed the streets empty? Do you not wonder where the people went? Many were admitted to the hospital when the fog broke. Some became quite ill. Like, ill enough that they weren't taken to hospitals, but to morgues, because they were dying while they were alive, their skins peeling off their bodies, and, I'm sorry...I'm sorry for bringing up these hideous images in your heads. But the thing is, we're in the thick of it, partner. And there isn't an easy way for me to say this other than put it as plainly as I can. It was a whole mess. The graveyard has so many unmarked graves. I've never seen anything like it."

"You mean to say our parents might be at the hospital? That's what the cop said too," Lucy said, tugging at her own sleeve.

"You guys met Cody, the living piece of shit?"

Damien shot Lucy a mischievous glance, not because the Other Man knew Cody, but because he'd said shit like it didn't mean anything. Damien giggled.

"Oh, my bad, kid. I forget I'm not supposed to curse, especially when there's children around." The Other Man chuckled. "But yeah, Cody's a bona fide bad seed. He..."

"There were dead bodies in the basement where he... He took our lamp and...he was going to do something terrible to us," Lucy said, and then retold the entire story, including how Cody died.

"That bird requires some serious firepower to kill," the Other Man said. "I'm glad you got out alive when you did. I've had my fair share of matches with that bird. Let's just say, one of these days, one of us is going to kill the other. Rot vulture, I call him. And I'm glad that the rot vulture did something useful. Cody was always a crooked cop."

"Why was he sleeping with his eyes open?" Damien asked.

"It could be the fog, the disease pervading through this town. It does strange things to people," the Other Man said, taking out a pipe from one of his jacket's many pockets. He proceeded to stuff it with tobacco and then light it. Almost immediately, the living room began smelling of chocolate and smoke.

"Can you take us to the hospital so we can see if our parents are there?" Lucy asked.

The man took his pipe out of his mouth and looked at Lucy gravely. "You must never go there. Ever."

"Why?" It was Damien who asked this.

"You think the town is bad? You think the animals and the birds and the maddened people are hard to deal with? Wait till you're at the hospital. That's the source of it all. The wards are filled with patients undergoing metastasis, spontaneous rot, and God knows what else. Anyone who so much as steps in the hospital is infected. The place is under quarantine. You know what quarantine means? It means those who are inside can't go out and those who are outside can't go in."

"But if everyone's sick, who's treating the sick people in there?" Lucy asked, her heart sinking at the prospect of her parents lying in a bed, unattended, rotting away, dying slowly. Something about this image also gave her a sinister sort of satisfaction that she was too afraid to address, even if it was just in her own mind.

"There are doctors there; doctors in quarantine suits. Of course, the entire order of the world hasn't collapsed upon itself," the Other Man said. "But I suppose that isn't saying much."

"What do we do? Do we stay put? What is in the lamp that you gave us? Is there really a pixie in there?" Damien asked, unable to stop himself from asking one question after the other.

"Pixie? What on earth are you talking about? It's a phototherapy lamp with strong ultraviolet light, but here's the kicker. The light that you see is yellow. That's because humans can't really see ultraviolet light. It's used in medical treatments, tanning beds, and by forensic teams to find traces of blood and other bodily fluids. I made the thing myself. I'm somewhat of a prepper, you know," the Other Man said, puffing his chest.

"I don't know what a prepper is," Lucy said.

"Well. Put it like this. I stocked up my house with all sorts of stuff preparing for the end of the world, and looks like the end of the world is here. And here we are."

"Err...sir... What is your name?" Lucy asked, deeply unsettled by all the end of the world talk.

"What do you call me?" The Other Man grinned.

"We just call you the Other Man," Damien stuttered.

"I'm going to trademark that. It's got that same Marlboro Man charm to it. I call you boy and girl. Do you really want to do names? It breeds familiarity, and in such times, familiarity is a weakness."

"My name is Damien."

"My name is Lucy."

"Well, I'll be." The Other Man whistled. "You know. I do like the name you've given me better than my original name. So let's call me Tom. Short for 'the Other Man.' How about that?"

The kids nodded at him, giving him feeble smiles.

"Now, I don't need to have some nutritionist degree on my wall to see you kids are mighty starved. Why don't you sit in front of the TV and wait for me? I'll make you something nice, assuming you have the ingredients for it in the kitchen. After that, I do have to go. But don't worry. I'm not leaving you without a gameplan."

Upon hearing the familiar word, Damien's eyes lit up. He said, "Lucy already has a gameplan!"

"Does she now? Your sister is wise, boy," Tom said, nodding at Lucy. "You best heed whatever it is she has to say. It might save your life."

The kids, a little calmed that there was an adult presence in the house, and that the adult in question wasn't some strange man, but quite a pleasant man given the circumstances, sat on the sofa and watched TV. The Other Man busied himself in the kitchen.

Outside, it rained, wetting the streets, drenching the trees and the grass.

In the dead of the night, with only one house's lights on, a trash truck rolled up. Two men got out of the truck and hurriedly threw the dead demonic dog's body in before going over to where the other corpses lay.

————

He made them chicken and vegetable soup, but that wasn't all he made. He'd also taken a packet of frozen chicken out from the freezer, thawed it, and then baked it. It was tender, well-seasoned, and quite delicious.

"You're growing kids. You need both your proteins and all the nutrients vegetables can give you. I made enough that you can have it tomorrow and the day after. I'll say one thing about your kitchen. It's well stocked."

"Lucy took us to the store and bought a lot of stuff," Damien said, helping himself to the tender baked chicken. He was so overwhelmed with choice that he'd have a spoonful of soup, then tear a piece of chicken next, then he'd chase it down with grape soda.

At the dinner table, the Other Man, with both elbows on the table, looked at the children and said, "Now listen here, children. I have been roaming around in this new and strange world of ours and I've learned something valuable. If you pretend like everything's normal, no one's going to bother you. Not the dogs, not the birds, not any of the other creatures that lurk. Hell, if you act like nothing's the matter, even the people will treat you like one of them. I don't know how long you're going to be stuck here, so my advice is this. It's going to come across as counterintuitive—that means something that doesn't feel right yet *is* right. You've got to put fear out of your mind. If you can't put it out of your mind, then at least put it somewhere deep within your mind where others can't smell it. Do things you'd normally do, but do them during the day. Go to school. Pretend everything is normal. Always take the lamp with you. And come back home before it's evening."

"We don't wanna go to school!" Damien said. "Have you seen our school? It sucks doodoo butt."

"You're not understanding what I'm saying, boy. This place is a nightmare, its residents paranoid, agitated, even crazy. If enough of them realize that there's two kids out there who are wise to the way of this world and are hiding in a house all by themselves, what do you think's going to happen? It won't be just a few dogs or a big bird that will come for you. It won't be that one cop either. It will be the entire town that comes for you, with all its mad people and hellish creatures."

———

The Other Man was wrapped in all his many pieces of clothing, his goggles back on, his cowboy hat floppy atop his head. He stood by the door, gun-staff in hand, and the empty bag in the other.

"What's that bag for?" Lucy asked.

"Sometimes, when I'm out about town, I find some really good stuff lying about, unattended," Tom said.

"Do you have to go?" Damien asked.

"Yes. You see, I am on a mission of my own. I have to go out and do something. I'd stay if I could, but how about this? You know the manor just outside of town?"

"Manor?" Damien asked.

"Big house," Lucy said. "With the iron gate."

"That's the one. That's where I'm staying. What's the point in being modest? That's my house. It's quite protected, and there are many rooms there. I've done a little something-something that makes the fog weak there, so you can even pretend like it's a normal day. Tell you something. I'll still be doing my nightly rounds and check up on you to see if you're doing okay. But if it all gets to be a little too much, just come to my house. And then you can stay there for as long as you need or until all this blows over, okay?"

Lucy and Damien stood by the door, trying to figure out what to say to him that would prevent him from leaving. Now that he was here, the sheer reality of just how horrific it was outside was.

When finally he opened the door and was all ready to step out, Lucy said, "Tom, will you look for our parents in the city?"

Tom stopped with his hand still on the doorknob. He sighed, then turned around, giving Lucy a smile.

"Sweetheart, if I find them wandering about, I shall grab them each by the ear and bring them right here."

That was all he had to say. Even after he left, even when the fog consumed him and he and his lamp were no longer visible, that one sentence stuck with Lucy. It calmed her thinking about it, that the great adventurer Tom would be out there searching for their parents.

MAKE BELIEVE

At least the school was still there.

Lucy stood with the lamp in hand, a second sun burning far brighter than the gray dusk-ball in the sky. There was something about the air today, something that made the fog feel thinner. Perhaps it was the exercise in self-delusion that both kids had been doing, pretending everything was normal. It was not easy, because nothing looked normal. Not the vacant houses. Not the constantly shifting bushes and the lingering eyes behind them. Not the cold that seeped in through their clothes and stung their skin.

However, the fact remained that they were children, possessing children's imaginations. It took a jump-start, but once they started to pretend that everything was normal, everything *did* start to seem normal.

And instead of a foggy, cold day, it was a sunny day with sunlight gleaming on the surface of green leaves.

The grass was freshly mowed on each lawn, cars straight out of the wash stood lining the street. Children laughed as they raced after each other on their bicycles. Men waved at each other from across the street as they got into their cars and drove off to work. Birds chirped harmonious melodies in the branches. A true microcosm of Americana.

That had been Pinebrook before the fog. And as terrible as their home life was, the life outside was not as dreadful, other than the bullying at school, which was occasional and not at all anywhere near the torment they bore at home.

Damien had Ted and Chris, his two buddies who always tagged along with him, and anytime Lucy would see them in the hallway, she'd find them immersed in meme talk (they'd look at her and go, "6, 7, 6, 7!" weighing their hands, and she'd pretend not to know what it meant) or videogame talk or YouTube video talk.

Lucy had Cassie, Rhea, and Elody, the four of whom had a group that was formed by being excluded from every other group in class. As a result, they were, all four of them, completely different. Rhea loved to pretend that she was not ten, but fifteen, and therefore dressed as such, acted as such, and pretended to know what words like *couture* meant. She was vain, but not a toxic level of vain. Cassie was a bookworm with the glasses to match. Once someone in class had called her "Cassie the beetle." It was another girl. That girl had gotten a punch in her guts from Elody, who was the group's muscle. Youngest sister to five boys, she was boyish herself and was the group's gearhead, talking about cars, motorbikes, and videogames featuring cars and motorbikes. She was the only one in the group with an interest in videogames, and was always playing *Call of Duty*, *Fortnite*, and *Valorant*.

It helped Lucy pretend that everything was normal by imagining that when she'd go to class, her friends would be there waiting for her. Some part of it was not pretend at all. They had to be there at the school, she reasoned with herself. After all, where else would they be? What were the odds that all of them would disappear.

"Come on. Ted and Chris might be waiting for you," Lucy said, turning the lamp off and stowing it in her bag. She figured that if she didn't bring her books, she could use the real estate in her bag to store the lamp. And she was right. It was a snug fit.

They walked through the doors of Pinebrook Elementary together, and what they saw inside immediately shattered the fragile layer of make-believe.

Grimmer than outside, the grayness pouring in through shattered windows, the main hall had flickering lights and trash all over the floor. Several of the lockers were open, their doors swinging in the wind.

Only one person stood in the hallway beside them. The janitor, Yuri. At school, people used to say that Yuri was an ex-communist from Russia. Some said he'd come from Sweden. He was taller than God and had a clean shaved face with pockmarks and scars. He didn't speak a word of English. All he knew was the bucket and the mop, and to stay out of the way when the classes let out. Lucy had seen him stand by the bleachers and smoke cigarettes. He'd wave at her, but she'd never wave back.

"What are you two doing out in the hallway?" Yuri said, making Damien's mouth hang open. He'd heard the same rumors, that Yuri was a mute Russian. "The classes have stared. Shoo, shoo, little children, to your classes. Or the principal will give you detention."

"I'll see you here at the end of school," Lucy said, holding Damien's hands. "You can take care of yourself without me for a few hours."

"I can." Damien grinned. "Don't you know? I run this joint."

She watched her brother step into science class, and then she hurried off for her first-period English.

There were only three other children in the class with her, and they all looked gray, gangrened. A teacher stood by the blackboard, but it was no one she'd ever seen at school.

"Well, look who decided to show up, little lady," the old man with a rim of long white hair on his otherwise bald and tanned head said. He wore photochromatic glasses that were black in the white fluorescent glow. He had an orange shirt tucked into beige pants and a brown tie.

Lucy thought that he looked like the living embodiment of shit. She held back a snicker.

"What's that?!" the teacher said, bulging his potbelly in her direction. "I didn't quite catch that. I've had a word with the principal about your long absence. You'll be pleased to know you have detention at the end of day."

"But...I was sick...Mr..."

"Duke. I'm the substitute English teacher," Mr. Duke said unaffectedly. "And if you were sick, why didn't your parents get in touch with us?"

"They're sick too."

"Uh-huh. Next you'll tell me the dog ate your homework. Sit down and turn your book to page three hundred and ninety-four."

"I don't have my book."

"Share with Beth."

One of the three students, the only other girl, Beth, had askew teeth and a thousand pimples on her face. She wore braces and a full-sleeved dress with a long skirt that made her look like one of those conservative girls that Lucy would see sometimes with the nuns by the church. Choir girls. Lucy groaned internally, not wanting to share a book with a choir girl.

Beth continued waving. Lucy groaned again and sat down on the chair beside her.

"Are you new? I haven't seen you before. Like, eversies."

"Eww. Nobody says eversies," Lucy said, chuckling. "I'm not new. I wonder where all the other kids are."

"But it's always been just us three. And now you make four. That's Brad Donohue. And that's Harry Bush."

"His name is Harry Bush?" Lucy found that hard to believe.

"Yes. Like the president," Beth said.

Harry and Brad were sitting in front of the two girls. Harry turned around and held his hand out to Lucy. "My name's Harry Davis. Don't believe everything Beth says. She's one of those messed up church girls. She'll say anything to get a laugh out of you."

Brad turned around and took a good look at Lucy, saying, "Where did you come from?"

"What do you mean?" Lucy asked.

"We've never seen you before," Brad said. He had long, wavy black hair and redness under both eyes. He had a very red nose as well. "Are you sure you're supposed to be in fourth-grade English?"

"Yes. This is my class," Lucy said, wondering whether to play along like Tom had said, or straight up confess that she didn't know what was happening.

She chose the former, and then busied herself with Beth's book.

"Today's lesson is about American grammatical syntax and how it differs from British or Australian English," Mr. Duke said, writing something on the blackboard.

Lucy remembered this lesson. She'd already gone over it in her regular class months ago. Rather than panicking, she thought she'd use that to her advantage and impress the entire class.

Sometime during the middle of the class, Brad turned around and leaned toward Lucy, saying, "Hey. It's fucked up everywhere, right? Like, we're not crazy? You're new here. You tell us."

Lucy reeled at the f-word, a word she'd only heard before, never used.

Harry turned around too, looking at Lucy with a degree of concern on his freckled face. "Do you see them too?" he asked.

"See who?" Lucy asked, having a great deal of difficulty maintaining her make-believe in the face of this peer questioning. The Other Man had told her to pretend everything was normal, and yet here they were, three kids her age, asking her if she saw what they saw.

"Do you see the fog monsters too?" Beth whispered.

————

Damien discovered that he, in fact, did not run this joint. The moment he walked in the classroom, he tripped on something he didn't see and fell face-first on the cold, hard floor.

Something crashed around the same time as he landed on the floor. Dazed, his head spinning from hitting the ground, he looked and saw that a long lamp had fallen and broken in two.

A hand shot out of the sea of pale students gathered around him. Not wanting to be embarrassed any further, Damien took the hand and pulled himself off the floor. It was a kid almost the same size as him, but paler. In fact, now that he was no longer sprawled on the floor, he could see that all the kids were paler than him. There was a tinge of blue about them. They all looked at him with hostile eyes and strange smirks, their expressions synchronized.

Damien frantically looked for his two friends, Chris and Ted, but did not find them in this class.

"You broke teach's lamp. Teach's gonna be pissed," the kid who had helped Damien said. "Don't you know Mr. Thompson's crazy?"

"I didn't know!" Damien sputtered. The kid did not laugh. He had dark hair that fell on his forehead, and darker eyes. He wore faded clothes that were two sizes too big for him, and his nose looked like it might be runny. His hand was cold when Damien shook it.

"Bullshit, you didn't know. You tripped on it on purpose," the kid said. Behind him, the rest of the class nodded. "You're fucked."

"You're not supposed to say that word," Damien whispered, afraid someone might overhear this conversation.

"When Mr. Thompson comes in, I'll tell him that you said the f-word and that you broke his lamp," the kid said, grinning now.

"Why would you do that to me? Have I said anything to you?" Damien asked, tears welling in his eyes.

"No, but you're new fish. And I don't like new fish. We're an even number. Twenty. You make twenty-one. Twenty-one is a messed up number. You don't belong here, Damien."

"How do you know my name?" Damien gasped.

"Oh, I know more than just your name, and I have

half a mind to tell all the class about it. How your mother's a miserable woman and how your father likes to beat you when he's drunk. I know other things too. Things you did. Things you'd rather people don't know," the kid said, his voice slick like oil, his gaze menacing, making Damien feel uncomfortably hot. Like the kid was burning him with his laser vision.

"I don't know what you mean," Damien said, looking at the rest of the class. The classroom was like the classroom he'd remembered. The same old stuff up on the walls. A bookshelf with several books missing. A crooked corkboard with drawings on it. The blackboard with half its wooden frame missing. This was his class, and yet this was not his class.

The kid's grin broke into a full sly smile. "My name is Ron. You'll learn the rest of their names in time. We look young, but we're real clever."

"I can see that," Damien said, his throat constricting. At any moment the teacher would arrive and observe the broken lamp, and then it'd be hell.

"Tell you what, I can make your troubles disappear if you do something for us," Ron said, rubbing his palms together. "I can say that the wind made the old lamp blow over. I can keep your secrets. But you, Damien, have to do something for me. For us."

"What do I have to do?" Damien gulped as the kids all ganged up on him, leaving no room for him to breathe.

"You," Ron said, poking Damien in the chest with his cold finger, "are going to get us a gun. And you have just three days to get one. If you don't, I'll tell the entire school about what your mom does, and what you've done. I'll even tell Mr. Thompson you broke his lamp and called his mother a bitch. We'll all enjoy seeing what he does to you. Mr. Thompson, he's got quite the temper."

————

At recess, Damien, breaking out in cold sweat, sought his sister, who was standing beside the swings with a girl he'd never seen before. They were talking in hushed whispers, their heads close together. Damien walked up to his sister and tugged at her elbow.

"Oh, you're here," Lucy said, giving him a smile. "Meet Beth. Beth's a new friend."

"Hi there," Damien croaked weakly. As despicable of a day as it was, it was nothing compared to what had happened to him in the class. The gray fog seemed so inconsequential now that he had bigger things to worry about. Mr. Thompson, the tall, obese man with the long moustache and the constant frown on his tanned face. He didn't talk loud, which made him even more fearsome, because his anger was quieter.

"What's got you all worried and tongue-tied, bro?" Beth asked, grinning at Damien.

"Kids from my class," Damien said, unable to utter a complete sentence. He was trying to figure out who to tell. The principal? Some other teacher? Maybe he should come clean to Mr. Thompson, and that way Ron wouldn't have a hold on him. But then again, the kind of person Ron was, he probably wasn't bluffing about the things he knew. After all, he'd known Damien's name. Damien didn't want things getting out. While young, he was intelligent enough to know that rumors, once circulated, tarnished your reputation like nothing else.

Chris was not a booger-eater, yet when someone had said this about him two years ago, it had stuck. Now, no matter whatever Chris tried to do, he couldn't shake off that reputation, and that was something quite harmless. If the truth about Damien's mother and Damien's own actions came to light, that wouldn't be harmless.

Except...what was it that he had done? He couldn't remember. Maybe he'd ask Ron kindly, and Ron would tell him.

"What did they do? Did one of them hit you?" Lucy asked, bending over to look at Damien better. When she was sure that he bore no signs of violence, she stood up again and looked at her brother worriedly. "What did they do, Damien?"

"They want me to get a gun for them."

"And why would they want to do that?" Lucy asked. Beth nodded quickly, as if that was exactly the question on her mind.

"They say they're gonna get me in trouble if I don't get them a gun," Damien said, his face suddenly very pale and green. He held his hand to his face. "I hate school."

"Let me go and talk to them," Lucy said, beginning to walk toward the school building.

"No!" Damien yelled, making several heads turn in

his direction. He held his sister's arm and pulled her back. "They said if I tell anyone, they're going to... they're going to tell Mr. Thompson I broke the lamp."

"Did you break the lamp?" Lucy asked, scowling.

"No!"

"Then why are you worried?"

"Because there are twenty of them, and just one of me. Who's Mr. Thompson going to believe? Them or me?"

"I'm not letting you get your hands on a gun!" Lucy snapped.

"These are second graders?" Beth asked. "What are they going to do with a gun? Hunt the fog monsters?"

"Shhh!" Lucy said, glaring at Beth. "I told you, don't talk about them!"

"I don't understand you," Beth said, shaking her head. "They exist and are a very real part of this world. Why pretend they don't exist?"

"Because if you notice them, they hunt you harder," Damien said, his face bearing the weight of gravity that belonged on someone much older.

"Ooh. Then you should have led with that," Beth said, her face growing red. She narrowed her eyes, looking at Damien with great curiosity. "How do *you* know of these things?"

"Because he's much wiser than he looks," Lucy said, puffing her chest proudly. "And he can take care of the kids in his class. They're eight-year-olds, Damien. They don't want a gun. They're just teasing you. And if they're not, well...I'll come in your class and twist their ears till they cry uncle."

Damien chuckled, his anxiety settling just a little. There was still the fog and the dreadful atmosphere all around him. Still the way back from school to home. Still the loneliness in the dead of the night when the world fell dark and the howls of the nightmare creatures rang through the streets and the dense fog. He stopped chuckling at this thought, his face turning back to its default grimness.

"Hey, Luce. Are we still doing that thing after school?" Beth asked, looking at her new friend eagerly.

"I don't know," Lucy said, watching the children on the playground half-heartedly interact with the jungle gym and the other playground equipment. There weren't as many kids as usual, and this was undoubtedly strange, but then again, there were probably a lot of parents who didn't want their kids out in this horrible weather. "I have to drop him home."

"He can come with. Come on, Damien. Won't you come with us? There's this strange thing under the bleachers that I saw the other day. I promised Lucy I'd show her. Do you wanna come with?"

"That depends," Damien said, sulking. "What kind of thing is it?"

"Only the best kind!" Beth said excitedly, stomping a foot and turning her hands into tight fists. "Like a fantasy thing. I think it's almost like a portal."

Damien's eyes widened. As did Lucy's. The two shared a look. Damien nodded at his sister briefly. Then

Lucy nodded back. Finally, she looked at Beth and said, "All right then. We have decided that after school we'll let you show us that portal fantasy thing."

"Perfect!" Beth squealed with a happiness that did not belong in such a desolate place. It felt so alien that all the kids turned to look at her, as if envious that she had something to be so happy about. Or perhaps angry that she was disturbing the mood with her misplaced glee.

PORTAL FANTASY

Brad Donohue, ten years old, stood by the chain link fence to the baseball pitch like a guy protecting a speakeasy. He stood nonchalantly, one foot on the fence, arms crossed, looking idly to one side and then the other.

When the other three approached, he looked like a strange stick figure against the immense backdrop of unending gray behind him. Only the bleachers were barely visible; the rest of the pitch was rendered obscured. It was late in the afternoon, and there was no one around.

Brad waved at Lucy and Beth, and frowned at Damien.

"I didn't know you were bringing another."

Lucy stared at Beth in incredulity, saying, "I didn't know Brad was going to be here."

"Are you kidding me? I discovered the thing!" Brad said heatedly.

"Can we all cool our jets?" Beth said, raising her hands in a placating gesture. "Brad, that's Damien, Lucy's little brother. She's in charge of him and can't leave him behind. Where else would he go?"

Brad sighed tiredly, then shrugged. "I guess it's okay. But do keep up. And don't touch anything, okay?"

When Damien nodded firmly, Brad turned around and lifted the chain link that had been cut so cleanly that one wouldn't even know. But Brad knew. He knelt and got through the little hole in the fence, then held it open for Lucy, Beth, and Damien.

"Couldn't we have taken the door?" Lucy asked once she was through. There was a door not far from the cut in the fence.

"Try it," Brad said roughly. "And get back to me after Yuri the janitor catches you and takes you to the principal. I don't trust that man."

"Yuri or the principal?" Lucy asked, a little apprehensive. The cold was beginning to bite her skin, despite all the many layers she was wearing. A little part of her wanted to turn the lamp on just for safety, but these two kids didn't know about the lamp, and what were the odds they'd ask her for it, and when she refused, they'd put her in an uncomfortable situation?

"Yuri. The principal is just a husk," Brad said without looking back. He crouched under the iron bars of the bleachers and disappeared in the darkness underneath the seats. "Yuri is like a weird guy, because this fog and the rest of it doesn't seem to affect him at all. He whistles. He stares at you funny. He laughs when there's no one around. And when he's certain that he's alone, he talks to himself in Russian."

The other three kids didn't say anything. They were too awestruck by the spectacle of this whole other world hidden under the bleachers, a world that was not visible from the outside. Strange bioluminescent mushrooms had sprouted from the ground, and around them, even stranger fireflies hung suspended in the air, glowing blue. Vines crawled on the underside of the benches, forming a convoluted canopy with flowers that shone in dangerous colors.

"Poison flowers, strange mushrooms, and vines," Damien whispered. "You know where we are, Lucy."

"Stop it with that fantasy stuff right now or so help me God!" Lucy snapped.

"Oh, don't be screaming at him. He's just a kid," Beth said, her voice breaking. "You can tell me, Damien."

"We're in the Underdark," Damien whispered in a hallowed voice. "It's this place underground where some pretty scary stuff happens."

"Sorry to burst your bubble there, bud," Brad said, standing by what looked like an effervescent pool at the end of the path. "But this is nothing like your Underdark. Or does your Underdark have portals too?"

"You don't know nothing about the Underdark if you think that there's no portals there," Damien said smugly. He had a hint of a smile on his face. What had he done to deserve all of his fantasies coming to life? Parentless, thrown into a dangerous fantasy land with strange monsters, a kindly warrior-like figure watching over him, a magic lamp, and now portals in the Underdark underneath the bleachers.

I could be a knight. A paladin. Ooh, ooh, ooh, I could be a freaking sorcerer, Damien thought with rising glee and excitement in his chest.

As for Lucy, who had no such predilections for the fantastical, fear weighed down each step as she walked up to Brad, to where the blue portal shone in the ground. She hated Damien for putting that image in her head. It could be something else too. A wormhole. Why couldn't it be a sci-fi tunnel? One that could take her back to the reality she remembered. A reality without fog. That old reality still had its fair share of misery, but at least it was familiar misery, and not this alien brand of misery that had no give.

When her parents would tire, they would sleep. Those long stretches, paired with the duration of the school day, would comprise a span wherein there was no violence. At least, not parental violence. Kids still bullied her sometimes, and the odd adult sometimes scolded her, but it was never anywhere as terrible as what her parents did.

Beth was on all fours beside the shining blue hole. Brad was looking at it with great intrigue. When Lucy walked up to it, she gasped. It wasn't water, that was for sure. But it rippled, and there was something visible underneath it. All around it were the same mushrooms and poison flowers that grew under the bleachers.

"What..." Damien gasped, looking at the moving imagery within the portal. It was like a thin layer of smoke had covered the entrance, and on the other side—

"It's another version of Pinebrook," Brad said with the air of a prophet. "One where there's no fog or fog monsters. I've looked through the portal for hours. There are more people in the parallel version. They are happier. The bleachers are always full of people watching the matches. There. Do you see?"

Lucy could. She could see a street. More precisely, her own street. Her parents' cars were parked in the driveway: a Prius and a minivan. It was a sunny day on the other side. So sunny and warm that Lucy was tempted to put her hand through the portal.

"Stop!" Beth called out, but it was too late. Lucy had already touched the portal. It rippled dangerously, emitting an angry sound.

Brad watched her with horrorstruck eyes, saying one word. "Run."

Before any of them could heed that advice, a cracking sound came from all around them, turning everything completely black. No longer was the portal or the underside of the bleachers visible. They stood in pitch darkness, unable to see each other.

"Damien!" Lucy called out.

"Be quiet!" Beth whispered next to Lucy. "You weren't supposed to touch it. Why did you have to do that?"

"I thought I could—"

"You thought you could travel through the portal?" Brad scoffed. "Please. That's not so simple."

A bright light shot out in the darkness. For an instant, Lucy thought it was maybe her lamp. But the light was white, unlike her lamp's yellowy glow. The light sped around them. It sounded like something moving through water.

"What is happening?" Lucy whimpered.

"It's a demon," Damien said. "When you stir a portal without permission in the Underdark, a demon—"

A hand shot out of the dark and grabbed Damien and shook him violently.

"There is no demon! This is not the Underdark!" Brad yelled, roughly yanking Damien.

What happened next, none of them were prepared for, least of all Brad.

The white light zoomed toward him, a snarling sound following in its wake. When the light was upon Brad, making him shine like he was standing under a limelight, the creature to whom the light belonged also came into view.

It was a giant angler fish, wreathed in black, its white teeth longer than swords, all of them jutting out as it opened its mouth and shrieked at its prey.

In his last moment, Brad saved Damien's life by pushing him so violently that Damien disappeared in the dark, along with Beth and Lucy.

Brad stood facing the fish, the bleachers gone, the gray world disappeared, leaving only the dark and the monster lurking in it.

The angler fish snapped its mouth shut, leaving Brad's legs standing there, his upper body gone, his innards spilling out, blood shooting out of what remained of him. With blood smeared all over its mouth, the fish swooped again and plucked Brad's legs off the ground, leaving no sign of him.

A few feet away, Lucy, Beth, and Damien sat behind cover with their mouths covered, their bodies shaking, their eyes spilling tears in the wake of witnessing a gruesome death.

The angler fish, now done with Brad, was swimming toward the other three. It could locate them with relative ease, given that what they thought was cover was actually not.

Lucy wished to be back in the fog-covered world. It was nothing compared to this pitch-black nightmare. With fumbling hands, she took out the lamp from her bag and held it up to the angler fish.

The angler fish's light shone white upon the three of them, and it opened its mouth once again, ready to devour. Lucy, at that exact moment, turned the lamp on.

The fish screeched in agony as the lamp's piercing light began to tear away its flesh. It backed away, biting the air, snarling, howling in pain, and as it retreated, the darkness it had cast all around started to disappear, revealing the Underdark, the gray fog, and the pulsating portal.

Lucy stood up and advanced toward the retreating fish. She stepped in Brad's blood. She sobbed loudly as she continued to advance despite fear trying to root her to the spot. The angler fish swam inside the portal, and for that one second, the portal enlarged to accommodate its size. And when the fish was back in the portal, it shrunk to its original size.

As it shrunk, it did so with a shockwave that sent the three children flying. Lucy hit her head against the metal scaffolding of the bleachers and was knocked out. Damien rushed to her side, screaming her name at the top of his lungs, shaking her so she'd wake up.

He did not notice that Beth had walked up to the lamp and picked it up. She was studying it most intently, as if the death of her classmate hadn't affected her one bit.

"Lucy, wake up!" Damien shrieked.

"The lamp..." Lucy stirred, her eyes still closed.

Damien looked at Beth. Beth stared back at Damien, the lamp in her grasp.

"If you'd told me you had a monster-repelling lamp, Brad wouldn't have died," Beth said, anger and loathing on her face. "You—"

"No!" Damien stood up and snatched the lamp away. "You and your friend were the ones who brought us here. You didn't tell us it could be dangerous."

"My friend is dead!" Beth yelled, tears running down her face. "And we're all still stuck here, in this horror!" She wiped her eyes clean, then turned around to face the portal. "You know what. I'm not sticking around. I'll go to the other side!"

"Beth, wait!" Lucy said, sitting up. But she was too late. Beth had already broken into a run, and was not concerned with what Lucy had learned of the portal. That it was not a portal, but a pocket dimension. Like a lake at the bottom of an ocean. That there was no other side. That the reflections were an illusion, a trap, just like the light dangling in front of the angler fish.

"See ya, chumps!" Beth said, sobbing, hysterical. She jumped into the portal. And then her scream could be heard.

Damien, knowing that he shouldn't, couldn't help himself as he walked up to the blue liquid pool and saw Beth's fate. There was no *other side*. She was sinking in the water, the angler fish circling her greedily. She swam up, reaching for Damien's hand.

Damien reached into the portal. Maybe he could save her.

Their fingers touched.

And then Beth was pulled back into the dark void of the endless water, the water's blue turning red as the fish had their way with the little girl.

Damien jumped back, staring at the red pool, then at his sister.

Lucy was crying, shaking her head, her hands covering her ears.

"We have to tell someone," she wept. "We have to tell the principal. We have to..."

"No," Damien said, offering his hand to his sister, and feeling great relief when she took it and lifted herself up. "It will happen again. We'll go to the principal, and like that crooked cop Cody, the principal will punish us or lock us in some closet. We don't have to tell anyone other than the Other Man. He'll know what to do."

"What is there to do? Beth and Brad are dead!" Lucy cried.

"I know," Damien said, mustering whatever shred of bravery he could. "But you're alive. And so am I."

"For now," Lucy sobbed.

The two of them crawled out from under the bleachers and went back to the school through the hole in the fence.

A tall figure was standing by the entrance, obscured by the evening and the shadows it brought.

When it saw the two children approaching through the deserted playground, the figure stepped forward into the lamp's light. He had a clean shaven, pockmarked face, and a toothy grin on his overlarge face.

"Yuri seen four go. Yuri see two come back. Is Yuri to presume the other two are dead?" the janitor asked, holding his mop like a staff. "That is terrible. Every day, more and more kids disappear. Yuri likes kids. Yuri hates seeing kids in this state. Come, come, younglings. I dry you off. There is blood on your shoes."

"There...there was a place under the bleachers!" Damien pleaded, wiping his tears off as they followed Yuri into the empty school.

"Ah, yes, yes, little brother. There are many places like that. Dead places with deader things in them. What was it Shakespeare said? Hell is empty and all the devils are here," Yuri said, abandoning his janitorial cart by an empty classroom at the end of the hallway. He opened the door and waved them in.

It was as if someone had preserved all the brightness

and vividness of the old world in this room, where all the posters and pictures on the walls were more crisp than in any of the other rooms. Here, in this room, the smells of pages, petrichor, and room freshener hung pleasantly.

There was also not a single table or chair in sight. There was a blackboard with a big bear drawn on it with chalk. A small CRT TV was propped up on a broken shelf on one side. A skillet, a gas cylinder, a single mattress on the floor, and a mini-fridge—this was a shelter room.

When Yuri closed the door, Lucy and Damien noticed that it was reinforced from the inside with metal rods and several locks.

"This place is not so empty, Yuri thinks. So, what does it make it? Not hell," Yuri said, scratching his head and opening a cabinet, revealing several children's shoes in neat rows. He turned around and looked sadly at the two kids. "Many children go missing. Yuri collects their shoes. Yuri is sad to see so many children go. Yuri tries to stop them. Yuri set up alarms on all the doors. But that Brad kid was clever. Too clever. He must have cut the fence. To think that his actions could have killed you two too. That would have been a real loss."

He estimated their sizes and took out two pairs of sneakers. "You can come get your old shoes from me. Yuri will wash them. Yuri will also close that fence so you can't go to the bleachers again."

"But...but Brad and Beth," Lucy whispered.

"They broke the rule. They stopped pretending that things were normal. They started investigating. They riled up this world. The world responded in kind. Yuri pretends that all is normal. That is how Yuri is alive."

Upon listening to this familiar instruction, Damien's ears pricked and he asked, "Do you also know Tom? Did the Other Man tell you to pretend things were normal?"

Yuri got down on one knee in front of Damien and ruffled his hair, a tragic smile on his face. "When you are old enough, young friend, you will learn that this is a rule all adults learn. To pretend that things are normal when they aren't. That is how we make our way through life."

"Oh. I thought Tom told you," Damien said, growing less interested. The two of them put their new, bloodless sneakers on.

"You better hold onto that lamp. I have one just like that too," Yuri said, taking out a big flashlight from his pocket. He flicked it on. Its yellow beam landed on the wall.

"Whoa! It comes in flashlight form too?" Lucy asked.

Yuri's eyes grew distant. He flicked the light off. Sitting there in a chair that was far too small for him, he spoke in a low tone. "Once upon a time there was a world filled with great dusk and dust. A world like this one. The people prayed to their gods for any kind of help. What they didn't know was that the gods had turned their back on this dying world. So none of the gods listened, and the people continued to dwindle in the dark. Until one day a trickster god on his many-legged horse flew past the dying place, and noticed just how many people were weeping and calling out for help. Intrigued—as he didn't have a lot of worshippers—he landed in front of the people, and upon hearing their pleas, gave them hair from his own head. Each strand coiled and shone and drove away the dark. They thanked him for his hair, falling at his feet and groveling, kissing, prostrating. The trickster god felt something. I don't know how to explain it. See, the trickster god was a vile god who was always punishing people. He liked to kill people for sport. He had even murdered other gods. But when he saw those people stuck in the dusk-world, he had a change of heart."

Yuri studied the two children intently listening to his story. When he was sure they were immersed and no longer reeling from the horrific experience they'd had under the bleachers, he told them the rest of the story.

"Metanoia," Yuri spoke, lifting his hand as if casting a spell. "A profound change of the heart and mind. A turning away from rot, dark, sin. Coming to the light. The trickster god experienced that when he saw the people earnestly worshipping him. He flew on his horse to the source of the dust and darkness. It was a volcano. He took off the rest of his magical hair and cast it into the volcano. The volcano stopped erupting. The smoke stopped rising. The world eventually cleared. People still held onto the god's hair strands. They made shrines of him. Statues, temples. Rosaries. Legend has it, the trickster god became a sincere god from that day. Some say that the modern Christian god and the trickster god who had a change of heart are one and the same. Some say that such stories are a waste of time and that there are no gods."

"But the light," Lucy said, utterly entranced.

"Oh. This," Yuri laughed, looking at his flashlight. "No, no. This doesn't contain any god-hair. It's... This belonged to my wife. We had many such lights like this in Russia. She died some years ago. Coming to America did not suit her. One night, many years after losing her, I woke up to the fog and the darkness, and there were strange dogs outside the school. I couldn't see anything. So I reached for the place where I knew she always kept the flashlight. And there it was, that light. Even in death she looked after me. I turned the light on and discovered that it wasn't ordinary light. I have kept it safe, and it has kept me safe. Why? Did someone give you that lamp?"

"Yes," Damien said. "The Other Man. His name is Tom. He told us to pretend things were normal because that's the way to stay safe and alive. He also told us to go to school."

"Hmm," Yuri said, looking out the window. There was nothing visible outside other than the gray sea of fog. He shook his head. "I am glad you have a friend. But if I may ask, children, where are your parents?"

Lucy and Damien shared a look, then shook their heads in unison.

"We don't know. We haven't been able to find them since the fog. Tom thinks they might be at the hospital."

"Oh, yes, yes," Yuri said, nodding vigorously. "Many people got sick because of the weather. The hospital. You must never go to the hospital, otherwise you will get sick. It's a very dangerous place. More dangerous than the bleachers."

"Have you been under the bleachers?" Lucy asked, feeling a little confident now. She walked around the room, looking at things but not touching anything. Yuri opened the mini-fridge and offered her a juice box. She took it gratefully. Surviving was thirsty work, after all. He offered one to Damien too. Damien also took it eagerly.

"I've been there," Yuri said, lighting up a fat cigar. "And I've seen the fish. I've seen the dogs and the birds. Have you seen the overlarge sentinel?"

"No," Damien shook his head fearfully. "What is that?"

"It's this big person who is as tall as a skyscraper. His glasses shine as he looks for people in the night. I saw him pluck a child off the street. What he does with them, I don't know. That's why people don't go out at night at all. If he finds them roaming, he just takes them. There are many ways to die, but none as horrible as being hunted by a giant and then taken to his lair."

"Err...Yuri...sir," Damien coughed to clear his throat. "Do you know where I can find a gun?"

"A gun? Now what would you do with a gun?" Yuri laughed, clapping his hand on his thigh.

"A kid in his class is bullying him. Ron, was it? He's given Damien three days to get him a gun," Lucy said, sitting beside her brother, putting her arm over his shoulder.

"Oh. I don't envy you your position. Ron and his classmates are... Oh boy," Yuri said, whistling. "They... I... You know, little brother. I guess you better find a gun and bring it to him."

"What if he shoots me with it?" Damien whimpered.

"Trust me. He won't shoot you with it. He's asked for a gun before. And when he wasn't provided with one, it was ugly. I am afraid I cannot help you there," Yuri said, standing up and opening the door. "It's dark out there. You need me to drop you off at your home?"

When the kids nodded, Yuri picked up his light and guided them out of the school. They were just at the entrance when Damien and Lucy spotted a familiar lamp-staff parting the fog.

Tom stood there by the entrance.

"Is he your friend?" Yuri asked.

"Yes! That's Tom!" Damien said excitedly.

Yuri nodded at Tom. Tom nodded back.

They didn't speak to each other. Yuri stayed by the school's entrance, Tom in the middle of the road.

Damien and Lucy walked over to Tom and looked back at Yuri, who stood with his flashlight on in the night.

"Who is he?" Tom asked.

"Yuri the janitor," Damien said. "He...he's okay. He's not a bad guy."

"If you say so, kiddo. Come on. I've been searching for you everywhere. When I said go to school, I didn't mean make the damn place your second home."

"We were attacked," Lucy clarified, then told Tom the entire story of the fish and the bleachers. She also detailed the deaths of Brad and Beth.

Surprisingly, Tom didn't seem shocked by the news. He guided them through the fog, and only said, "I've seen people die for less. You are lucky you survived. Next time a kid offers to show you something, have the wisdom to refuse them. Now come on. I was just by your street. There are more animals there than usual. It's prowling night apparently. I'm taking you to my home for the time being. I can keep an eye on you that way."

"Do we have to go to school? After everything that happened?" Damien asked tiredly.

"You've lived another day, haven't you?" Tom grumbled. "Count your blessings."

Damien tried. He could count only two. One, that he was alive. Two, that his sister was alive. That was it.

They walked through the menacing night, their lamps lighting the way, splitting the fog just wide enough to give them way. They walked for an hour. Lucy and Damien had never been to this part of town before. In fact, they weren't even sure that it was Pinebrook anymore.

When Tom stopped ahead of them, Lucy lifted her lamp and saw why he'd stopped.

She gasped.

And then, a second later, so did Damien.

There was no more fog around them. Warm lights shone from every window of the immense manor.

"Welcome to my humble abode," Tom said as he swung the wrought-iron door open. "You will be safe here for the night."

A Strange
Manor of Things

The wrought-iron gate was thirty feet tall with sharp edges. The iron rods were close enough that nothing could pass between them, almost like the bars of a jail cell. Vines and ivy ran up the gate, thick with thorns and flowers. Around the entire manor, there was a twenty-foot-tall stone wall with a ten-foot fence atop them riddled with barbed wire. The manor's defenses were impenetrable.

A net was cast from the roof of the house and connected to the fence, making it impossible for anything airborne to enter the premises as well. But it was not a hideous net marring the beauty of the house. It had fairy lights, flower vines, grapevines, and flowers hanging from it at several points, giving what were otherwise defensive measures an aesthetic appeal.

Once they were in through the gate, there was a fountain greeting them, spouting water. Around it was a flower bed and a few benches. To either side was a garden. Here, the Other Man grew fruits and vegetables. Chickens clucked somewhere in the distance. Lucy peeked and saw that behind the manor there was a back garden with cages and coops. Goats grazed in the night, sheep bleated, and the rooster crowed at uneven intervals.

"You have a whole world here," Damien marveled.

"And that's all one needs, despite wherever it is one finds. A man is defined by how self-sufficient he is. You will discover that this place is a monument to sustainability."

"Do you have a gun?"

Tom grinned at Damien, saying, "If you think I'm going to let you borrow one of my guns to humor a classmate, you've got another thing coming. Who cares what that kid says or thinks? He's got nothing. Kids his age bluff like their life depends on it. Pay him no mind."

For some reason, this bit of reassurance did not land. Damien recalled the menacing way he'd been trapped in that classroom, how the rest of the kids had ganged up on him, and how they were all seemingly under the spell of Ron, the puppet master who knew the world's dirty secrets. His heart started beating irregularly at the thought of showing up two days later without the thing that had been asked of him.

Lucy had no such concerns at the moment. She was struck by just how gorgeous the manor looked, with its many windows and its red bricked building and the enormous mahogany door. She felt like a princess who had finally arrived at her castle. At this moment, the fog and the despair were the last thing on her mind. Here, in and around this manor, there was no fog. Here, there was no despair. The Other Man was not a stranger, but a dear friend, and he would keep them safe forever.

"Do you have a library?" she asked, barely able to contain the excitement in her voice.

"Oh, do I. You will have a blast. I ransacked all the bookstores in the area. They were abandoned anyway. I have so many books that you can spend the next couple of decades and still won't be done. I think this is life's greatest irony that there are so many excellent books and not enough time. Perhaps death is a library. Endless time, and all the books to read that were ever written."

Lucy rather enjoyed the idea of death being a library. Damien, on the other hand, wondered if this library would come stocked with comic books and fantasy novels.

Tom opened the vast door to his manor and walked inside, holding the door open for the children. The moment they walked in, the door closed automatically. The inside of the manor was richly decorated. Dozens of sconces shone warm light on portraits, gilded décor, and intricate woodwork. Beneath their feet was a red carpet that extended to every room.

"Make yourselves home. Wander wherever you may, just don't go in the basement. That's off-limits. I presume you already know why. When hungry, wait for me in the dining hall. I shall attend to your needs. As it happens, there's a pheasant waiting for me in the kitchen. Maybe I'll roast it for you. Or...are you more fond of nuggets and fried chicken?"

"Roasted pheasant sounds amazing," Lucy said, who had been taught not to present too many requests when being hosted as a guest.

———

The house smelled delicious as Tom busied himself in the kitchen. Damien, in his excitement, ran from room to room, studying the map of the whole place, admiring the decoration pieces and ornaments. Presently he was lying by the fire in the living room, enjoying a Patrick Rothfuss novel that he'd plucked from the library. Lucy was still in the library, roaming from aisle to aisle. The aisles reached the ceiling, and had moving stairs along them so that one could travel as high or as far as needed.

There were so many books here that her head was spinning. She had already stacked a few favorites on the table in the library, and was fishing for more. She would ask Tom if she could borrow them, and then she'd take them home.

Music came from a gramophone in the living room, playing Bach. Lucy loved the tone. Damien didn't care much for it. But he found that reading the book with classical music playing in the background helped greatly.

Half an hour later, Tom carried a tray to the dining room and rang a bell. The children ran with a book in hand, and watched the glistening roasted bird with their mouths watering. Vegetables, French fries, iceberg lettuce, and fruit slices were arranged all around the roasted bird.

Tom beckoned them to sit and poured them Coke in their glasses. In his own glass, he poured some wine. He cut a leg piece each and gave it to each kid. For himself, he kept the pheasant breast.

"I wish we could stay here forever!" Lucy chirped.

"I would like nothing more to host you and have two pairs of helping hands at the manor," Tom said, smiling at her. "It gets very lonely here. And in those moments of loneliness, I discover that all the books in the world fail in doing for me what the company of another living human being does."

"Overrated!" Damien said, then put a hand on his mouth for speaking without thinking.

"Huh?" Tom chuckled.

Lucy kicked Damien under the table. Damien blushed red.

"Oh, come now. You don't have to be all that formal with me," Tom said, taking a bite out of the pheasant breast. He didn't use a fork or a knife. He lifted the meat in his hands and tore another bite off. "When was the last time you let your hair down? Have you ever eaten meat with your hands like a caveman, juices flowing down your hands? It's liberating!"

Damien didn't need telling twice. He picked up the large leg piece and bit into it, caveman style. His cheeks and chin smeared with the juice from the pheasant. Tom looked at him and laughed. Then he nodded at Lucy, who finally ditched the fork and the knife and did the same thing. She tore an even bigger bite, juice squirting out of the meat and running down her hands.

Damien laughed loudly. Tom clapped in approval. Lucy grinned as she ate, feeling like this was the first time in her life she was eating so relaxedly. She laughed louder, and the entire dining hall rang with their mirth.

"Now what was it that you found overrated, Damien?" Tom asked, pouring himself some more wine.

"Other people. Other people are doodoo. Give me videogames, internet, and books and you'll never see me interact with another human again."

"So you say," Tom said, looking longingly out the window, as if remembering someone or something. "But then you get old. Your hair starts turning gray. You wish you had said yes to that girl thirty years ago. Maybe you'd be married. Maybe you'd have divorced. Maybe you'd have children. When one too many maybes stack, it's a recipe for endless remorse. And between me and you, little brother, regret ain't nothing if not bitter and hard to swallow."

"You may be right," Damien said, digging into the rest of his food. "But I'm just a kid, and what you're saying sounds sus to me."

"Sus?" Tom asked, looking at him confusedly.

"Suspect," Lucy clarified. "Gen-A slang. Don't ask. He says some of the weirdest things. Even I can't understand some of it."

"So I'm suspect?" Tom chuckled, hands on his inflated stomach.

"No, you're all right, Tom. You are an unc though," Damien said.

"Unc as in uncle?"

"See, you're catching on!" Damien giggled. "Unc also means uncool, but you're not uncool. You're the coolest person I've ever seen. Yuri comes at a close second."

"Yuri is the janitor," Tom reminded himself. "Is he like me?"

"No. He's really strange. He started telling us this strange story about a trickster god and something called met-meta-met-metano..." Damien struggled to remember the world.

"Metanoia?" Tom asked, his mouth hanging open just a little.

"Yes! Do you know what that means? He said it was someone bad turning good," Lucy added. "But we didn't understand the story."

"Tell me what he told you," Tom said, putting his forearms on the table to lean closer.

So Lucy did, and wherever she paused, Damien filled in. When they were done, Tom's eyes felt like they'd glazed over with thick glue. "I wonder why he didn't tell you the whole story," he whispered.

"What's the whole story?" Damien asked.

"Well, you see, the world that Yuri talked about, that was certainly affected by a similar fog and darkness as ours. And when the trickster god came running on his many-legged horse, it wasn't because he'd overheard the people praying. It was because he was there to hunt those people. He wanted to kill them for sport, but he found them praying, already defeated. Hunting, if you know a thing or two about it, is fun when your prey runs. When your prey doesn't run, it kills the fun. The trickster god took pity on them, but that doesn't change the fact that he'd come to hunt them for fun. But since he wasn't having fun anymore, he chose to turn over a new leaf. Show them his benevolent side. Gave them his hair. Smote their volcano. Ended their suffering. But the change of heart didn't happen because he wanted to be good. It was because there was no more fun in being vile. Have you ever seen a cat play with a mouse? Most of the time, the cat eats the mouse after playing with it. But sometimes, just sometimes, the cat becomes bored and lets the mouse run away, live to see another day. Gives it a fighting chance so that next time, it would come to her stronger, bigger."

Lucy sat in silence, mulling over the story. Damien sat staring at the rest of his food, thinking of cats and mice. Finally, Lucy spoke, "I've never heard this story before, and I've heard so many stories."

"Well, sweetheart, that would be because most of the useful stories of this world have been erased by evil men who wish to further their own agenda. That is why whenever witches are mentioned in modern tales, they are mentioned as evil beings casting spells upon vulnerable people. The stories about witches being saviors of communities, witches being benevolent goddesses unto themselves, witches being mothers, lovers, wives, friends—you won't read much of them. And you won't find much stories about pagan gods, gods before the Abrahamic God took center stage. You won't find instances of female priests in history, female prophets. They burned the library of Alexandria. They razed Babel. They destroyed the archives under the Vatican. Evil men think burning books is the easiest way to censor information, but they are idiots on top of being evil. Wanna know why?"

Lucy nodded.

"Because every time a book is written, another copy of it is written in the ether, in the quantum realm, in the Akashic Records. Do you want to know a secret, Lucy Bessemer?" Tom's face was so close to hers that she could smell the wine on his breath, but oh, how she wanted to know the secret.

"The secret is that despite the libraries being burned, the literature of past civilizations being destroyed, all of it exists in the Akashic Records. Think of it like the internet before the internet. If you meditate and really focus inward, you can access a library that has billions of books. Not hundreds, thousands, or hundreds of thousands. Not millions. Billions! And when you access that knowledge, you realize just how much bullshit we've been made to ingest, and what the truth really is!"

"Can you access the Akashic Records?" Lucy whispered.

Tom retracted back into his chair and sat sullenly, shaking his head. "Alas, but I am no shaman or wizard. I'm just a man trying to survive this nightmare."

They ate what remained on their plates in silence, then emptied the remaining contents of the tray. When the last bone was picked clean, and even the lettuce gone, Tom burped and said, "Between the three of us, we've eaten an entire pheasant and then some."

"Where did you get a pheasant?" Lucy asked, stretching her arms and yawning.

"Oh, I had a flock. Only a few remain. There was a time when I used to find animals very easily. Now I have to travel far and wide. I don't know for how long this place can sustain itself. There are less and less resources with each passing day," Tom said.

While Lucy and Tom were talking about food and provisions, Damien asked what had been weighing heavy on his mind.

"Tom. Did Beth and Brad really die? Did a fish really eat them? Did they die like that cop?"

Tom realized what Damien was asking, and there being no easy way to say it, Tom nodded. "Death is an indisputable reality. And yes, those two did die. I want to say that it serves them right, for luring you into danger. But I cannot say that. They were just kids, like you. They didn't know any better. The cop did know better. He deserved his death every bit. But enough death talk. It's time I took you to your bedrooms. Remember, you can roam around the house, but please don't go in the basement. That's where I keep my weapons."

Both kids promised that they wouldn't ever go in the basement. Tom was glad to take their word for it. He took them to a bedroom with two single beds. Then, once he was sure that they were tired and would surely go to sleep, he left them, saying something about going out to run an important errand.

"I don't know why we can't stay here forever. Our

house is so mid compared to this," Damien said, pulling the blanket over his face.

"You know why. Our parents might come back and find us not there. They'd freak out," Lucy said.

"Man, I don't care about our parents. And if they cared about us, they'd find us. We don't even know where they are. Yuri and Tom have been better parents to us than our own mom and dad," Damien said, each word stretching as he grew sleepier.

Lucy didn't reply. Naturally, she disagreed. Her parents weren't entirely bad. There had been good times, times when her mother would treat her to a trip to the mall and buy her the things she wanted. Times when Damien would play catch with Dad. Times when the entire family would watch a movie together. Granted, those times were very few and very far between, but it would be a disservice to the memory of her parents if she didn't recount those instances.

Perhaps, in those moments, her parents had their own metanoias, and wanted to be good parents for a change.

———

Lucy woke up with a start as the door closed. The lights were on in the room. But Damien wasn't in his bed. The clock showed that it was four in the morning. Lucy groaned and got out of bed. The door had only just closed, meaning Damien would've just gone out. She had to keep an eye on him, and maybe twist his ear for disturbing some much needed, dreamless sleep.

"Damien!" Lucy hissed as she saw her brother turning a corner in the hallway. She didn't have enough time to put on her shoes, but she wasn't entirely worried about that. The house was carpeted. The hallways were warm. The rooms were vast, the way to them familiar, intuitive.

Lucy ran around the hallway and intercepted Damien as he was about to open a door that presumably led to the basement.

"Stop, Damien!" Lucy reached for his sleeve, but he was quicker. He was already through the door. Lucy gritted her teeth and raced after him. She wondered wildly why Tom hadn't locked the basement if he had explicitly forbidden them to go down there.

She climbed down the steps after Damien, her heart sinking as she realized why he was going down there in the first place. He was not deterred by anything that Yuri or Tom had said. He would get his hands on a gun and he would deliver it to Ron and the other kids of that class.

She also knew why Damien was so pressed to do that.

There were skeletons in her parents' closet that she had the misfortune of being privy to. Skeletons that were closer to real corpse remains than social stigma. She knew Damien knew too. What she didn't know was how Ron knew.

"Damien!" Lucy whispered, reaching the end of the stairs.

Now she regretted not wearing her shoes or slippers. The carpet ended with the wooden staircase. The floor of the basement was cold stone.

"Damien?"

"What is it?" Damien scoffed. "Why did you have to come after me? Can't you ever leave me alone and let me do something? You know I need to do this. Go back up and pretend that I'm sleeping in bed."

"You know I can't let you do that! And you better not give me any of that lip. I'm your elder sister," Lucy said, trying to feign bravery against the utter dark of the basement. There were no windows nor any light sources. They were standing by the stairs, and the only light that came was from the ajar door upstairs.

Damien reached for the switches and turned them on. Almost immediately, there was a sound of loud buzzing, and several light bulbs turned on. They were not fixed in the ceiling or in the walls. They were hanging from wires, swaying idly, casting oscillatory shadows in the basement.

It was by no means a small basement. In fact, now that Lucy could see, she could also understand that the basement spanned the entire length and breadth of the house. Along the stone walls of the basement, there were racks upon racks of weapons, including rifles, pistols, shotguns, and machine guns. There were crates of ammunition, grenades, and other manner of firepower stacked along the walls.

Broad columns, twelve of them, formed the foundations of the house. They were made of the same stone as the floor and were dug deep into the ground. They reminded Lucy of ancient trees with enormous trunks.

And yet, now that she stood there, holding her brother's arm so that he wouldn't run freely about the basement, she could see that this place wasn't as innocuous as met the eye. There was, in the far distance, a table with bloodied equipment. Razors, saws, pliers, knives. She had once spied her father watching an action movie where the hero was being interrogated with such tools.

Her eyes followed the swaying light and came to the large splatters on the other side. Splatters of red on the floor, on the walls, on the stone pillars.

Lucy gripped Damien tighter, who was, all of a sudden, in no mood to explore the basement candidly.

"Come on. Let's go. We're not supposed to be here," Lucy said.

"I... Okay," Damien whispered.

Lucy's eyes caught something hidden behind a pillar. She knew she shouldn't step into the basement, but she couldn't help herself. After all, now that she was here... She stepped to the side to see what was hidden behind one of the pillars.

It was a large rusted cage, and now that she had taken a step to the side, she could see that a similar cage hid behind each pillar, and it wasn't mere rust on it that was giving the corroded metal that color. It was blood. She looked at the floors of the cages and saw bones. Bones and entrails that did not look like they belonged to animals.

The door to the basement closed shut with a loud bang.

Lucy gasped and sped up the stairs, trying to open the door. It didn't budge. Damien raced up to help her. Together, the two of them turned the knob, pushed the door, and when nothing worked, they started kicking it and screaming at the top of their voice.

"I think I saw a trapdoor leading out of the basement," Damien whimpered.

"Now you're being useful?! Whose idea was it to come down here?!" Lucy slapped his shoulder, hard. Like her mother would.

Damien's eyes glistened with tears of fear and guilt, his lower lip quivering. "I'm sorry. I had to get the gun."

"Well, take your sorry and shove it where the sun don't shine," Lucy said, repeating something she'd heard her father say when he'd been on a call with someone. She didn't know what it meant.

Resigning herself to a fate of being trapped in the basement, she climbed down the stairs again and studied the strange place, looking for trapdoors.

What she found were chains wedged in the walls, as if this was not a basement but a torture dungeon. There was more dried blood on the walls.

"I don't think Tom is a good man," Damien spoke low, staring at a wall studded with axes, daggers, and other such medieval weaponry.

Something suddenly shrieked in an inhuman way, making Lucy jump. She turned around and saw that there was a large crate by the wall next to the stairs, a crate that she hadn't seen up until now. It had holes in it and was taller than them.

The cage rattled. Muffled screams came from it.

Lucy stepped closer and saw that an eye was staring at her from one of the holes. From other holes, bruised fingers peeked out, their nails missing, their skin ripped.

"Run!" Damien yelled, taking her hand and rushing toward the trapdoor that he had sighted earlier. It was at an angle with stairs leading up to it. It was their best bet for escaping the dungeon.

Lucy ran, screaming, her mind unable to comprehend what this basement was being used for, what was in the crate, and who the dead body parts in the cages belong to.

Damien leaped up the stairs and pried the trapdoor open. He pushed it with both hands.

It opened into the side garden.

But there stood someone barring the way.

A blood-drenched robe-wearing man with a red hood over his entire head, with just two slits for eyeholes. He was grotesque, deeply scarred along his forearms, and holding a long, curved sword that was the same size as him. The sword was covered in dried blood.

He was an executioner, Damien realized, and this was his dungeon.

The hood over his head was triangular. It dangled forward as he swung his sword and aimed to slice Lucy in half.

Damien threw her back. She fell on her back and hit her head against one of the pillars.

Damien, knowing that this was his fault and that if they were to die, the blame would be entirely on him, ran to the side and picked up a revolver from a weapons rack that only had revolvers and pistols. He didn't know that the gun was loaded. Nor did he know that the safety was off. He most certainly didn't anticipate that when he'd pull the trigger, the gun would fly and hit his face.

His aim was terrible. The executioner turned in his direction and strode while Damien recoiled from the brutal force with which the revolver had hit his nose.

But now Damien knew, and knowing what to anticipate, he, with his bleeding face and broken nose, aimed the revolver with both hands and pulled the trigger.

This time he did not miss. The bullet soared through the air and hit the executioner, but nowhere that counted. It struck his sword and deflected into the room, its echo resounding in the basement.

The executioner closed the distance and grabbed Damien by the throat, lifting him up in the sky and pinning him against the wall.

This blood-drenched, red-robed nightmare of a man aimed his sword's point at Damien and pressed the tip against his throat, drawing blood.

Damien cried out in pain. Behind the executioner, Lucy was unmoving but still breathing.

Damien started crying, but no voice came out of his throat. It was being crushed by the merciless murderer.

"Please," he croaked. "Don't do this."

Eyes went wide behind the mask, the tight grip loosened. Damien collapsed on the floor, his body badly hurt and throbbing with pain.

The executioner raised his sword to strike Damien.

Damien held up his hand, tears streaming down his face. The nightmare executioner was taller than any man he had ever seen, and there was no escaping him. He might well be the cause of the fog and the evil animals prowling about.

"Don't do this to us, please," Damien wept, holding his hands up. "You don't know just how much we have been through." As he pleaded, barriers that had been built around old memories started to break from stress. "Our parents tortured us. Our parents starved us in the basement. They broke Lucy's arm. I have a scar on the back of my head where my dad hit me with a whiskey bottle and broke it against my skull. You think you're tough shit, scaring us, hunting us? We're miserable enough as it is. Go find our parents and kill them if you want. They're the evil ones! What have we done to deserve this?"

The sword came down with brute force and landed with a clatter next to Damien.

The executioner roared gutturally and punched the stone wall, then lifted his sword again and walked to the large crate. He tore it open with his arm and pulled out the burned, scarred, blood-soaked, stripped-to-the-muscle body of the person trapped within.

The person could not form any word. He lay down on the floor, begging wordlessly, screaming, yelling, and the executioner kept bringing his sword down upon him again and again, chopping away limbs, splitting his torso open, tearing his legs into bits, until the tortured man was certainly dead.

Damien got up, crying, sobbing, and went to Lucy, who was beginning to stir, her eyes fluttering.

"Come!" he cried, and pulled at her. She rose to her feet, screaming as she saw the torn corpse behind her and the executioner standing over it silently, sword in hand. He was staring dead-eyed at the two kids as they ran up the stairs and escaped through the trapdoor.

Going back in the manor was out of the question. Damien held onto Lucy with one hand and flailed the gun with the other.

"Do you have the lamp?" Damien yelled.

"No!" she cried out.

Damien didn't care. He had a gun and he knew how to use it. Besides, the light of day was beginning to creep through the fog.

When they reached the wrought-iron gate, a blood-soaked Tom appeared out of thin air, panting, bruised.

"What did I tell you about the basement!?" Tom cried as he fell on his face. Lucy's lamp fell from his hand and rolled on the ground. Lucy immediately picked it up.

"Tom!" Damien reached out, but Lucy held him back.

"Run and don't ever come back here!" Tom panted. "I don't want to see you here again!"

"We can't leave you alone!" Damien protested. "The executioner is still there."

"I'll deal with him!" Tom said, getting up and

pushing Lucy and Damien out the gate. "Go home. Keep to the roads. Don't come back to the manor. I shouldn't have brought you here. I'm sorry."

"Tom!" Damien called, but it was Lucy's turn to pull her brother. He broke into tears at the thought of leaving Tom alone with the butcher in the basement.

"At least you got what you wanted!" Lucy scolded, her hand on the scruff of his neck as she pulled him violently.

Damien, in tears, his breath hitching, looked at his hands.

True enough. He still held the revolver. It still had four bullets in it.

The two children walked back to town in the light of their lamp. Around them, things snarled, shadows lurked, eyes peeped from behind trees, but they didn't stop. They went home and locked the door.

Suffice it to say, they didn't go to school that day.

Uncle Tommy

Everywhere she looked, she could see the executioner. He was always standing there, an inch away from where the periphery of her vision ended. When she walked, she could hear the rattle of his breath behind her. If she closed her eyes, she could imagine his blood-soaked hands upon her, choking the life out of her.

This won't do, she tried to tell herself as she jumped at the sight of someone standing in the kitchen behind the ajar door. When she turned the light on with shaking hands, she saw that it was just the mop that she'd placed there herself. The mop's shadow had been cast into a disproportionate length, the inverted mop head looking like the hood of the executioner.

Oh, this won't do at all, she repeated as she grabbed a banana and a glass of cold milk—her breakfast. The desire to tend to her stomach by way of making something delicious had been driven out of her and it did not look like it'd ever come back.

Damien, it appeared, was going through something similar. He had not gotten out of bed, even though there was no fog outside today. The sky was still gray, and the cold was still bitter as ever, but at least everything was clear.

She sat there at the lonesome dining table, eating her banana, drinking cold milk, running last night through her mind. Before the basement, things had been going what her mother sometimes liked to call "peachy keen." *Peachy keen, Avril Lavigne,* her mother used to say when she was in a good mood. Whatever that meant. Lucy didn't know who Avril Lavigne was and what she had to do with things being peachy keen.

But the manor of Tom had been peachy keen, indeed. The rooms had been like those of a palace. The food was warm and expertly cooked. None of the amateur cooking that Lucy had recently started doing.

Why did Damien have to do that? And would his not doing so have changed the outcome? Would the executioner still have come? Would they have been in their beds, sleeping soundly, when he attacked them?

She shuddered at the thought. Her eyes strayed to the gun on the coffee table. She had wanted to throw it into the fog, but Damien had put up a fight. Not with his hands or with his body, but with his pleading. She couldn't understand just how much and how deep the kids in his class had hurt him, terrorized him, to warrant him smuggling a firearm into school. When he was inconsolable, she met him halfway. He couldn't take the gun into the bedroom. It had to be somewhere where they could both see it. They wouldn't touch it. And when he'd take it to school, they'd take the bullets out of it. The other students might have asked for a gun, but they had said nothing about bullets.

The gun's bore was a sentient eye, inspecting Lucy.

When she couldn't take it any longer, she went over to it and placed a cushion on top of it. Once, she'd spied on her parents watching a movie called *Nick of Time*, some strange old movie where the guy used to silence his pistols by placing pillows against them. Lucy had stood in the doorway for a good twenty minutes watching the movie before her mother realized that she was there and dealt with her with a prompt slap across the face and a warning that she'd not get her next three meals if she kept this up.

There had been many movies and TV shows that she'd snuck glimpses of over the years. Sometimes, she saw things that she'd rather not have seen, things that kept her awake at night. They were fond of horror movies, her parents, and sometimes invited friends over to watch the latest horror flick with them. When they had friends around, they couldn't openly beat Lucy or Damien if they found them sneaking around. And by the time their friends were gone, her parents were either too tired or too drunk to care if anyone had snuck around.

Sometimes Lucy wished there were tunnels underneath the house that led all over the world. A tunnel to China. A tunnel to Europe. A tunnel to Africa.

Wouldn't that be the coolest? That way she'd get to explore the world and be back home without anyone finding out that she'd gone.

She chuckled depressively as she walked away from the cushion-covered gun. She was standing by the door, wondering why Tom had given free reign of his house's basement to a murderer, when there was a hurried knock at the door. The knock was familiar. Four quick raps.

"Come on, come on, or else Uncle Tommy's gonna freeze out on the porch!"

Lucy's eyes lit up with joy as she recognized Uncle Tommy's voice. He was her father's younger brother. Almost too young. He was still in his thirties. Uncle Tommy was always a good time, and whenever he was around, the kids felt protected, because he'd never let anyone so much as raise their voice at the kids, let alone hit them. He'd take the kids out and show them a good time around town. They'd slam bumper cars at Fun Land, Pinebrook's conservative idea of an amusement park. He'd hit all the metal plates in the middle with the air gun and win them each a teddy bear. The memory of Uncle Tommy was inextricably linked with the smell of cotton candy, hot dogs with plentiful mustard, and 7-Eleven Slurpees. He insisted they were better than anything sold at Fun Land, and always argued with the guy at the entrance to let them bring outside food in. When nothing worked, Uncle Tommy would slip the guy a twenty and tell him to look the other way. The guy would.

She ran to the door and opened it wide. It banged

against the wall. She jumped at the man standing in the doorway. He already had his arms open to receive her.

"Oh, Luce!" he said, squeezing the air out of her as he hugged her. She didn't care. Breathing was not as important as being in Uncle Tommy's comforting presence. She had her arms around his neck and had him in just as tight of a hug.

Uncle Tommy hugged her for another full minute before walking inside and putting her down.

He had long hair that curled in regal locks. A permanent, good-natured smile danced on his face. He always sported the same five o'clock shadow on his face, but it seemed to work in his favor. It gave him a devil may care look that Lucy associated with fun times, as opposed to the clean shaven, all business no pleasure look of her father. Despite them being brothers, Uncle Tommy was nothing like her father.

"Hey there, kiddo," he said, beaming at her, fishing for something in the pocket of his overlarge hooded puffer jacket. He looked like a walking, talking parachute in that jacket. Underneath, he wore torn jeans, a fashion choice that Lucy never understood, these jeans having gone from cool to uncool way before when she was born. "Dreadful weather we're having, isn't it?"

"Uncle Tommy!" Lucy's eyes brimmed with tears as she clung to his legs and buried her face in the warm part of the jacket. "You don't even know what is happening."

"Well, I did find out that your parents went and did a runner. Typical. Can't understand them. I never did. I'm sorry it took me this long to come back. I told you I had business in San Francisco, didn't I? I think I did. Well, the VCs sent me on a trip to China. Can you believe it? Man, I don't even like China, but apparently they needed someone to consolidate the Chinese market, and they couldn't think of a better person than yours truly."

"You were in China?!"

"Yes, Lucy Goosey. Well. I wasn't just in China. You know me. When I'm in China, of course I'm going to Hong Kong. I got college friends who live there. And, of course, when we college friends get together, we kinda have to go to Singapore, because guess what? You think Los Angeles and New York are a good time? You haven't seen how they do things in Singapore. It's like another world there. And once I'd concluded business in Singapore, I came back here and called your father. I wanted to give him an earful for not responding to any of my calls. And then I find out that Pinebrook's been hit by this epidemic. Some localized climate catastrophe that blew over from Lake Michigan or something. I'm not sure I understand it. But they're saying it's happened before in other parts of the world across history. It just sucks that it had to be Pinebrook, you know? Place looks like hell."

"You have no idea," Lucy said, bursting into tears.

"Oh, sweetheart, oh, no," Uncle Tommy soothed her, going down on his knees and wiping her tears with his palm, giving her a kiss on her forehead, and then offering her the familiar comfort of his hug. "It's gonna be okay, I swear. These things happen. That's life. It's not like we're all here living out our utopic fantasies. We're braver for it, wiser, stronger. You know? Suffering ain't just arbitrary. And it's never eternal. This storm will end. The town will go back to normal. Your parents will come back from the hospital."

"How do you know they're at the hospital?" Lucy asked, wiping her eyes.

"Oh, the hospital got in touch with me once I was stateside. They told me they'd been trying to get in touch with me, what with me being your father's emergency contact, but they were so overstretched and under-manned that they were only getting a chance to do it now. I came as fast as I could."

"Uncle Tommy!" Damien hollered from the stairs and then raced down to fling himself at his favorite and only uncle.

"Hey there, Buster Scruggs!" Uncle Tommy had the air driven out of him as Damien collided into his chest. "You're getting real tall and heavy, kid. Damn near killed your uncle with that tackle. Gonna be a great football player one day. I'm thinking linebacker or quarterback. Whaddayasay, Lucy Goosey?"

Before either of them could respond, Uncle Tommy began procuring the goods he'd stowed in his jacket. Candies, jellies, and chocolates by the fistfuls. Soon enough, the children had their hands full, but Uncle Tommy wasn't done. He took out two more things. A strange box with markings upon it and a golden bracelet.

"This box here, Damien," Uncle Tommy said, handing him the box, "is a real special thing. See, it's got this viewing hole inside and this other hole that brings in light. If you peek inside, you'll see all kinds of shapes. It's like being on DMT."

"What's DMT?" Lucy asked.

"Oh, don't mind that," Uncle Tommy said, chuckling, scratching his head awkwardly.

"DMT stands for don't mind that?" Damien asked as he put the box next to his eye. He exclaimed and laughed, "Oh, holy moly, there's like a billion colors in there! They're moving, Uncle Tommy!"

"That's a kaleidoscope, kiddo," Uncle Tommy said, grinning. "And this, young lady, is a mood bracelet. It looks gold, and sure enough, it is twenty-four karat gold, but do you see that line in the middle? Now that line is entirely made of thermosensitive crystals. I'm sure it's quartz. It's almost like magic, you see. Put it on and I'll tell you what it does."

The bracelet was beautiful. It clung comfortably to her skin once it was around her wrist. The gold glimmered as she twisted it, but then there was another light. A pink light emanating from the middle of the bracelet. Lucy gasped.

"Pinks means you're happy. White means you're bored. Yellow is for excitement. Red is for angry. Purple is for mysterious. And if it's black, that means you're stressed. It should go green when you're feeling nothing at all. These were big when I was a kid. We called them mood rings. Each color for each mood."

"It's glowing blue now!" Lucy said.

"Oh, yes, that means you're at peace. You're calm," Uncle Tommy said. "It's a good way to keep in check with how you're feeling. You know, we human beings, we often feel confused at how we're feeling. Well, now you got one less thing to worry about. Oh, and if it glows extra red, it means you're hangry. Which is a mixture of angry and hungry. Just saying."

The children, excited with their gifts and snacks, momentarily forgot that they'd almost died last night. It was only when their uncle went to the sofa and propped his legs on the coffee table that both of them turned to look at him taking the cushion away from the table, exposing the gun lying there.

"Kids? What is that thing doing here?" Uncle Tommy asked warily, holding one hand to keep the kids away, and the other picking the gun up. "Why do you have a gun at the house? Whose is it?"

Damien and Lucy shared a look, instantaneous telepathy taking place between their minds. Tell him or don't tell him? It's only so long that we can't tell him. We have to tell him. He's the one person to trust. More trustable than Tom, whose real name wasn't even Tom, it was the Other Man. The Other Man who was harboring a freaking executioner in his mansion's basement. There were bones in cages. There was a man trapped in a box. The executioner killed him.

Their faces went white. They nodded at each other. This had to be shared. He was their way out. He was the guy who'd take them out of town and away from this hellhole.

So they did.

They told him things in quick succession, beginning

with the mist, then the monsters, then the cop, then the Other Man, then the birds and the beasts, the lamp and its magic, the angler fish that killed two children, Yuri, and finally, the mansion with the executioner.

"You're not lying," Uncle Tommy whispered, the fingers of both his hands dug into the side of his head. "This really happened. I can see it on your faces."

It was relief beyond any relief they'd ever known to have Uncle Tommy believe their stories so readily.

"I'm so sorry that you had to go through all of that. But don't worry about none of that. I'm here now. I'll take care of you. This...this has happened before. There was a time some years ago when a pandemic forced everyone into their homes, and you know what happened? Tigers started roaming the streets of India. Markhors descended from the mountains and started skittering around Swat. In America, you saw bears and reindeers roaming abandoned towns. Dogs too."

"It's not natural," Lucy said, shaking her head. "It's not like that. There was an angler fish, swimming out of water. It was...dark magic. It was something out of a nightmare."

"Yeah. That part doesn't make any sense to me. And the bird tore off the cop's head, you say? That isn't natural either. Hmm. If I said I've seen stranger things, I'd be lying," he said, rubbing his palms together. "None of this made it to the news. Whatever the heck's happening here, they're keeping it hush-hush. It's almost like *Resident Evil.* I wouldn't expect you kids to understand."

"About the games?" Damien blurted out before realizing he'd snitched on himself. He clasped both hands on his mouth, his face burning red.

"Damien! You've playing the *Resident Evil* games?" Uncle Tommy asked, bewildered. "Those are not games for kids."

"Yeah, but...they're fun!" Damien said, grinning.

"I don't condone this behavior, young man," Uncle Tommy said, wagging his finger. "Seeing so much blood and gore at such a young age—"

"We've seen more blood and gore in real life than in those videogames," Damien said, crossing his arms.

"Fair enough," Uncle Tommy said. "But since you already know the story, here's what I'm thinking happened. There must've been some kind of government experiment happening here. Like, you know, the terrible sort of research they do. Animating corpses. Trying to open portals to other dimensions. Time travel. Maybe something to do with nuclear fusion. I don't know. Maybe it's one of those experiments gone awry and all those anomalies that you're observing, all the people getting sick—all of that's just part of it."

Lucy thought that it was certainly a good explanation for everything that had happened. This theory also explained the angler fish. If a government experiment had failed, then there could be pockets of other dimensions hosting nightmare creatures all over Pinebrook. Maybe all the strange fog monsters had come out of similar dimensional pockets.

"But enough of this depressing crap!" Uncle Tommy

slapped his hand on his thigh and got up. "It may be bleak, but there's people outside still, which means it's not *that* dangerous to go out. Come on, kids. We're going to paint the town red. This town looks like it desperately needs color! And if we come across the executioner or anything dreadful like that, we're going to run them over with the car! How about that? Nothing's going to harm you while Uncle Tommy's around!"

The kids chirped with gleeful excitement, getting ready to head out into town with Uncle Tommy. Even though the day was gray as ever, there was none of that fog outside.

It was as if Uncle Tommy was a walking, talking lamp.

Lucy's bracelet glowed hot pink as she stepped into the living room some fifteen minutes later, her hair done, her best clothes on, and a bright disposition on her face, a sign that she'd somehow put the recent harrowing memories out of her mind. Uncle Tommy had that effect on people.

Somehow, he always did.

Try as she did, she couldn't remember a single bad thing about him.

FUN LAND

Lucy and Damien were both racing to see who'd fill their Slurpee cups faster. Lucy had gone with cherry, and Damien was filling his with blue raspberry. This 7-Eleven was on the other side of town, as were most good things—finer restaurants, the KenTacoHut, and Fun Land. All of these things were on Neibolt Road, which just a few miles ahead merged into the highway and then became part of the interstate. The richer suburb of Pinebrook was also on Neibolt Road, as were several choice designer shops that were expensive for the rest of town, but not for the people who lived in the neighborhood.

Most of Pinebrook pretended that Neibolt Road didn't exist except for when they'd get their paychecks or end-of-year bonuses. Then, Neibolt Road not only existed, but thrived for all of the town. As such, Lucy and Damien had only been here a few times, and those, too, were few and far between.

Despite the dismalness outside, the 7-Eleven retained its nostalgic, bright aisles packed with snacks and other gas station grocery. Uncle Tommy was by the counter, talking to the shopkeeper about the sorry state of Pinebrook.

"Oh, that's nothing. You tourist types think that's bad. Where were you a week ago when the fog was so bad that—" the shopkeeper said, pointing a finger at Tommy.

"Yeah. Yeah. Go cry a river about it. You're stuck here. I'm not. Call me tourist all you want. I'm not the one who can't leave this place at a moment's notice," Tommy said, then nodded at the two children. "I'm only here for them."

"Them? Who are they to you?" the shopkeeper asked, eyebrow raised, both forearms over the counter, inspecting the kids closely.

Uncle Tommy pushed him away, saying, "Important."

The kids came back with their Slurpees, sporting wide grins on their faces. They also had their arms full of things that had caught their fancy in the store. Uncle Tommy never said no.

He ruffled their hair and paid the guy with a fifty, bidding him to keep the change.

"You're so rich," Damien commented casually, all the while slurping from the enormous cup that was more the size of a jug.

"True, true," Uncle Tommy chuckled, opening the door of his Ford Raptor. "All because I bought all that crypto in 2011. Eh. More people need to know how easy making money is. You just make it. That's all there is to it."

"I wish you would teach that to Mom and Dad. They're always arguing over the bills, and then Mom..." Lucy began, but for the life of her could not remember what it was her mother had done that had deeply troubled her.

"Don't you worry about your mom just now. I'm in charge of you young'uns while they're gone. What else is family for? We're going to Fun Land, and when you're at Fun Land, you hang your troubles at the door. Capeesh?"

Laughing, they got in the truck and drove off toward Fun Land. Since there was no fog outside tonight, the moon hung in all its lunar splendor, a giant crystal ball on the horizon, so close and humongous, yet hundreds of thousands of miles away. Moonlight fell on Lucy's face, who sat shotgun in the truck, sipping away at her Slurpee, making a mental note to brush her teeth extralong after she got home. Every few seconds, she'd reel from the sourness of her drink, but it was sourness that she derived great pleasure from.

And then the magnificent, colorful, monolithic board lit by hundreds of LED lights and bulbs proclaiming the name *FUN LAND* jutted out from behind tall oaks and maples. There was an image of two children hysterically laughing at a jester donning red and black juggling several bowling pins. The children were laughing so hard they had tears in their eyes, and their cheeks were pulled so far as to show their gums and their epiglottis on the billboard. The jester had bells on the many points of his hat. Behind him, there was a Ferris wheel, a carousel, and arcade machines bumping into each other in place of dodgems.

Carnival music and the smell of cotton candy traveled inside the truck, making the children giddy with excitement. The forty-foot-tall Ferris wheel had multicolored LED strips and fluorescent tubes all along its length. It was dizzying to look at all its many colors as it spun. Damien recalled that this was how it had looked in his kaleidoscope box. A giant octopus ride rose into the sky, all the miniature octopi whirring as the ride rose into the air and tilted at a dangerous angle.

A log flume traveled down the slope, throwing water everywhere. A tiny train with its track well above the rest of the amusement park zoomed at dangerous angles. There was no one sitting in it, just like there was no one in the rest of the rides. The park was completely empty.

Uncle Tommy parked the truck right beside the entrance and jumped out.

"I may have twisted someone's arm to open the place," he said, grinning at the kids.

"No way you did that," Lucy said, her mouth hanging open at the regal medieval carousel with knights on horses, unicorns, centaurs, and a very happy minotaur shaking hands with a mermaid.

"Of course I did. Anything for my niece and nephew. You know, when you were born, I wanted to name you Denise, but your mother insisted on Lucy. And I wanted to call you Denephew. But your dad was like, enough with your jokes, Tommy. He's Damien."

The kids understood it a second late, but when they did, they burst out laughing. Uncle Tommy ushered them through the pink and white iron gate of Fun Land. Two life-sized statutes of humanoid labradors in mime costumes stood frozen at the entrance, bowing with their little red mime caps in their paws. There were all sorts of animal statues in whimsical costumes all over the park. Monkeys wearing suits. Owls wearing robes. A goat in a German frock holding two beer mugs. Pigs in overalls chewing on hay.

"Your tickets, my lord, my lady." Uncle Tommy procured two tickets that said, *Express entry to all rides, all inclusive.*

"But there's no attendants..." Lucy said, realizing that there was no one at any of the rides' entrances.

"Oh, I don't see how that's going to be any issue," their uncle said, promptly whistling. Much to their surprise, a very old man in a red uniform and a cap appeared out from the main ticket booth.

"Meet Reeves. Reeves used to operate this park when I was a kid. How long's it been, Reeves?"

"Fifty years."

"When God made this guy, he forgot to put in the quit, if you know what I'm saying. He opens the park, closes it, and knows how to operate most rides. And the ones he doesn't... Well, we're intelligent people. I'm sure we can figure it out."

The kids looked at the pale, old, gray man with his

white beard and bags under his eyes. He gave them a weak smile, revealing yellow dentures. Damien smiled back nervously. But that was the start and the end of his nervousness.

This was a dream come true for him and Lucy. To have the entire park to themselves. They could go on all the rides without ever having to wait in line.

As the kids got on the pirate ship, each sitting on their own side to keep the "balance," Uncle Tommy fetched himself a cowboy hat from the kiosk and ate a corndog. No rides for him, he'd insisted. They gave him vertigo, he claimed.

Damien yelled at the top of his lungs, as did Lucy. And at the apex of the pirate ship's swing, they felt infinite. Like things were going to be okay. In fact, things were already okay. They were having fun. The horrors they'd faced were just minor inconveniences. In fact, they might not even be real. So thought Lucy as the ship swung and she likened herself to a strong, young pirate captain who was put in charge of this whole ship, and if she so wanted, she could veer it into the sky and soar away as far as she liked to.

After enjoying seven of the rides, the kids caught their breath on a bench overlooking the Ferris wheel. Uncle Tommy sat in the middle, helping himself to the popcorn and cotton candy he'd bought them both. Now that they were all out of Slurpees, they were making do with Coke to wash down the buttery popcorn.

"So...what are we thinking, turkey legs or hotdogs next?"

"Hot-diggety-dog!" Damien cackled, biting a large piece of the red cloud that was his cotton candy. It tasted like raspberries. Everything tasted of raspberries after the enormous drink he'd finished. Even the popcorn.

"Know what I think?"

"Tell us, Uncle Tommy."

"I think that love, fame, money, and power are the four quadrants on the graph that dictate a man's life. And that innocence is the greatest of powers. That once it's lost, it can never be regained. That's why Buddhist priests and Sufi mystics alike revere the holiness of children. You know what I'm saying? It's okay if you don't. It's just that I don't have someone I can actually talk to about these things without them judging me. I don't want to be invited to podcasts and sound like a conceited know-it-all. It's just...talk. Before podcasts and social media and all this nonsense, when two people talked, they just talked. You're out there monetizing conversations. What's that about?"

That was the best thing about Uncle Tommy. Both children thought so. He never talked down to you as if you were a kid. He talked to you like you could understand. Some of their previous conversations had been about topics too complex for them to understand, such as Big Pharma, the actual reality behind climate change being much more worse than the news let on but also quite easily reversible if the bigwigs actually gave a crap, and how legacy media was a psyop that was being dismantled by social media, which was a different kind of psyop. Needless to say, Lucy and Damien didn't listen to him for the purpose of understanding; they listened because it sounded nice when he talked, and because he gave them respect when he talked more than any respect their parents had ever given them.

"I think some people are quite stupid," Damien said, staring into the distance, thinking about the kids in his class, and the fact that the deadline for showing up with the gun was tomorrow.

"I think you've summed up the human condition and human experience on this here planet earth as succinctly as one could. Some people are quite stupid. And other people are more than just stupid. They're dangerous. Far more dangerous than a clever and dangerous man is a stupid and dangerous man, for the clever man aims his danger with precision. The stupid man is a ticking time bomb, destroying all those around him," Uncle Tommy said.

Lucy, who was beginning to get a little bored with the high-brow nature of the conversation, changed the topic ever so subtly. "Is it true you're leaving? I think I heard you say something to the shopkeeper."

"Leaving? But I only just got here. Besides, if I leave, who's going to take care of y'all? The Other Man? You wanna know what I think? I think he's a delusional homeless person squatting in the manor, trying to make sense of this madness with his own internal brand of madness. No. I'm not leaving. Not until I know you're safe and your parents are back. Well, I might stick around some even after they're back. They need their ears twisted and a hard conversation about how to handle their children, and that if they don't need 'em, well, I'll take 'em. You'd come with Uncle Tommy, wouldn't you? I'll take good care of you both. I promise."

Damien, too overcome by the extending of such a warm gesture, hugged his uncle and said nothing. Lucy gave him a sad smile and then nodded.

"Hey now. There's no need to cry at Fun Land," he said, wiping her tear away and pulling her close for a hug. Both children were now under his arms. "Lookit. I'm mother hen."

Lucy laughed, and then wiped the other tear away from her face. She wanted to tell him that no one had ever cared for her like he had. That his being here made Pinebrook feel less dreary. That when he left, she'd very much love to take Damien and go with him. Wherever he'd go, they'd go. It'd be the perfect life.

"All right then. One more for the road, and then we gotta go home," Uncle Tommy said, getting up and heading over to the hotdog stand. The old caretaker of the park was there, making hotdogs. He took three hotdogs from Reeves and brought them over. "What? Aren't you gonna protest? I thought kids protested when—"

"This is more than enough," Lucy said, gratefully taking the hotdog. "We've been out for hours, it feels like. Besides, Uncle Tommy, we have to go to school in the morning. Can't skip school two days in a row. I think that he's a little crazy, the Other Man, but he's also wise. See, we're pretending that Pinebrook is fine, and it almost looks fine. I can hear people talking to each other somewhere close by. The sky's visible, and it's blue. I think if we keep pretending that all's well, we'll attract more normal stuff. Like you. We didn't know you were coming. We just...hoped for things to get better. Maybe tomorrow things go better at school. Maybe the murder of Beth and Brad—"

"I wouldn't worry too much about...you know... murders. I got the lay of the land in the time I've been here. I think that people here know that death lurks around every corner. And that death is to be expected. You know, like with that cop guy who tried to chase you but then got killed by the bird. I suspect it has something to do with the cell towers. Mind control of the masses— or, you know, whoever remains. But we can have this conversation later. Have you decided on the last ride?"

Damien and Lucy, glad to be free of such a burden-some topic of conversation, grinned eagerly and nodded their heads at the Ferris wheel.

"All right then. Reeves?"

Reeves shook his head and pointed at the Ferris wheel.

"So, the whole thing has been spinning on its own, is what you're trying to say?" Uncle Tommy asked confusedly.

Reeves shrugged.

"All right. You know, I actually interned at Disneyland when I was taking a gap year. I think I know how this works," Uncle Tommy said, heading over to the control booth of the Ferris wheel. After much tinkering with the knobs and the lever, he got the wheel to stop.

"Come on then. I've got it," he said, hunched over the controls, studying them curiously.

Lucy and Damien trusted the man to the point that they got in the nearest cabin and locked the door shut. The whole cabin was made of metal, even the chairs. It was quite uncomfortable to sit on. But their excitement was so profuse that they didn't mind. With their hotdogs half-eaten, they sat down on the seats. Beside the wheel, there was a large lake that had perfectly still water reflecting the night sky and all the many wonderful lights of the amusement park.

"All right, strap in! We're going!" Uncle Tommy yelled from the booth and pulled the lever.

The Ferris wheel went really slow the first time around, giving Lucy plenty of time at the apex to look around town, at the few cars that drove down Neibolt, and at the dim orange lights of the restaurants and shops that were still open at this time of night. But it was the park beneath her, sprawling all around her. Hundreds of blinking lights, the warm and fuzzy music, and the smell of food traveling to her nose.

"Uncle Tommy, go faster! We can take it!" Damien said, holding the metal rods of the cabin tightly.

"Lucy Goosey?" he called out.

She nodded and followed it up by saying, "We can take it. Full speed ahead!"

Lucy was more of a thrill seeker than Damien, but people often overlooked her because she was a girl. But she enjoyed fast rides, and had always wished for the Ferris wheel to be faster.

But nothing had prepared her for just how fast it could get. She hadn't any time to hold onto the rods like Damien, and so when the wheel spun violently, she hit her head against the back of the cabin, and the entire world swirled out of existence, leaving her only one realization as all the lights went out, the fog creeped back in, and the moon—a mere illusion—disappeared with the rest of the sky.

She didn't have an Uncle Tommy.

There were no uncles on either side of the family.

So who was this?

And more importantly, why did she think that she'd always known him? Why had he been so familiar until the moment she hit her head on the railing?

The entire amusement park had gone dark. None of the rides other than the Ferris wheel were working. The Ferris wheel had gone dark and was slowing down. Damien was laughing gleefully, clapping his hands and looking out the cabin's window as they descended.

"One more time, Uncle Tommy!" Damien yelled at the top of his voice.

Lucy's chest squelched with pain, and when she saw that no one was operating the booth, her heart stopped beating for four seconds. She clutched her chest, and then looked at Damien, who was still blissfully ignorant.

"We don't have an Uncle Tommy!" she said, but he

wasn't hearing her. He was still entrapped by the same spell that had worked on her. If it *was* a spell. Whatever it was, it had brought them both out into the middle of the night to this abandoned amusement park. Fog weaved through the metalwork, turning each happy statue into a faceless silhouette.

"What are you talking about? He's standing right there!" Damien pointed at no one in the booth. There wasn't even old man Reeves manning the hotdog cart. Lucy could see the gate of the park from up here, and it was locked and bolted with a padlock and chains. Beyond its perimeter, violent dogs lurked, howling and snapping at each other.

No cars on the road. No lights in the windows that were lit before Lucy hit her head.

With no more music playing in Fun Land, the rusty creaking sound of the Ferris wheel haunted her ears as she realized that the ride was over. The cabin door swung open of its own accord. The lake water was rippling, bubbling.

Damien was looking blissfully at someone who was not standing there.

With terror dissolving Lucy's rationale, she quickly did the only thing that made sense to her fear-maddened mind.

She grabbed Damien's head by a fistful of hair and banged his forehead against the metal rods as hard as she could.

Psyop

Blood dripped from Damien's forehead, bathing his vision in red. As his head spun, the lights that had enamored him all went out, leaving him in darkness. He touched his forehead and looked at the blood on his fingers, then at his sister. Lucy's eyes were red from fright.

"Psyop," Damien whispered. It was the only word that came to his mind. He didn't know the word "irony" just yet, but he felt the emotion just the same; that the person who had taught him all about psyops was never real. Nor were any of the memories associated with him.

"Do you see him still?" Lucy asked.

Damien shook his head, sending blood droplets flying. He opened the cabin door and stepped out, holding his sister's hand.

"Home is miles away. How are we ever going to go back?" Damien asked, his hand shaking, his voice even worse.

"I don't think we're going home. I think whatever brought us here is going to kill us. We're meant to die in this park," Lucy said. Her head throbbed painfully where it had hit the cabin bars.

"It's not just this place playing tricks on us," Damien said. "It's..."

"The Dark Presence," Lucy finished for him. She wasn't one for videogames or movies, but the concept of the Dark Presence had always intrigued her. It was the stuff she couldn't get enough of when it was three a.m. and she had the tablet all to herself. Her TikTok algorithm was composed entirely of creepypasta videos about Slenderman, liminal spaces, backrooms, the blood-stained bride, and the wandering orphans of Roanoke. Amongst many such creepypastas, there was one that she'd watched several videos on, videos that had kept her awake for the rest of the night.

The Dark Presence, a malevolent supernatural and sentient force occupying the Dark Place. The Dark Presence could morph into different creatures, inhabit inanimate objects, corrupt living beings into being its thralls, manipulate reality, and control your thoughts.

Granted, most of these videos were regurgitated fan fiction from the famous *Alan Wake* franchise, but gradually this topic had gained quite the cult following.

Shadows shot across the fog, curling it into snide shapes. Snarls approached them. Lucy held Damien's hand tightly.

"The lamp," she said. "We didn't bring the lamp with us. The Dark Presence is affected by light. We need the lamp. And if we don't have one, we have to create one. The Dark Presence can't get to us."

"I..." Damien stuttered, looking around. Then, just as the distorted shadows closed the distance, he tugged on his sister's hand and ran toward the kiosk. It was wreathed in black vines and devoid of light, but it had a retractable gate. It was the closest structure to them. As claws and arms shot out of the gray mist, Damien shoved his sister into the kiosk and then jumped in after her. He slammed the retractable gate shut and bolted it from the inside. They stood in the middle of the kiosk, amidst abandoned gift items, knickknacks gathering dust, and broken tchotchkes. Lucy slammed the shutter shut.

Charred hands shot out from the space between the retractable gate. Morbid eyes glowed crimson and bore into the children. Smoke rose from the burnt bodies that were trying to get in. They spoke a language of grunts and snarls, roars and growls.

"Something! Anything!" Damien shrieked, looking around the dark kiosk.

Lucy also helped in looking. Underneath the counter, there was a wooden box. She opened it. Inside there were several things laying scattered, but a note lay on top. She squinted as she read what was written on it.

Hey Yuri.

Thanks a million for all the good shit. But I don't got it in me no more, brother. I got no more fight. I can't let these bastards keep terrorizing me every single night. It's lights out for Reeves. I lived a good life.

Fuck this place.

She rifled through the belongings, finding a strange plastic gun with a very short yet wide barrel.

"Damien!" she screamed as she realized that one of the scorched arms had gotten its fingers on the bolt and was turning it open. In another minute, the kiosk would be flooded by these burned beings.

"Flare gun!" Damien said, taking the gun from her. He checked inside. There was a flare already in it. "Stand back."

She stood back and watched as Damien held the flare gun in both hands and aimed it at the door. The door contracted and opened as the arm pulled it. And now they weren't just arms hanging suspended in the dark mist. They were entire bodies rendered black and red from whatever fire had claimed them. They shrieked and stretched their arms out, nothing standing between them and Damien anymore.

Damien pulled the trigger and closed his eyes.

A bright red light shot from the flare gun and threw back the dead crowd as it exploded, the light burning them, blinding them, and driving them away, shrieking, their arms and legs on fire. For a few seconds, the flare shone, driving away the mist, but then, weakened by the impact with the immolated corpses, it snuffed out.

But in the meantime, Lucy had found more useful things in the wooden box. She had found another lamp, one that flickered as it shone, but still worked. There were handheld flares in there as well. Several packs of cigarettes. A lighter. Bottles of vodka. A long roll of cotton.

"I have an idea," she said, giving the flare gun ammo to Damien. He hung it around his shoulder.

She lit the cotton roll with the lighter and let it burn in the wooden box. She turned the lamp off and ran out with Damien.

All around them, the dead were swarming once more, and they were not alone. They had brought with them the unnatural animals that lurked all over town. The commotion had also drawn the attention of the overlarge bird, which sat perched atop the kiosk, its beady eyes studying the bedlam below.

Damien put another round inside the flare gun and shot it into the sky as the madness surrounded them.

The flare burst above them, showering red light all around them, making each of the burnt bodies reel and howl. The bird put its feathers over its eyes to protect itself from the blinding light.

The two kids took advantage of the momentary confusion and ran through the dazed crowd of assembled nightmares.

They paused only when they'd reached the gate of the amusement park, and then they turned just in time to see the wooden box catch fire, making each of the vodka bottles explode, the liquid content inside them bursting into a brilliant ball of flame, setting fire to the entire wooden kiosk and every manner of creature assembled around it.

The bird's wingspan caught fire. It tried to fly away, cawing and screeching, but somewhere near its ascent, it died as a result of its injuries and fell upon the rest of the fire like a crashing airplane.

There was no Ford Raptor parked by the entrance. And as such, no sign of Uncle Tommy.

"WHERE ARE YOU?!" Lucy cried out as the flames died down, leaving nothing but fog monster corpses in their wake. They only lay there aflame, the smell of their burning flesh pungent and revolting.

"WHY DID YOU BRING US HERE? DO YOU WANT TO KILL US? BRING IT!" Damien screamed. His voice vibrated with rage. Fear had become his new normal. Survival was the only way he knew how to live. Instead of crippling fear, he felt agitated. His mind had reached the threshold for misery and terror. The new uncharted territory it was discovering was vengeance.

Vengeance against the forces that had conspired against him and his sister.

"They're all the same," he said, wiping blood and tears from his face and looking at his sister, who seethed with a similar rage. "The fish. The bird and the dogs. Cody too. The executioner. Uncle Tommy. They're all the same."

"I think we can trust Yuri," Lucy said, producing the note and handing it to Damien. "It's because of him we're alive, after all."

"Then maybe we talk to him tomorrow," Damien said, holstering the flare gun. "I think I'll go to school. What are those kids compared to all this crap?"

"For that, we need to get home first," Lucy said, crawling under the gate and appearing on the other side.

Damien did the same. "It's gonna take us hours to walk home."

"Or we can just go to school. It's closer," Damien said. "It's midway between this place and home. We can go there. Yuri will be there in his cozy room. We'll tell him what happened. He'll know what to do."

As they walked away from the amusement park, a lone figure hidden in shadows, still bearing the shape and form of Uncle Tommy, stood watching them go.

He no longer had the warm brown eyes that the children had associated with familial kindness. His eyes were red.

Two tears spilled from his face as he watched the children go. And when they disappeared in the fog, Uncle Tommy receded in the shadows, but not before whispering, "I'm sorry, kids."

————

It was as if the kids had taken care of most of the population of the harrowing creatures that dwelled in town, for the rest of the way they didn't encounter anything out of the ordinary other than the fog itself. The flickering lamp they'd found in the kiosk made quick work of the fog, parting it for them to walk safely through it.

Damien was right. In another forty minutes, they had reached school. And just as he'd assumed, the light was on in one of the rooms. The rest of the school was shrouded in darkness.

Damien knocked on the door. No one appeared. Yuri didn't show up for the next ten minutes.

Lucy pushed the door. It swung open.

"That's strange," she said, looking at Damien.

"He's old," Damien said.

They walked toward Yuri's room.

Lucy opened the door and walked inside. How she wished she hadn't.

Yuri lay there, torn to pieces, his clothes in tatters, his blood sprayed all over the walls. His face was unrecognizably mauled, and there were deep claw gashes in his chest. She could see the ribcage housing his still heart.

Damien wasn't looking at Yuri's mangled corpse. He was staring at the trail of blood leading up the wall. It was splattered as if Yuri had been cut open with a long blade. The blood arced up the wall in long splashes.

It was still wet to the touch.

———

Ron looked pale and tired. The rest of the class bore similar fatigue upon their faces. When Damien walked into class, they discovered that he, too, looked insanely drained.

What they didn't know was that he'd spent the entire night cleaning Yuri's room with his sister, and after they'd cleaned the room, they'd put Yuri on a tarp and pulled his corpse outside of the school and laid him next to the bleacher's entrance. They'd meant to bury him, but neither of them knew the first thing about digging a grave or burying a body.

"We must put some kind of cloth on him. As a sign of respect," Damien had said. "I can't look at him like this."

"We can burn his body," Lucy said, staring in the dead man's eyes. Damien didn't object. So they set fire to his corpse and stood there silently by all the burning wood consuming his flesh.

Then they went back in to clean the rest of the room.

When they came out again to check if the fire was going, there was no sign of the fire. And there was no sign of Yuri's burned corpse being there at all. Lucy and Damien were not surprised. They had already lived through a day's worth of fatal gaslighting. What was one more body disappearing after all they had experienced?

"You brought the gun?" Ron leaned toward Damien as he sat down.

"Yeah."

"Good. I was worried you weren't going to make good on your end of the deal. It would have been a shame if I'd had to spill all the shit I know about your mom."

Damien's eyes turned dark as he reached forward and grabbed Ron's face and squeezed it.

"You don't want to mess with me," Damien growled. "Not now. Not ever. Got it?" He shoved Ron's face back harshly.

To his surprise, Ron, despite his fatigue, was smiling.

"There he is. There's that fire that we've been looking for. I was wondering when you'd grow a spine."

Damien scoffed and crossed his arms, snapping, "Are you even real?"

"What the hell's that supposed to mean?" Ron scowled.

"Silence, you twerps," Mr. Thompson said without turning away from the blackboard.

So they remained silent. They remained silent until the class was over, and Mr. Thompson had gone.

"Show it to me," Ron said, standing up. The rest of the class ganged up on Damien, standing all around him.

Damien took out a gun, but it wasn't the gun he'd snatched from Tom's house or the flare gun. It was a new gun, one that he'd taken from Yuri's room after they'd gone through all his belongings. This gun had a full magazine and plenty of spare ammo. He showed Ron the gun, then shoved the bag toward him.

"You delivered," Ron said, his face turning red, his mouth hanging open. He took out the ammo, inspected the magazine, and ran his fingers along the gun admiringly. "You did it."

"What are you going to do now, kill me with it?" Damien asked.

"Kill you?" Ron looked surprised. He put the gun back inside Damien's bag. "Now why the hell would I kill my friend?"

"You can save it," Damien said, looking away.

"Well, if you want to see something cool, I suggest sticking around after school's let out. We're going to try something," Ron said, grinning at Damien and the rest of the class. Other than Damien, they all smiled back.

———

When school let out, the floor was dirty with footprints and trash, but no janitor came to clean it. Lucy had attended her classes, and to her surprise, Harry was completely unperturbed about the fact that Brad and Beth were no longer attending. When she asked him about it, he said that such things were the rule, not the exception, and then he went back to chanting something under his breath that she couldn't understand.

Lucy watched the principal and the rest of the teachers leave. They left the lights on. No one turned the lights off. No one even asked around about Yuri.

When all were gone, Lucy went to Damien's classroom and found him standing there facing the rest of the class. They were not paying any attention to him. They were all gathered around Ron, who was whispering something so quietly she couldn't overhear.

"You! Are you the one who's been threatening Damien?!" she snapped.

Ron turned away from the class and faced her, holding the gun in his hand. "Oh, look. He brought his sister."

"What do you know about our mother, huh?!" Lucy said, striding over to Ron.

"Oh, you soon won't have to worry about that," Ron said, turning the safety of the gun off. The rest of the class stepped back. "Please step back and join your brother." He waved the gun at her, ushering her to back up.

She looked at Damien, who shook his head.

"Are you okay?" she asked.

"I'm fine," he said flatly.

"So what do you know about our mother?" Lucy asked, her back to the blackboard. Ron stood in the center of the classroom. "And what are you going to do with the gun?"

"Like I said, you don't have to concern yourself with any of that," Ron said. "I won't harm you with this gun. I promise. And as for what I know about you and your mom, well, see, it dies with me."

Before either of them could do a thing, Ron closed his eyes and put the gun under his chin. He had the calmest smile on his face as he pulled the trigger.

The entire school rang with the roar of the gun.

Dead Kids Tell No Tales

Ron lay on the floor with a bullet hole under his chin, and smoke coming out the top of his head where the bullet had exited. He lay there with both eyes open, the gun still in his hand. A tendril of smoke trailed out of his open mouth.

Damien was hyperventilating, his face red and hot, and his heart feeling like it would stop beating at any given moment. Lucy was too shocked to see a kid killing himself with a gun. She had her hands around Damien, trying to hold him in place. Some kind of grim understanding was beginning to dawn upon her, but as to what it was exactly, she didn't know.

"Did it work?" one of the kids standing there asked. "Is he dead?"

"I think so," another kid said, poking Ron's rib with the edge of his sneakers. "Does this mean we get to go next?"

A sudden gasp followed by a loud, high-pitched scream, and Ron was sitting up again, holding the gun in his hand, looking at it with tears in his eyes. "It didn't work! I thought it would work, but I can't kill myself." He glared at Damien, as if this anomaly was somehow his fault.

"You!" Ron yelled at Damien, pointing the gun at him. Ron slowly got up from the floor. Lucy was surprised to see that not a single drop of blood had spilled from where he'd shot himself. "Come here!"

Damien quivered as he broke free from Lucy's grip and walked over to Ron as if spellbound.

"You shoot me. Come on. Clearly the rules of this place dictate I can't kill myself. It must be you. You have to kill me and then the others. You don't understand. It's..." Ron started to cry. "It's been hell, being trapped here for so long. We can't leave this classroom because the motherfucker killed us here."

"Who?" Damien asked, the hair on the back of his neck standing up. He noticed that the overhead lights were flickering. Were they always flickering?

"Mr. Thompson, who else? Come on, kid. You never read the news?" Ron asked. He shoved the gun in Damien's hands and made him close both hands around it, then pulled his hands up to his head such that the gun was now against his forehead. "What do you think this place is? Who do you think we are?"

"I don't know! I don't wanna kill you! I can't!"

"Do it!" Ron screamed. Behind him, the rest of the

kids of the class were sullen, their faces a strange shade of cyan. When Damien focused on them, it wasn't just their faces that were this shade anymore. They were more or less cyan in color. And then his eyes went back to Ron, who was light blue and green all over. "It will be a mercy. Please. I beg you. Don't you think I'd get the gun for myself if I could leave this classroom? We're not even in the classroom all the time! Just for around the same time as when Mr. Thompson came in the class and fucking killed us."

"And then he killed himself," one of the kids said quietly from the back of the class. "Sick fuck."

"Now we're stuck here in a loop, attending the same class over and over. We can't leave. We don't know what we're waiting for," a girl said. "We've tried to kill ourselves with the means at our disposal. We thought that would help us be free of this place. But it didn't."

"We didn't want to die the first time around," Ron sobbed, wiping his entire forearm along his eyes. "We were kids, for fuck's sake. How were we to know that the chocolate brownies Mr. Thompson brought for the summer break celebration were laced with cyanide?"

"He remembers killing us. He's talked about it several times over the decades. Says it was the best thing he did. That it felt like nothing else. That he'd endure the rest of eternity reliving the memory of seeing us choke and bleed and pass out and scream as he watched with the classroom door locked from the inside," another kid added in a mournful voice.

"I called out for my mom," another girl said. "I had

blood coming out of my eyes and nose, and I was calling for my mom. The principal banged on the door. The security guards tried to ram it open. Mr. Thompson had placed his table and the rest of the chairs against the door. It wouldn't budge."

"I was the last to die," Ron wept. "And I watched the smug grin on his face as he took the last brownie and ate it like a mad bastard. The year was 1976. We don't even know how long it has been since we died."

"But we're not dead," Lucy said quietly, taking the gun from Damien. "I don't remember dying. I think I would remember my own death. What you're saying makes no sense."

Ron looked at her pitifully. "This is not your world, sweetheart. This is not anyone's world." It felt strange hearing the word sweetheart from his mouth, but Lucy realized that if he were alive, he'd be a fifty-eight-year-old guy. "That's what's wrong with it. This is no place at all."

"We didn't die," Damien insisted. "Like Lucy said, I think we'd remember something as important as dying."

"Oh?" Ron laughed. "This town then. Has it always been like this? Fog and fog and fog and fog as far as the eye can see? Unholy beasts roaming the streets? The giant Lurker with the lit-up glasses? Killer fish flying in the air? Okay, let's suppose all that's the norm, and I'm just one crazy old guy stuck in the body of a child forever. Where the fuck are the people? There are buildings, but no people. Classrooms and schools aren't supposed to be this empty. Tell me you know that this is not Pinebrook."

"I..." Lucy began, her finger curling around the trigger. She didn't want to hear this anymore. "But people are sick. The hospital…"

"The hospital?" Ron laughed. "I hear other ghosts passing through the school. The hospital is not what you think it is. I suppose some kindly man has spun some kind of tale that your parents are in the hospital and that everyone in town is sick and therefore the town is empty?"

"The Other Man…." Damien whispered.

Ron started clapping his hands, his moroseness replaced by an unsettling madness. "The Other Man. Oh, I envy your naivete, you stupid kid. What has he done? Saved your life a couple of times? Is that what he's done? You're not the first person to be lulled into a false sense of security. It's how Stockholm Syndrome works. You think he's your friend?"

"He's not like that!" Lucy said, hot color rising in her cheeks. "And if you so badly want to die, let me do it!"

"Go ahead, girl. Do it. I'm ready. I've died a thousand times. I can die once more. Here's to hoping it sticks," Ron said, stretching his arms, closing his eyes.

Lucy pressed the gun against his forehead and pulled the trigger.

The gun blared, red sparks coming out of it. Ron was thrown back by the force. The other children stepped aside to make way for his body. Ron lay there, breathing heavily, the hole in his head healing up.

"Fuck it!" Ron yelled. "If you can't kill me…then how do I die?!" He stood up and kicked a table, toppling it over. Then he banged his fist furiously against the wall.

The rest of the classroom shared his sentiment. The kids wept, huddled in corners, consoling each other with hugs and pats on the head, strokes on the back.

When no one spoke for a long time, Damien finally asked, "Are we in hell?"

"Hell? You really think that children deserve to be sent to hell? Do you see flames, demons, devils, and inferno anywhere? This place is so much worse than hell. There are no attendants. There is no torture. There's only the endless wait. I call this place the Forgotten World."

Damien squinted against the overhead lights. They were beginning to flicker wildly. Outside, it had grown dark.

"That's our cue to disappear," Ron said, pointing at the fog. "We'll reappear in the morning."

"I'm sorry I couldn't help you," Damien said.

"You tried your best. And in return, I'll do you a favor," Ron said, putting his hand on Damien's shoulder. "Every boy, unless he's an orphan, cares about his mother. I don't know jack-shit about your mother or your father. I just wanted you to do my bidding. I was so sure that I'd die. I'm sorry for lying to you."

Damien shrugged and looked at his sister with a *What now?* expression on his face.

"I don't understand. I'm not dead. I am a hundred percent certain of that. I went to bed one day..." Lucy began, but by the time she was about to say the next thing, she wasn't so sure that she'd gone to bed. What had she been doing?

Ron smiled at her and said, "Stay long enough in this place and you'll mix up your facts and your fictions. For instance, I, for the life of me, can't remember if it was Mr. Thompson who brought the brownies or if it was me. Maybe we killed him because he was a piece of shit, but then we got overwhelmed by what we'd done, and so we ate the rest of the brownies. Who knows?"

There was none of that sadness on Ron's face. He was smiling snidely at Lucy. "You look like fun. I guess that's how we're going to pass our time. Let's see if we can't kill you."

To her horror, the other kids blocked the door, all of them smiling, their eyes darkening in unison. Ron snatched the gun from her hand and aimed it at her.

Damien was more concerned with the lights. They had flickered so violently that several of them had sparked shut. The few that worked bathed the room in a cold, dim light, and in that light, the dead children looked every bit like the ghosts that they were.

Ron moved toward Lucy, gun in hand.

"Let's see if we can't kill you. Maybe that will reveal something about the rules of this place. Maybe it's a sacrifice that I need to make, and you did say that you weren't *dead* dead," Ron said.

"You're sick," Lucy said, backing up against the door, but the children blocking it pushed her toward Ron. "You're—"

"I'm what? Please tell me. I'm *dying* to know. I've been here for years, and there's not a combination of insults that I haven't already heard. What novel piece of verbal banter are you going to grace me with?"

"Lucy!" Damien yelled, pointing to the pool appearing in the middle of the classroom. A dark sludge had appeared out of nowhere within mere seconds.

Ron, distracted by Damien's shout, turned back to see what the commotion was.

The sludge rose from the ground, and now it was evident that it was congealed blood rising in a heap, taking the shape of a tall person dressed in bloodied clothes and a matching hood to go with it. He held a broad blade that was nearly the same length as him. He lifted it and made it slam on the ground, cracking the floor.

"Oh..." Ron said, lowering the gun and looking at the executioner. "Now where did you come from?"

The executioner gave him no response other than the burning gaze from his eyes, and then he slashed his blade in a wide arc, gashing Ron's chest.

This time, blood *did* spout, and it sprayed across the floor as Ron gasped and clawed for breath. He first collapsed onto his knees, clutching his chest, whimpering.

"No..." Ron begged, raising a hand toward the executioner.

The classroom was filled with the shriek of the trapped kids. As they ran from one end of the room to the other in hopes that their movement might save them (seeing as how they were not able to leave the confines of the room), Lucy and Damien grabbed each other and darted for the door. Lucy swung it open and hurled Damien through. She closed it tightly and stayed just for a brief second to catch a glimpse of the executioner tearing through the ghosts of the children. Only, as they died, they did not feel like they were ghosts.

They just looked like dying children.

The executioner skewered two kids through his blade and pinned them against the wall.

They were laughing as they were dying.

———

They didn't wait around for the executioner to get out of that classroom. Within five minutes, Lucy and Damien were already stomping across the road, the lamp held out in front of them.

Everything had changed.

The executioner wasn't just some deranged murderer confined to the manor. He could appear anywhere at will.

And if half of what Ron had said was true, then this place was not home, and they were trapped in a nightmare.

It was nighttime when they reached home, but there was little comfort left waiting for them. Lucy closed the door behind her and locked it, knowing that it was futile, that any sense of security she had was a blatant lie.

"If he didn't die when you shot him, or before when he shot himself, why did he die when the executioner killed him?" Damien asked.

Lucy wanted to slap Damien out of frustration. Instead, she slammed her hand against the kitchen doorframe.

"Enough!" she shouted, her unkempt hair falling all over her face. "I don't want to hear anything about the executioner or Ron or this place! I've had enough! This has gone on long enough! I'm going to the hospital. If Mom and Dad are there, I need to see them. And if they're not, then I don't know what the hell I'm going to do!"

She collapsed weakly against the doorframe, tears clearing lines on her dirty face.

"I'm scared. I don't know why we're here. I don't remember anything."

"Maybe that's just the thing. Have you considered?" Damien asked, sitting beside her, offering her comfort as only a younger brother could—by holding her hands and putting his head against her shoulder. "Maybe we *are* dead. And if that's the case, it isn't so bad."

"What do you mean?" Lucy rested her head against her brother's head.

"At least I'm not alone. At least you're here with me. And as long as you're here, I know that you'll keep me safe," Damien sobbed.

The two children clung to each other in the kitchen doorway.

When they had exhausted their scarce supply of tears, Damien looked up at her and said something that Lucy couldn't get out of her mind, no matter how hard she tried.

In fact, hours later, when she was sure that Damien was fast asleep, this question was what prompted her to walk out into the night with nothing but her lamp, headed toward the hospital.

"Did it...did it, for a minute...did it look like the executioner had come to save us?"

THE LURKER

Nothing made sense. Not the way her memory leading up to the current state of Pinebrook was blank, nor what Ron had said. She couldn't be dead. Unlike Ron, she didn't disappear after a certain time.

She needed to eat, sleep, go to the bathroom. When the executioner had thrown her against the ground, she got cut in several places and had bled from there. The cuts still hurt. She didn't have the best understanding of death in the world, but from what little she knew, she knew that you weren't conscious. That your body stopped needing things.

"I'm not dead," she told herself, holding the lamp up. It was good that there were two lamps now, one that they'd picked up from the park, and this one that Tom had given them. She was starting to think of him as Tom again, and not the Other Man. There was a problem. She didn't know if Tom had disappeared because he'd been hunted and killed by the executioner, or if it was just shame on his part that he'd let the children get in harm's way.

She didn't believe what Ron had said. But the disbelief part didn't sit easy with her, because they *had* tried to kill Ron. Why hadn't he died? Why did he die specifically when the executioner killed him?

Why were the children laughing as they were being killed? Was there some kind of sick, twisted pleasure in death only the dying knew?

The town had ceased shocking her. It just was. With its mist and its silhouetted buildings and its stinging cold, Lucy had brought herself to believe something that was far more palatable than whatever conspiracies Ron had been spinning before his death.

Far more palatable than the reality "Uncle Tommy" had imposed upon her.

She decided that the first truth was the entire truth, and that Tom had not been lying to her. Because if Tom had wanted them dead, he'd have let them die any of the several times when they were in danger. He didn't have to save them. He didn't have to kill the fog dog in the basement. Nor did he have to bid them to stay away from the manor.

He'd said that their parents were in the hospital, and he'd given her the lamp, the first one. Two and two equals four. Tom was not a bad guy. And maybe that's why he had disappeared. To make things right.

Yuri wasn't a bad guy either, but Yuri was dead now. As were Beth and Brad. Were they dead too, or just finding ways to die? Was there a connection between the angler fish which had killed them, the bird which had killed the cop, and the executioner who had murdered an entire class full of kids?

It hurt her head to think about it.

"I'm not dead," she whispered, trying to make herself believe it. "I'm still breathing."

The mist thinned above, giving her a glimpse of the moon. Only, it was strange. In the distance, there were two more full moons. It couldn't be that there were three moons. The other two moons were in close vicinity to each other, and much lower. They hovered behind the water tower in the distance. Lucy shrugged and pulled her coat tighter around her. It was unbelievably cold. The streets were completely empty and pin-drop silent. There were no dogs or animals prowling tonight. Not a leaf stirred in the stillness, nor did any movement come from the underbrush. The only sound was the patter of Lucy's feet on the asphalt.

All around her, empty cars stood in driveways gathering dust and dead leaves. Rust crept up lampposts. Wet opacity gleamed on all the windows of the houses, the glass panes that constituted sunrooms that had not seen the sun in ages. Opaque, too, were all the windows of all the cars. Leaves lay scattered on the road as Lucy walked resolutely toward the town square, from where she knew the way to the hospital. She'd consulted the map from her tablet, memorized it, and was certain that she'd reach the hospital and find her parents within the next hour.

It was optimistic, at best, the outlook of this plan of hers, but it was the only plan she had. The other plan was no plan at all but a death wish. She had considered going back to the manor, climbing down into the basement, and confronting the haunter, the executioner, and asking him why he had spared them that day.

That plan required a whole lot of courage that she was certain she didn't have. She'd run out of most of it, and what little of it remained, she had mustered for this death march to the hospital. She was aware that she could be attacked at any given moment. But the payoff was huge, potentially. If she was successful in going to the hospital, one of two things would happen.

Tom would reappear and tell her to stay away from the hospital. This would be good. Tom knew things. She intended to find them out. Moreover, Tom, if he was alive, needed to explain why he'd done this disappearing act. Why wasn't he looking after the kids? Where was he when they needed to be saved from Uncle Tommy? Where was he when they were being ganged up on at the school?

There were more questions pounding at her brain than answers. And that was the other reason she needed to go to the hospital. If Tom didn't show up, then he was a liar from the get-go. And if she was able to get inside the hospital and find her parents in there, in whatever condition they were, then she'd try to talk to them. If her parents were not cognizant, she'd talk to the nurses. She'd try to find someone rational and reasonable in this bizarre place.

Lucy was so immersed in her own thoughts that she did not notice the twin moons blinking behind the water tower. A minute later, when they disappeared from behind the tower, she didn't notice either. She was busy thinking that if the executioner was somehow their guardian angel—or guardian demon, more like—then there was a good chance he was lurking in the shadows, and he had made all the town quiet.

She was wrong.

———

Pinebrook was, like most small towns of America, built around the town center. There had been a great many tales about Pinebrook's founding. The mayor, Thomas Caulk, had written a book about Pinebrook's history, amongst other things that weren't exactly history but certainly historical.

It was the most detailed book on the subject, but it wasn't the only source of stories on this topic. The University of Urbana-Champaign's Literature and Anthropology departments had several research papers and dissertations in their archives on the subject.

But it was Thomas Caulk's book that still retained the most popularity on the internet, in niche groups, on Reddit, and even had a cult following outside of America. For it wasn't just a history book to those who studied it intently.

It was a book of the occult.

In this book, Thomas Caulk talked at length about the Illiniwek tribe that called this place home nearly six hundred years ago. The surviving descendants of the tribe still lived around Pinebrook.

They had told Thomas that when the settlers came, they found this place abundant in natural resources. It was in close vicinity to two rivers with branching streams. Not only was there plenty of shade, but the landscape was diverse. Forests, plains, little hills, creeks, and farmland, all here in this little microcosm of America. But what struck the settlers strange was the name that the local populace called this place.

Niitawenepici.

The settlers weren't able to understand the word, nor were they able to pronounce it. The locals tried failingly to tell them that the word meant *the crossing where new breath arrives* and that this land was holy for that purpose.

Three centuries later, the name, mistranslated, mispronounced, was all but lost to those who still retained history by way of passing traditions down from father to son. The town wasn't named after the scientist who had birthed calculus.

It was named with reverence, a place of death, life, and the crossing of these thresholds.

Thomas Caulk's book explored the strange things he'd heard happened in Pinebrook. The things that people had told him. Red lights in the thickets. Spectral reindeers with glint-stone antlers wandering in the woods.

Sightings of a hooded man in red wielding a massive, blood-soaked sword. The hounds of hell walking in stride with him.

Unbeknownst to Lucy and Damien, there was a copy of this book at their home, locked away in a cabinet in the attic, along with the rest of the forbidden literature that their parents consumed, including but not limited to smut, vintage *Playboys*, copies of *Cavalier* magazine, books from the golden age of horror, from the silver age of porn, books that you wouldn't want to be caught dead with.

———

Lucy had reached the town center. Or she thought she did. Four roads went in their separate directions. Traffic lights and cameras hung off horizontal rods, the lights going red, yellow, green upon timed intervals.

Shutters were drawn across all the storefronts and windows. The awnings of all the stores were drenched in wetness and shadows. They looked like black funeral shrouds.

The hospital stood separate from the rest of the smaller buildings. The lights were on in most windows. It was a cubical building, ten floors high and just as wide. A marvel of brutalist architecture, it was a dark gray building with the windows small and barred. Eight pillars propped the building's front, with the ER entrance, the main entrance, the driveway for cars to pull up to the building, and a series of trashcans with ashtrays atop for all the nurses, orderlies, doctors, and patients who came out to smoke.

Caution tape, cones, and plastic barriers were placed all around the hospital. Lucy didn't dare walking up to the hospital. There were two cops prowling, talking to the security guards stationed at the entrance. An ambulance was parked in the driveway, its back open, two EMTs attending to a dying man in the stretcher.

The cops turned around and pointed at something in the sky. Lucy turned back to look at what it was. She could see nothing behind the buildings, no matter how hard she squinted. Just the three moons from earlier. When she turned around, no one stood at the hospital's entrance.

She sped up, hoping to cross the street and get into the hospital.

Something clattered to her left.

She stood still.

There was another lamp hanging suspended in the fog up ahead.

"Who's there?" she called out into the silence.

The fog didn't stir. No shape came out of it to greet her. The other lamp turned off. And now there was only her. She shivered and retracted her steps to the town square, where all was just as quiet.

This was a mistake.

She squinted against the blinding light that shone

from the sky. Three moons. Except, the other two moons were nearer, bigger, and—

They were not moons.

They were glasses, shining on the blank face of a being taller than all the buildings around it. It took extremely slow steps, avoiding all the buildings and coming into view. Its glasses were like floodlights, lighting up the place where Lucy stood.

Fifty feet tall—taller than most buildings in the town square; taller than the hospital—it looked like a gray boy, his lips blue, black hair falling over his forehead.

He wore a full-sleeved shirt tucked into cotton shorts. The shorts were held by suspenders the size of bridges. He had tall black and white socks, and black boots that quaked the entire ground when he stepped.

A hand shot out of the dark and grabbed Lucy by her arm, digging into her skin.

She screamed.

The Lurker's eyes shot where the scream had come from.

There was no one standing there.

The Lurker resumed its quiet earthquake gait through Pinebrook, minding the buildings.

———

"Are you out of your mind?!"

Lucy was out of breath, gasping, clutching her chest with both arms. She was against the wall of a small alley that she'd been pulled into.

Damien stood there with the lamp, glaring at his elder sister.

"You thought I wouldn't notice you sneaking out of the house?! Do you want to die? Is that what you want? Do you know how stupid that was, going out into the city all by yourself? And to the hospital?! There's a reason Tom forbade us from going there! And now look at the mess you've landed us in. The Lurker almost caught us!"

"How do you know he's called that?" Lucy whispered.

"Did you not listen to Ron?" Damien snapped.

She suddenly recalled in crisp detail what he'd said.

This town then. Has it always been like this? Fog and fog and fog and fog as far as the eye can see? Unholy beasts roaming the streets? The giant Lurker with the lit-up glasses? Killer fish flying in the air? Okay, let's suppose all that's the norm, and I'm just one crazy old guy stuck in the body of a child forever. Where the fuck are the people? There are buildings, but no people. Classrooms and schools aren't supposed to be this empty. Tell me you know that this is not Pinebrook.

"Now we can't leave until he leaves," Damien said, poking his head out of the alley and looking for the Lurker.

"But don't you want to go in the hospital? See Mom and Dad?" Lucy asked, then realized that this wasn't what she was supposed to be asking. He was out when he was supposed to be sleeping. "Why are you following me?"

"One of us has to be the sane one," Damien said. His voice was unnaturally deep. "And since you've decided to be the idiot, I have to do the responsible thing and take you home."

"Damien, no. I need to go inside and find out the truth. No one's telling us the truth. I'm done with this place. We go inside. If our mom and dad are in there, then at least some of what we know is true. If they're not in there, then we've been lied to and this place actually isn't what it is. Then we'll have to figure out some other way to escape. But you can't stop me from going into the hospital. It's right there. I didn't come all this way for nothing," she said. What occurred to her next wasn't an epiphany, but a suspicion. Once it had taken root, she couldn't look at Damien the same.

"We're not going in. Don't you remember Tom saying that there are horrors lurking in the hospital?" Damien asked.

"How did you come here? We both know you don't know the way," Lucy said, taking a step away from Damien. If he was Damien, that is.

"What do you mean? I saw you get out of the house. I followed you," Damien said, his face innocent, confused even.

"That's funny, because I looked behind me several times and I didn't see any lamp," Lucy said, stepping back two paces, till she was out of the alley. She held her lamp up to Damien.

"Stop it. It's not funny. I'm your brother and I'm not

going to let you make this mistake," Damien said, reaching forward.

She stepped away, slipping from his touch.

"Are you?" Lucy asked, her eyes darkening. "Or are you like Uncle Tommy? See, that's the thing. I didn't see you leave the house. I've been wandering for an hour. I didn't see you anywhere. You just appear when I'm at the hospital? You... You're not Damien."

Damien had tears in his eyes.

"Don't you realize this is what this place wants you to think? It's tearing us apart, Lucy," Damien said, holding his hand out for her to take it.

"I don't think so. I think this place is trying to give me signals that I haven't been picking up on. It was you who went lurking in the mansion. You who went in the basement. You put me in harm's way. Then you went on this whole quest with the gun thing. You're not Damien. You've never been Damien. You're this place, and everything wrong with it."

"Lucy, snap out of it! I'm Damien!" Damien wept.

But Lucy didn't listen. She'd already turned around and was running away from the alley, toward the hospital.

Damien stood in the cover of the alley, holding his lamp up, calling after her as she crossed the road. "Lucy, don't do this!"

Lucy had reached the hospital and was standing in the driveway, looking up at the gray pillars that merged into the building.

There was no one standing behind the door. No

nurses, orderlies, or doctors. The reception was unmanned. She didn't care. She just needed to be away from the creature posing as her brother. This place had played its fair share of twisted jokes and tricks on her, but none had been as cruel as pretending to be her brother.

Had he ever been here, or was this nightmare just hers?

She stepped forward, under the shade of the building. She was ready as she'd ever be.

Blinding light shone upon her, light that burned her skin. Her little lamp was no more than a candle against the solar intensity of the two glasses that were boring into her.

He was face to face with her, having appeared so quickly out of thin air, hunched over so he could see this trespasser better.

Lucy screamed as she stared into the eyes of the Lurker. His face remained expressionless as he reached out his giant hand, each finger as long and thick as the supporting pillars of the hospital building.

"Lucy!" Damien yelled from somewhere far away, and it was only then that Lucy realized that the trick this place had played on her was that it had made her believe that Damien was not real.

It really was Damien in that alley. He'd tried to stop her. It was too late to admit her mistake.

"Damien, run, please!" she cried as the Lurker's fingers wrapped around her, crushing her. The pain and the terror was so intense that it instantaneously drove her unconscious.

———

Damien wept with his hand covering his mouth, watching the Lurker pick his sister up and walk away into the fog.

How could he let this happen?

He immediately turned his lamp off, realizing that the Lurker could change his mind any moment, and could come back around and pick Damien up with as little difficulty as he'd picked up his sister.

Was she still alive? He had heard her scream excruciatingly, a scream that had all but told him that his sister had breathed her last in this dreadful place.

With hot tears running down his face, he watched the Lurker disappear into the fog, his heavy steps shaking the road, making the windows clatter, setting off car alarms.

And then the noise, the rumbling, the shaking ceased, as did the light that shone from his eyes. The night was dark once more, with the spectral moon hanging low above the fog.

"Help me," Damien wept, his eyes closed. "If you're there, help me. The Lurker's taken my sister. She might already be dead. But if there's a chance—"

A hand touched his shoulder.

Damien was too afraid to open his eyes and see who it was. Some part of him already knew who it was that he had called. His rattling breath was all too familiar.

Slowly, Damien opened his eyes and looked up to see

the blood-drenched hood of the executioner and the broad greatsword hung over his shoulder.

"Are...are you here to kill me?"

The executioner did not move.

"Will you help me save Lucy?"

The executioner gave the briefest of nods and bid Damien to follow him in the dead, dark night.

WATERWORKS

Damien had skipped school that day because he had been feeling ill for two days. Something he'd eaten around the house, something that he was not supposed to eat. There were cupcakes in the kitchen, eight of them. Damien had eaten three. He had been puking for three days. Her parents had not taken him to the hospital. He had been paling when she'd last seen him. He'd soiled his pants and was too weak to get up and change his clothes.

Lucy, for the life of her, hadn't been able to understand what was in those cupcakes. Later, the rest of the cupcakes had disappeared and neither of her parents had gotten sick. She assumed they had eaten the rest. They often made food that they prohibited the kids from eating. Mommy and Daddy's special relaxation treats, they called them.

Lucy had never wanted to eat them. She'd always found the smell off-putting, like cat piss.

Earlier that morning, her mother had woken her with a violent slap across the face.

"I suppose you'll beg me to drop you off at school? I'll make you walk, you little shit," she'd said.

Lucy had been told by other kids in her class as well as her parents when they were sober that a parent's anger was a gift, a privilege, a sign that they cared, and that one should not question it but accept it whenever your mother or father beat you. It was their way of caring for you. So, too, was when they screamed at you. It was character building stuff.

She'd tried to tell herself that her mother screamed at her out of love, but the vengefulness in her voice didn't feel like love. Nor did the harsh slaps.

"Get up! Get ready! Leave!" her mother screamed. Her eyes were red and her breath smelled of alcohol. The bags under her eyes indicated that she had been up all night. "And if you're late from school, you can forget lunch."

"All right, Mama," Lucy had said, and had gotten ready for school in record time. Ten minutes. In another five minutes, she stood outside the house, waiting for the bus. In her hurry, she hadn't been able to check on him. She'd been up most of the night taking care of him. That's why she hadn't woken up when her alarm had rung.

She watched her mother and father staring at her from the living room window. They were talking to each other. She didn't want to leave Damien all alone there with them. Who knew what they'd do to him. It was their fault he was sick in the first place. Them and their drug-laced cupcakes.

He was feverish last night, his eyes traveling up his skull, sweat all over his deathly white face. "I'm dreaming of this place," he'd said. "It's...it's a funny place. There's no school there. And you're there. We're going there soon. Our parents won't be there. I know it."

This was not the first time she'd heard drug-induced ramblings. It tore her heart that her younger brother was hallucinating from the effect of whatever drug of choice was in those cupcakes. She had made up her mind. Later that evening, she'd call CPS for good and tell them everything. Maybe that was the place Damien was dreaming of. A foster home where this kind of nonsense wouldn't be tolerated. Lucy had slowly come around to the idea. Whoever they'd be placed under the charge of, they wouldn't be as bad as her parents.

There were empty alcohol bottles strewn across the living room floor. The house perpetually smelled of weed and other ranker stuff that stung her throat whenever she breathed the air, leaving her feeling lightheaded and breathless.

The laundry hadn't been done in days. Piles and piles of clothes lay all over the house. At night, there came fighting and grunting noises from her parents' room. They beat each other up, she was sure of it. They often came out with bruises on their faces. They just as soon forgot all about it as well.

Lucy knew they were almost never sober.

She didn't know the reason for it. She wasn't sure she

cared to find out. Even though she was just ten years old, she had assessed the salvageability of the situation and discovered that her parents, their mental health, their drug addictions, and the financial quagmire they were stuck in couldn't be helped.

If there was a way out, it was CPS. They'd see the mess in the house. It'd be a surprise visit, of course. There would be cops. Soon. All she had to do was attend one more day of school.

She suffered through her classes, thinking about Damien, and if he'd soiled his pants again. She'd have to change his pants, give him some of that oral rehydration solution that her mother drank whenever she was sick. And then she'd call CPS.

She'd have to do it while they were asleep.

She sat through each class, not talking to anyone, nodding absent-mindedly when the teachers said something of note. She stared out the window, thinking about all the ways she could escape. Outside, the sun shone on the football field. A coach was guiding football players through practice. Some kids were sitting on the bleachers, laughing, clapping.

She envied those kids, and how they could afford to laugh so carelessly.

She thought about going to the principal's office and feigning sickness. She also thought about going to the principal's office and telling him that her parents were being dangerous in the house. He was a principal. He would expedite the CPS process. Maybe she wouldn't even have to go home.

But she had to. Damien was there. She wasn't going to do anything unless she knew he was okay and that he could go with her. She had the whole thing planned. When Child Protection Services would arrive, she'd go on her knees and beg them to take them away. She'd beg with all the words she knew. She'd cling to their coats and ask them to put Damien and her together.

To not separate them.

It was that thought that stopped her from going to the principal's office. She bore patiently through the rest of the classes and was the first to get on the bus.

When the bus dropped her off at her home, she was certain that they must be sleeping. After all, they were up all night shouting, banging against the walls, grunting, moaning.

She opened the door to the smell of ammonia, cat piss, and a harsh chemical that hung suspended in the air. She stopped herself from choking. She didn't want to announce her arrival.

They were already there in the living room, smoking something out of small glass pipes. Their faces were gaunt and sunken, eyes red, flakes in their hair, and rashes all over their skin. They didn't notice her as she snuck in the house.

Lucy crept through the living room, watching them aggressively smoke the dangerous-smelling chemical from their glass pipes.

"Motherfuckers don't know who they fucked with, firing me. I got them the clients, the big-paying mother-fucking jackoffs who have millions to throw. Fucking get the fuck out of here!" her father yelled and slapped his mother across the face, then began kissing her aggressively, pinning her hands against the sofa.

Lucy couldn't watch. There were whimpering sounds coming from close by. She needed to check on Damien right now. She crept up the stairs, hearing her mother yelling from below.

"Fucking do it now and be done with it. Where's the bitch? She has to be there for it! Motherfucking stretch mark-giving, youth-sucking whore. Stop it! Get off me! It's this shit you pull that put two kids in my fucking body."

"Two's better than one! What would you have done with one?!" her father yelled. She heard the sound of glass shattering. "Imagine if it all goes right, fucking island parties. Fucking Gucci, Prada, fucking Versace, Louboutins, all that motherfucking Fifth Avenue shit. They'll suck my dick. You can watch or you can join."

"Fuck your shitshow. I'll be parading with those skeleton-thin bitches on the walkway. We'll have so much we won't know what to do with it," she said, scratching her cheeks furiously.

Lucy heard the sound of them kissing each other. It sounded as if they were biting each other's faces off. She closed her ears to that sound and to their high-talk. They often talked like this, especially when they were sure that the kids were asleep. But this was much worse. They were agitated, dangerous.

Lucy opened the door to Damien's room, only to see

that he wasn't there. She checked the rest of the floor, the bathrooms, but her brother wasn't there.

She went down the stairs, where she could hear the sound of whimpers. She saw that the door to the garage was open.

There was blood on the garage floor.

Damien's feet were visible.

"There you are, fucking bitch!" Her father was on his feet, holding a poker. He shot a mad look at his wife and said, "She's here, and you didn't know!"

"You didn't know neither!" she yelled at him.

"Come here, Lucy! Daddy wants to talk!"

Lucy ran to the garage, slipping past her father.

Damien lay there on the floor, covered in blood. He was wheezing and whimpering.

"Run," he croaked. "Lucy... Go."

But by then it had been too late.

————

Her cheeks were cold and wet. Her entire body hurt, but she discovered that she could move, although not without undergoing mortal agony. Lucy opened her eyes. It was not a dream that she'd been having. It was pain breaking past the barriers of her memory, making her recall a memory before the town had gone to hell in a handbasket.

It had been a sunny day. There was warm, idle sunlight teeming through the leaves on the street when she'd come home that day. But the memory was fragmented. She could recall that her parents had been high, and that Damien was lying injured in the garage. Maybe he'd rubbed them wrong or tried to come down for a drink of water. Maybe they'd found him standing there, and in their daze, they'd taken to him with the fire poker.

She couldn't remember the rest. Only smaller fragments.

"Stop, Mom!"

"You'll turn on me? Your own fucking mother?!"

But she could remember where she'd been before where this dark place was. The Lurker had grabbed her, squeezed her in his hand—and then she'd passed out.

A sliver of moonlight came from somewhere, lighting up her immediate surroundings. The cold, wet things next to her face were bones. Lucy gasped with a start and sat up, the pain coursing through her body sharpening her sight.

She lay atop hundreds of bones, none of them small enough to be from animals. When she saw the human skulls scattered in there along with the ribcages and the femurs and tibias and fibulas, it became evident that she lay amongst human remains.

It took everything she had to not scream. She looked up at the missing rafter from where the moonlight was shining through. The room, if it could be called a room, was spherical and wooden.

When at last she finally could, she poked her head through the missing slate, and saw that she was suspended in the fog. The metal latticework of the water tower's railing and walkway was all around her, rusted, broken off in several places, and creaking. Lucy pushed her body through the slit, wondering how the Lurker had put her in there in the first place. When she was standing on the walkway, she saw that the roof of the water tower was battered and dented. That was how.

He'd lift the roof, put the victim in, and then leave them to die.

But why just leave them to die? Where was he?

As her eyes adjusted to the fog, she saw the enormous pool of water below. Its surface was black and still, reflecting the fog and, somehow, the moon. Just the one moon.

Her heart wrenched with guilt as she realized that she'd left Damien all by himself in the alley in front of the hospital, where it had smelled like medical refuse. Just like she'd left him all by himself that day when she shouldn't have gone to school.

And to think that she'd assumed he wasn't Damien.

"How stupid can you be?" she asked herself as she placed her weight against the railing. The entire water tower creaked.

She walked a circle around the tank, looking for signs of the Lurker. She could not see his shining eyes anywhere. What kind of creature was he that he was so tall and silent? It was as if this place had an unending reserve of sick and twisted beings all hellbent on finding her and her brother and subjecting them to torture; if not the physical kind, then the worse one—the one inflicted upon her mind and soul.

"My lamp," Lucy whispered, realizing that somewhere between losing consciousness and being trapped in the water tank, she'd lost her lamp.

As if Pinebrook had also picked up on this little yet important fact, wings flapped above her, and she saw vultures circling the tank. Dead, eyeless, flesh-covered carrion feeders cawing, waiting for her to falter.

She walked around the tank once more, ignoring the caws of the birds, the threatening creaking sound of the entire tower as its weight shifted. There were metal stairs leading down to the ground, but they were broken along the middle. She would have to jump at the halfway point and catch the stairs below. She could easily get impaled on the broken metal jutting out. But she had to get off the tower before the Lurker came back.

She'd only begun thinking of pulling this impossible feat when the pool of water below stirred. The water that had seemed black up until a few seconds ago turned darker, if such a thing was even possible. Underneath the surface, two lights shone, blinding lights with large radii.

Then he emerged from the water, climbing out of his slumber, rising till he was at eye level with the water tank atop the tower, staring at Lucy. His hand climbed up, reaching for her.

She screamed and ducked, her sore body reminding her that she wasn't able to afford such mobility.

The fog birds flew away, seeking refuge in faraway trees.

Instead of grabbing Lucy, the Lurker grabbed the water tank and pulled it. The entire tower screamed as it toppled. Lucy clung to the railing for dear life, closing her eyes as the tower fell into the water.

When she hit the water, the coppery taste that invaded her mouth made her aware that whatever this was, it wasn't water.

The Lurker's eyes shone through the water. All around her, human bones dove, sunk, and floated, covering the pool's surface.

Underneath the sinking wreckage of the tower, the broken water tank, and the bones, Lucy sank. She sank for a good minute, the last of her breath giving out as bubbles. This pool was endless, it seemed. She flailed her hands and legs in a helpless bid to swim up, but her clothes were heavy and her body was weak.

An enormous arm shot through the water, fingers closing around the rubble and the broken metal. Finally, the fingers found purchase around Lucy and pulled her out of the water.

She came out screaming as the large fingers dug into her body, threatening to break her bones.

The Lurker was smirking as it held her up like she was a lab specimen, his eyes shining bright white light on her that singed her skin.

———

More memories. More snippets of violence and the stench of death, smoke tendrils unfurling in the living room as her parents flanked her, her father holding the poker, all of the madness of the world in his eyes, her mother scratching her jaw and her elbow as she shook her head violently and leaped forward.

"Stop, Mom!" Lucy raised her arms to stop her mother from hitting her in the face. But Lucy's hand struck her mother.

"You'll turn on me? Your own fucking mother?!" she yelled, holding her face, and then kicked Lucy in the stomach, sending her hurtling through the doorway and into the garage.

———

Damien was all out of breath as he reached the Pinebrook Waterworks. The executioner was faster, two paces ahead, running with the sword in hand. When he reached the waterworks, it was to the sight of the tall Lurker pushing the water tower into the pool.

"Lucy!"

He saw a brief glimpse of his sister clinging to the tower's railing as the whole structure splashed in the water and sank.

"She's still alive! You have to save her, please. I'll do anything," Damien screamed at the executioner. The executioner was already on his way. He strode toward the giant and swung his sword at him.

The Lurker fished Lucy out from under the water and was far too busy inspecting her with his lit eyes. He did not notice as the executioner walked up to him and swung his blade.

The blade met the Lurker's calf and wedged in deep.

Blood gushed out from the spillway made in the giant's body. He opened his mouth and screamed, but no voice came out. The Lurker threw Lucy across the ground. She rolled and came to a skidding halt by Damien's feet.

Her eyes were closed, and she was not moving.

Damien knelt beside his sister, putting his head next to her chest. He could hear her heart beating fraily.

"Don't you die on me, Lucy!" Damien wept, holding her in his arms and cradling her tight.

She opened her eyes with a start and rasped in pain.

"Damien!" she cried. "It's you! I'm so sorry. I thought..."

"It's okay," Damien said, kissing his sister's forehead, smearing it with his own tears. "You're okay. I've got you."

"—how—"

"Never you mind how. We have to get out of here while the executioner fights the Lurker."

"Worst wrestling match ever," Lucy chuckled as she tried to sit up. But when she turned her head to see the spectacle, all mirth and relief escaped her body.

The Lurker's blood had spilled and formed a deep layer on the grass. The executioner had taken his sword out of the giant's calf, and stood against the tall monstrosity dressed like a European schoolboy.

The Lurker lifted his bleeding leg and aimed it at the executioner, trying to crush him. He brought the foot down fast and hard.

The executioner lifted his sword. It pierced through the Lurker's boot, impaling his foot, coming out the other side bathed in more blood. The Lurker lifted his foot again, screaming silently, his gaze shedding a spotlight on the fearless executioner, who had taken his sword out at the last moment, and now stood wielding it with both hands.

The Lurker was fast this time around. He didn't give the executioner a chance as his hand clawed through the air and squeezed him. The executioner screamed.

"We have to do something!" Lucy yelled.

"Against *that?!*" Damien screamed. "We need to run!"

But it appeared that the executioner had a few tricks up his sleeve. He somehow freed his arms. He held in each hand a dagger, and he dug those daggers into the Lurker's fingers. The Lurker let go of him as he retracted his hand and pulled back.

The executioner fell to the ground, but landed and rolled to avoid breaking his body in the fall.

The Lurker, agitated, knelt and reached for the executioner, grabbing ahold of his head this time, bearing all the sword slashes on his arm. He closed his fist around the executioner's head and slammed it against the ground repeatedly. When he let go, he also pulled the executioner's mask off his face.

From this far away, the children couldn't see who it was. Just that he had long hair and that his whole face was covered in blood.

Somehow, he got up and wielded his sword once more, slashing away at the Lurker's hand, cutting it clean off his forearm. Blood gushed like a waterfall from the stump. The executioner stood in its path, digging his sword in the ground to stop himself from being blown away by the bloodstream. When the Lurker pulled away, the executioner was entirely red, entirely drenched in blood; not a human, but what remained of a human when you took away all the humanity and left all the horror.

This horror jumped on the Lurker's bent knee, then leaped into the air with his sword, bringing it down into the Lurker's chest. The entire blade went in.

The Lurker backhand-slapped the executioner with his remaining hand as if he were no more than a fly. He crashed against a tree trunk and fell to the ground, unmoving.

As for the Lurker, he tried to get up and failingly tried to take the sword out of his chest. But instead, he toppled over and fell on his back into the water pool.

First his head sank, taking the light with it. It still shone from under the water, making visible the rest of his sinking. His handless stump was next to go. He flailed with his remaining hand, but was unable to hold anything as he fell deeper into the water.

The last to go were his legs.

The water splashed with each impact of his body, and finally, once he had fallen whole, the water waved violently. If at first it was black, now the water was crimson.

Finally, the light went out, and the water became still.

Once Damien and Lucy were certain that the Lurker wouldn't jump out of the water, they got up. Damien helped his sister to her feet. He flung her arm over his shoulder as they walked up to the tree where the executioner had fallen.

He had fallen on his face, his entire body drained in congealing blood. He was still as he lay there.

"Is he dead?" Lucy asked.

Damien let go of his sister. She leaned against the tree to hold herself steady as Damien bent down and pulled the executioner, turning him over.

His chest heaved as he took a sharp breath and opened his eyes.

Underneath all that blood and the violence inflicted upon his body, his face was not recognizable.

He drew another breath, harsher, infused with pain. He stared at the kids, then grabbed at his head, where he realized he wasn't wearing a hood to mask his identity.

He sat up against the tree and ran his hand across his face, drawing some of the blood away. He looked up at Damien, and only now was his face recognizable.

It was the Other Man.

House of Leaves

"I suppose..." the Other Man wheezed, blood dripping from his mouth. He was haggard, the opposite of how he appeared to them usually. His beard was long, his mustache weighed down, covering his lips. He held a shaking hand on his stomach, as if to quell the pain and stop the bleeding at the same time. "...you want an explanation for all of this."

Damien didn't know what he wanted. The shock of discovering that the executioner and Tom were the same guy had put him in a state of catatonia. Dams of memory were beginning to break, little snippets of recollections beginning to gush through.

Such as the fact that Damien had seen this man before exactly in this appearance in an illustration in a book in his house's attic. It was shortly before both of them came looking for him. He'd thought they might punish him.

But there was something else.

They'd made cupcakes.

"How about you begin by telling us why you've tried to kill us?!" Lucy snapped, her loud voice bringing Damien back to the present.

"Are you Uncle Tommy?" Damien asked.

The executioner raised an eyebrow at Damien, nodded shortly, and then coughed blood. "I've been many things, depending upon what the situation called for."

"You're sick," Damien cried. "I trusted you. We...we thought you were a friend."

"That was the idea, kid. That's always the idea. Lull 'em into a false sense of safety before you harvest their soul. Have you ever eaten game? Game meat tastes gamey. It's hard, rough, bitter, and no fun. The hunt overfloods the deer's body with chemicals. Puts it into fight-or-flight. A good hunter kills the deer such that the deer doesn't even know it's been shot at. It dies tenderly. Its meat is sweet, soft, and a delight to eat. A brace of coneys is the same. People think that all rabbit meat is shit. Ever tried catching the rabbit by surprise? You'll notice that it's quite the delicacy then," the Other Man said. He put his hands on the ground and pushed himself to his feet. While there was blood on him, there wasn't any spilling from his body.

He walked around the tree, and what appeared from behind wasn't the executioner any longer. It was Uncle Tommy, long hair, lively face.

"You wouldn't have been fun to me if I took your life in throes of fitfulness," Uncle Tommy said, circling the tree again, and reappearing as Tom, in his hermit-nomad getup. "I wanted your final moments to be those of peace. I worked hard to make it so. I...tried many things. After all, that's what the hunt is about," he said, without going around the tree a third time. He stood in his Tom form, grief upon his face. And shame.

"I am sorry that I did that..." he continued, bowing his head.

"Did you kill Yuri?" Damien asked.

"Yuri's not who you thought he was. He was just like the Lurker, like myself, one of the many fetid creatures out for souls. He would have killed you if I hadn't killed him first. I've killed two now. Yuri and this Lurker. I went into their territories when I shouldn't have. Worse yet, I've got a reckoning on my hands now. When someone like me breaks the rules, this place sends the Reapers. They're going to come for me. I done broke the rules. Best I get you someplace safe, possibly back to your own world, before that happens."

"What are you talking about?" Lucy was wary of Tom, standing back, arms crossed, eyes unblinking.

"There's a lot to tell," Tom said, looking at the still water in the water treatment pool. "And I'm not sure if we have the time. Come. We must away."

He didn't turn back to see if they were following him. They weren't. The two kids stood by the tree. Only after Tom had taken several steps did he look over his shoulder and find that the kids stood in the same spot.

"What makes you think we're going to come with you? You damn near killed us in the basement. Not to mention we saw you kill someone down there anyway. Like you were having fun doing it! You lied to us. We're not coming with you! And what was that whole deal with being Uncle Tommy and putting false memories in our minds?" Lucy's voice seethed with rage, her hands closed into fists.

"Need I remind you I also saved your life just now. And I saved your life when the dead kids had you cornered in that classroom. Not to mention Yuri. I took him out before he could take you out. A little gratitude would be nice, seeing as how I'm your only way out of this place," Tom grunted. "If you want to leave, that is. By all means, feel free to stay. This place and those who call it home would love nothing more than you staying."

Lucy and Damien shared a look. Tom wasn't bluffing. And he was right. Lately, he had protected them. But the kids couldn't bring themselves to trust him. What if this was yet another ruse?

The surface of the treatment pool bubbled, light flickering from underneath it.

Lucy broke into a run, her nails digging into Damien's hand. They followed Tom as he walked out of Pinebrook Waterworks. But they kept their distance from him, keeping within the glow of his lamp yet far enough that should he try something, they'd be able to run away at a moment's notice.

"You can walk closer. If I wanted to kill you, I'd have done it in your sleep. But that wouldn't have been any fun," Tom said. "And if there's one thing the wretched like me want, it's fun. But I've had enough of that now.

Enough to last me a lifetime, whatever little of it remains. Come along, Damien. Hop to it, Lucy. I've made two mistakes, and that's not counting you two. Soon, they'll notice. Four mistakes rids you of your head. That's a shame. I quite like mine."

Not understanding a word of what he was saying, the two followed him closer. By the time they were back on the road, it started raining.

"That's a first," Tom said, pulling the hood of his jacket over his head. They were just passing by Zyn's. He guided them toward the store. There was no one inside. Tom battered through the glass door, saying, "Mind the glass."

They walked inside the dark store. Luckily, what Tom was looking for was right there by the entrance. He took two umbrellas and opened them, handing them each to Lucy and Damien.

"Hungry? Need some snacks?" Tom asked, waving his hand around as if he owned the place. He might as well have.

"Just get us home," Lucy said tiredly.

Tom nodded briefly and then went out into the rain. The children with their umbrellas followed him into the night.

———

The air near their street smelled of rain and fallen leaves, but it also smelled of gasoline and decay. Tom trudged on with his lamp and his waterproof jacket, his goggles repelling the rain, allowing him to see farther than the children could.

"I thought you were not Damien," Lucy said, holding fast to her brother's hand. "When you followed me. I'm sorry about that."

"Don't be," Damien said, giving her a tired smile. "I wouldn't have trusted me either. I'm just glad you're alive. When the Lurker grabbed you, I thought that was it. That you'd died. It was worse than anything, that feeling. I can deal with this place. I can live to see another day even after fighting with these fog monsters. But what I can't do is lose my sister. The only one who's ever cared for me. I..." Damien's voice broke. His face was wet, and that had nothing to do with the rain. "I..."

"You're my brother from the same mother," Lucy chuckled. "There's no way I'm leaving you."

"Sister from the same mister," Damien laughed. Such a carefree laugh did not belong in this world. As it traveled, it gave the world just a momentary sheen of warm light that was too instantaneous to see. But the world felt it regardless.

And that was not a good thing. The denizens of this world felt it too. And now they knew where the children were headed.

"You'd best be quiet," Tom said, stopping dead in his tracks. He looked around the street, and when something felt amiss, he immediately turned his lamp off. Now they were standing in the dark downpour, bathing the dirt and dead leaves off the houses, making them travel down the road. Someone's paper boat swam past Lucy's foot.

Tom grabbed each kid by their shoulder and frantically ran to the house opposite theirs. The house belonged to Mr. Hersham, a widower who lived with his huskies. Every morning, they raised a ruckus, those five huskies, as Mr. Hersham took them out on their daily walk. Lucy loved those dogs. Ernie, Husko, Bernie, Mr. Bernard, and Cinderella. Mr. Hersham used to let her pet the dogs whenever he'd pass around their house. He was a pockmarked man who wore thick glasses and a brown turtleneck. He was always smoking cigarettes and coughing. He'd let Lucy take the leash of one of the dogs and have her walk with him. He was as neighborly as neighborly got. Whenever he saw a new bruise on Lucy's face or arm, he inquired about it, never buying any of her lies about falling down stairs or hitting herself on the cupboard door.

Thrice, he'd even rang the doorbell and had shouting matches with her father. Her father would then proceed to threaten with lawsuits and tell him to do a little something called minding your own business, and if that was proving especially difficult, then why didn't he try sticking his head where the sun didn't shine?

After the third altercation, Lucy's mother had given her a stern beating on her back with a walking cane, prohibiting her from ever talking to the neighbor again. And so, Lucy hadn't, even though he still walked the same dog-walking route every day.

His house smelled of dogs, but not in the bad way most dog-inhabited houses do. There was a smell of warm, shampooed fur, and dog food. Tom lit his lamp, promptly closing each curtain so that no one outside would see that they were hiding here. In the light of the lamp, the two children explored the living room. Five dog beds lined the sofa, adjacent to the TV. This was where Mr. Hersham sat down each night and watched movies with his dogs. Sometimes, he forgot to pull the curtains, and Lucy and Damien could see inside his house.

All the dogs lined up, wagging their tails, heads resting on their paws. Mr. Hersham with a beer in hand and a fistful of dog treats that he'd toss every five minutes or so. He'd always watch some kind of happy, fun-time movie like *Home Alone* to keep his dogs engaged. Lucy suspected that those were the movies of his childhood. He was not so old, after all.

He looked old, but he'd once told her that he was in his late thirties. That his wife had died because of something called ovarian cancer. He went to her grave every weekend with the dogs. Husko and Bernie were the older of the pack, and they remembered her, he told her. They got morose whenever they went to the graveyard.

"Something about a dog is downright holy in a nonreligious way, if you know what I mean. They're almost like sentinels, protector spirits. I know mine have stopped me many a time from making some terrible decisions. It got real lonely after Eileen died. I...considered following her," he'd once said. "And then I looked at Mr. Bernard, who was no bigger than a puppy at that time, and his sad eyes reminded me that while my wife was gone, they still needed me. I think people give cats a little too much credit. I think dogs are much wiser. Not that it's ever a debate. Husko and Bernie whimper terribly when they visit Eileen's grave. Ever seen a cat do that?

"Now you best make like a tree and leave. Tell your dad to clean up the front lawn and the roof. It's practically a house of leaves. So much dead, dry leaves. One spark and the whole thing catches fire."

Instead of telling her dad, she'd gone and cleaned all the leaves herself, even the ones on the roof. The thought of her house burning down had kept her awake for several nights. From that day, she'd never let a stray leaf remain on the lawn or anywhere on the house. It could be kindling in the case of a house fire, after all.

And now, how ironic, that Mr. Hersham's house was a house of leaves, with leaves all over the front, leaves covering his car. She peeked just an inch from behind the curtain to see some of those leaves being dragged away by the torrential rain.

"When it rains, it doesn't mist," Damien said, standing close behind her, keeping an eye on Tom. "Is that like scientific?"

"This place doesn't exactly follow the rules of science. Hell, most of the time, science doesn't follow its own rules," Tom said, taking off his wet coat. "Photons, wormholes, quarks, blackholes, gravity, time. It's all a multifaceted mess that we've led ourselves to believe is an infallible system. Take this house, for instance. Do you smell the dogs and their sweet, wet fur? Listen close, you'll hear them bark. Listen even closer, you'll hear the man who lived here and his wife, laughing, fighting, crying. Then you'll hear the man alone, mourning his wife. You'll hear his dogs whining. Listen."

Lucy and Damien closed their eyes, and while they could not hear anything, they could *feel* it. In some part. As if the past, present, and future were somehow the same. They couldn't describe it. This feeling stayed for just a moment, and then it was gone, and they were back in the cold, dark house, Tom looking out the window, whispering something under his breath.

"Shit. They're here," he whispered, and then stepped away from the window. He hastily turned the lamp off. Now they were standing in complete darkness. Even the little parting through the curtains was of no avail. There only came more deadlight from outside.

Lucy took the risk of pulling the curtain open a little more, so she'd see who was here.

There were four of them, standing in front of the children's house. Two of them carried flames in their hands. The other two were far more distorted to hold something. Like creatures in anguish, they crawled on all fours, looked rabidly from one side of the street to the other, and put their twisted arms on the tree trunks to balance themselves. Beyond them being four humanoid shapes, she could not see much.

But the way Tom was terrified, those four had to be something far more horrific than the Lurker.

"Reapers," Tom whispered. "They play by no rules. They have a fondness for torture. And for killing their prey with vehemence. Remember how I said that you lull a soul into safety, and then harvest it? They're not Soul

Harvesters. They reap it with all its bitterness. The coarser the reaping, the better. I've lived this long by making sure never to cross paths with them."

"They're not that big," Damien said. "They don't look that scary."

"Looks aren't the thing to focus on here, boy," Tom said. "They're older than I am. Stronger. They've been here longer. And they... Well, let's just say that they enjoy their exclusivity of being rulebreakers. I broke the rules, and now they'll want to kill me. It's almost tempting. You see, I haven't died before. I don't know what follows. If anything follows at all, that is. I've dealt death aplenty. But I've never been on the receiving side."

Two of the Reapers flung their flames into the house. The other two howled and cackled like hyenas, slamming their hands against their heads, shrieking and roughing each other up. Lucy didn't want to imagine what would happen if they caught her. They were faster than she could follow. One second they were here, and the next, they zoomed out of existence, appearing somewhere else.

Now that her eyes were adjusting to the darkness and its many spectacles, she could see that they, too, wore similar blood-stained clothes as Tom's alter-ego.

The windows broke as flames hurled through glass and frame. There was no end to the fire that the two Reapers wielded. They threw fireball after fireball at the house in their frenzy.

The fire was red without a tinge of any other color. Dark red, and bathed in blackness, this unnatural fire roared, howled, and shrieked, exploding each room with deafening sounds.

The kids could only watch helplessly as their house was set on fire, and the Reapers stood around it with their twisted faces contorted into snide laughter.

"Worst thing about them is...they don't honor the harvest," Tom said, turning away from the window.

Damien was far too fearful to say anything. All he could think of was how all his clothes, his toys, his books, his favorite movies from his father's DVD collections, the food that he ate every day, and his warm bed, all were up in flames, the whole house a beacon in the rain, the fire unaffected by the downpour. It rose and rose, billowing smoke into the air.

Flames crackled as the house turned red, and then black.

Finally, when the woodwork had weakened and sparks were beginning to fly, the beams and rafters beginning to crackle, the house collapsed upon itself with a loud implosive thud, the fire still as insatiable as ever. It traveled horizontally, burning the trees all around their house.

But that is where it stopped. When it reached the fences, it ceased its spread and stayed there, as if it was sentient and knew exactly what its task was.

"So this is how it feels when the hunter becomes the hunted," Tom said to no one in particular.

Lucy watched as the Reapers stood around the charred remains of the house like funeral attendees. She could hear them over the rain and the last of the flames.

They were laughing.

The Limn

It was when the last of the embers had died in the downpour that the four Reapers finally dispersed. Lucy hoped that they'd all go in the same direction. At least that would mean they were like a pack of dogs and could be tracked and avoided at the same time. Her heart sank when she saw each of them go in their own separate direction.

"They intend to draw us out," Tom said, his voice shaking. "They might call for reinforcements. They're not the only Reapers out there. You stay long enough in this world and you forget the sweet taste of soul. You forget you ever craved it. You diminish over time, and after all reason and desire has left you, what's left of you is a Reaper. I was almost a Reaper. I'd have been a Reaper. And now that I am not, does it make any difference?"

"I don't understand anything you're saying!" Lucy

said, stomping her foot frustratedly. "I need you to tell us what this entire shtick is."

Tom chuckled. "Shtick, you say. Where'd you pick up Yiddish?"

"How is that relevant?" Lucy snapped.

"He's changing the subject," Damien said, rubbing his arms in the cold.

"No, it's just... I'm not changing the subject. I eventually need to tell you what this is, why you're here, and how you came to be here. It's not a pretty story, nor is your role in it pretty either. Least of all mine. In fact, I believe I was supposed to be the villain in your story. I can't quite tell it here. The Reapers are out and about, and they're quick to pick up scents. We need to go. We'll head to the hospital, but we have to travel real cautious. Take breaks. Make stops. Throw them off if they're on our scent. If one finds us, we can fight him. If two find us, we run. If four find us, it's too late. Let's hope that doesn't happen."

"Our house burned down, in case you didn't see!" Damien pointed outside with his shaking hand. "Everything we had was in that house."

"No! No! I forget you're a child. This was not your house that burned down. It was a version of it. Your real house is out there. Beyond the Limn," Tom said. Instead of explaining what he meant, he put on his waterproof jacket once more, lit the lamp again, and went outside into the downpour.

Lucy and Damien stared after him, and then,

knowing they had no choice but to follow, took their umbrellas and ran after him.

For once, Pinebrook looked close to normal. This was how it usually looked when it rained. The entire town turned into a bluish hue, the sound of rain accentuated by every kind of surface it fell upon. Tin roofs. The roofs of cars. The gravel. The grass.

Even though they knew that they were being hunted, that the Reapers might appear at any given moment, the rain made them feel calm. It was as if it was calling them home.

Tom walked really quietly, and from time to time turned the lantern off. After walking for several minutes, once he was certain that nothing was lurking in the shadows, he turned the lamp off entirely, providing the explanation that their chances of going undetected were better if they had no light.

"Besides," Tom continued, "the Reapers aren't affected by the light. They might be agitated by it. That may cause them to be more violent. And as for the dogs and the birds and all that thriving animal life here, I think you took care of most of it when you burned down the amusement park. I haven't seen a dog since. But that's not saying anything. These things spawn out of thin air when they want to."

They walked behind the cover of parked cars and tree trunks. The snarls of the Reapers came from close by from time to time. When they did, the children and Tom became still as statues. When all was quiet again, they walked slowly.

It took them twice as long to reach Zyn's.

When they reached the store, Tom pulled two wooden boards and put them against the door that he'd broken earlier.

"We ought to stay here awhile. This place is big enough. Maybe they'll get tired after all and leave for the night," Tom said. "Don't turn any lights on."

They didn't. Instead, they went to the fridges and took out cans of Dr. Pepper, which they drank with Lays and Cheetos. Surviving was hungry work. Tom went behind the counter and helped himself to something strong and dark. He sat down by the window, looking out, drinking cheap vodka.

"Rain's dying down."

They reappeared from behind the aisles to see this phenomenon. Indeed, the rain had died down. A gray light was beginning to pour into the sky. At the center, the gray gave way to deep purple and red.

"Is that the sun?" Lucy asked, unable to believe her eyes.

"Aye. How does it feel, having the sun on your face?" Tom asked, taking another swig of vodka. "Burns, for me."

"It hasn't really risen yet," Damien said, drinking his Dr. Pepper. "Isn't it about time you explained everything?"

"All right," Tom said, looking disappointed. "I cannot delay it any longer. And it looks like I'm running out of time. Follow me. And please try not to judge me. I was made this way. This was my role. No different than the roles humans play on earth."

"You're not even a human?" Damien asked.

"I appear in front of you out of clotted blood. I take different shapes. I mess with your mind. I take my nourishment from harvesting souls. You really think I'm a human?" Tom asked. "You'd still bestow me that honor?"

"Well. A really messed up human, but a human anyway," Lucy said. "What are you then, vampyre?"

"No. My source of nourishment isn't only blood. Its life force, what the religious of the world call 'soul.' It's...difficult to explain. Let's see. It's like an electromagnetic force that's the same stuff as what makes stars hang suspended in space and planets orbit their suns. It's...what gives you life. Call it soul, call it your qi, call it what you want. It's the thing that makes you alive. I live off of it. That's what we do."

"Are you a demon then?" Damien blurted. "Like one of those crossroads demons from *Supernatural*?"

"In a manner of speaking, though it's not like we're ever portrayed accurately by your lot," Tom said. "The word *Daemonium* is Latin for evil spirit. That's...laughable, subjective. You call us evil spirits and then supplicate to us on altars made of your sins. Who's the demon here?"

"I still don't understand what we have to do with this. We're children," Lucy said, crossing her arms.

"Don't you know children are the best of sacrifices?" Tom smirked. The glint in his eyes, the red hue that was no reflection but a source of light in itself, confirmed to Lucy that he was indeed who he said he was.

A demon.

Which meant this place was hell.

"And before you go thinking this place is hell," Tom said, wagging his finger at her. "Let me remind you it's not. It's not Limbo either. One must find Milton, Dante, and T.S. Eliot and hang them by their necks along with all the clerics for their tall tales and assumptions. Hell is not the only hell out there. There are hells that have nothing to do with Satan or God. Hells that are abandoned, cold landscapes that were never designed for any kind of punishment, but lands that were forgotten after they were made. And this place...well...this place is one of the many hunting grounds on earth. Places where we 'demons' are given free rein to hunt souls, devour them raw, and then fulfill our end of the bargain. It's how humans have thrived for thousands of years. They offer their offspring, their virgins, their celibate pious men, and then they ask for this mercy or that mercy, this boon, that favor."

"We're sacrifices?" Damien asked, his eyes growing dark and wide.

"I'm afraid so," Tom said. "And if you're looking for the culprit, look no further than your parents. They're the ones who had the wonderful idea that offering their kids as sacrifices would solve all their worldly woes. Your mother would cease aging, grow beautiful, and become the famous, influential socialite who'd be invited to galas, fashion shows, sit side by side with famous designers and stars. Your father would find himself in immense wealth, wealth that would afford him all that his heart desires. That was the deal. This demanded two sacrifices."

Damien wanted to say something, but he was not able to. So Lucy said it on his behalf. "My parents are shitty people. But they wouldn't sell our souls. Even they'd have their limits."

"Again, I ask you. Who's truly the demons here? Is it us spirits, or is it you humans, whose greed for money, lust, fame, and power knows no ends, and for these pursuits they'd do anything? Offer innocents to Moloch and Baal. All for what? Momentary pleasure? The horrors that humanity pulls in such short lifetimes baffles us all," Tom said.

Now the sun was well up in the sky, but for some reason its light didn't reach Pinebrook. It was as if it was being refracted away by the clouds and the reappearing mist. Lucy groaned out of desperation as the mist descended down the street.

But that momentary glimpse of the sun was enough. Enough to give her hope.

"You're part of the problem then!" Lucy snapped. "To even entertain such offers."

"And be deprived of food? I ask you again, another question. What good is the offering of a soul to a spirit such as myself, a spirit whom your kind refers to as demon, djinn, devil? Do I contain them in vaults as if they were gold? I have no use for such currency. I consume souls, and I survive. If I cease doing that, I die. Think as your kind might, you're not at the apex of the food chain. Neither am I. There are worse things out there than I. Those who would prey upon me. I dare not name them lest I invite them. For me, souls are sustenance, and if humanity is so bent upon offering them to me, it makes my job easier to have them delivered right to my doorstep rather than having to go out and hunt them. In that regard, I am somewhat of a pacifist. In fact, you will discover that many of my kind don't actively go out to hurt your kind. It's only what's blatantly offered to us that we take," Tom said. He got up and put the empty vodka bottle on the counter, helping himself to another one. This time it was whiskey.

"Can we go back?" Damien asked. "To our home?"

"By law, you cannot. And there's a good chance that even if you do, other demons might continue to hunt you, seeing as how you're offerings," Tom said ruefully. "But the mathematics of it holds. If you can escape through the Limn, you can go back to your reality."

"What's the Limn?" Damien asked.

"Come, let me show you," Tom said, taking the whiskey bottle with him and heading to the back of the store.

"Luce, I have to tell you something. Things are coming back to me," Damien said. "I'm remembering what they did. I think Tom's right. We were sacrificed—"

"Not right now. We'll have that talk, and we'll have it properly. I'll tell you what I've remembered, and you can tell me what you do. When we're both sure we remember the same thing, we'll form a theory. Got it? For now, let's look at the Limn. Maybe we can cross over through that," she whispered and squeezed Damien's hands reassuringly.

Tom opened the door to the storage room.

"Mind the smell," Tom said, holding the door open.

Nigel Clive, the shopkeeper, lay there, dead, his eyes gouged out, his tongue torn from his mouth. What remained of his face was pulled back in the last expression he had upon dying—abject horror.

"Someone took this guy's soul. Was he offered as a sacrifice? I don't think so. There are many who roam this place who are only lost but can't find their way back. Comatose patients who have been in their comas for years. People overdosing on drugs. People on trips that last longer than they should have. This place is rich with souls. And someone just took this guy's."

"Nigel. His name was Nigel," Damien said. It looked like Nigel had been repeatedly stabbed across the chest, slashed along the neck, and then rammed against the wall. His head was bent out of shape and didn't look entirely solid.

Damien took his jacket off and put it on Nigel's body, covering his face.

"There. He could be resting now," Damien said.

"I'm afraid not. If your soul's consumed, you're gone forever. No living on after death in another realm, no nothing. There remains nothing of your friend Nigel. I would not lie to you again," Tom said. "As for who it was that took his soul so viciously, I would think that it's the Reapers. Soul Harvesting and Soul Reaping are two separate things. A Harvester such as myself takes great care when taking someone's soul. A Reaper, on the other hand, well, you can see for yourself."

"Where's the Limn?" Lucy asked, looking around the storage room but not finding any signs of it.

"Look closer. It's right there," Tom said, and shut the door behind them.

———

In the dim light coming from just the one fluorescent tube in the storage room, Lucy squinted hard to make out the Limn. But no matter how hard she looked, she couldn't make out anything other than crates, boxes, and Nigel's blood on the floor.

"Look beyond it," Tom said, waving his hand in the air. His hand stirred something in the air, like an invisible film of some thick, translucent liquid.

And then, slowly, it started to become clear.

She could see through to the other side.

"Mr. Vikram!" Damien cried out as he saw the kindly Sikh coming into the storage room to pick up a crate of cans. The lights were all on in this other version of the storage room.

Damien and Lucy looked around and saw Mr. Vikram leave, completely oblivious to their presence. In the store, there were customers going through the aisles. Mostly moms and dads on the way home after dropping their kids to school. The door that Tom had broken was not broken. There was ample sunlight coming in. It was the most normal sight in the world, the complete opposite of the Zyn's where they were standing, which was abandoned, torn down, and dark.

"Can we cross over from here?" Lucy asked hopefully.

"You can't," Tom said. "This was Nigel's limning point. He crossed over here. I suspect that this gentleman was some kind of transient, trying to hide in the storage room for the night. He must have overdosed on something to find himself here, not quite dead, not quite alive. See, this place is tricky, and when your soul untangles from your body, such as when you're in a drug-induced stupor, it may find itself here. Think, truly, about the people you have come across. Some were offered as sacrifices. Some simply traveled here by mistake. Some nearly died and wound up here, and after their bodies died, they couldn't leave. Like those kids in that classroom."

"Ron?" Damien asked.

"Yes, Ron. He...poisoned his classmates and his teacher. He was a real sick kid for doing that. Sick, but not really astute when it came to mixing quantities. He found himself trapped in that classroom with the rest of the people he'd killed. There are rules to this madness. If you die in a place, and your death is final, then you cannot leave. If, however, your death is a natural passing, such as in the case of Beth and Brad, the girl and boy that you saw getting eaten by the fish —in that case, you can roam around as long as you're in close vicinity of where you died. While I do not know how they died the first time around, I do know that it was within the school premises," Tom said. "And then the Soul Harvester in the form of the angler fish got to them."

"Harry too?" Lucy asked.

"Everyone you see here. That's why this place looks abandoned. And this place is always abandoned. Most of the sacrifices offered are consumed quite quickly. Like I was supposed to consume you," Tom said, opening the door once again and letting them out of the storage room. "Your parents invoked me by name from that book they own. Named me, named you two, and named their desires. At first, I thought nothing of it. When you're like me, someone who's been around for centuries, this business numbs you. I was supposed to kill you the first day you appeared here, but then I actually witnessed you," Tom continued, walking through the aisles, looking uninterestedly at all the merchandise laid out.

"Why didn't you?" Lucy cried. "What are we to you? Why did you spare us?"

"This version of Pinebrook is no place for someone as bright and full of life as you two, little ones," Tom said wearily. "The more I got to know you, the more I learned of what kind of life you lived, the more I found myself asking, 'What if I didn't consume you?' You made me undergo a change in my nature that I hadn't anticipated happening in a thousand years. It is no mere sympathy that moves me. My kind are not keen on sympathy. It is your perseverance and the way you retain your innocence. You could have surrendered to the nightmare. Most people do. They scream and scream and weep till they pass out, and then they're dealt with. You...were pragmatic. You tried to live here, in this place that is unfit for any human to live. No, it's not pity either. I am moved by you, by your courage, by your will. That is what brought on my metanoia. You instilled in me some of your innocence, and for those moments I felt what it was like to be human. For you have taught me that, I cannot kill you. Even though I receded into my old ways and tried," Tom said, and now he was weeping.

He held his face in his hands and cried.

"I'm sorry for that," Tom sobbed. "For luring you to the manor. For mesmerizing you as an uncle that did not exist. For stalking you in this form for days. I fought with myself. And I should like to think that I have won. That you stand here and draw breath, safe, is evidence that even one such as myself is bound to change if he's introduced to the light."

He wiped his eyes and looked lovingly at the two children. "Damien, Lucy. May you live a long life and eventually find this out for yourself, but until you do, take this demon's word for it. You are light incarnate. And if you hold true to yourself and each other, there's nothing that can dim that light."

Lucy wanted to say something. As did Damien. In fact, Damien wanted to go up to the man and hug him.

But before either of them could act, the wooden boards barring the broken door flew across the store. Damien and Lucy ducked to avoid them. Lucy ducked in time; Damien was not so quick. The edge of the board caught him in the head. He was thrown back against an aisle.

"Damien!" Lucy cried out after her brother. He was stirring, but his eyes had closed. She held onto him, watching the spectacle unfold by the store's entrance.

There he stood in the shattered entrance, a bloody-bandaged, hooded creature hunched over, wielding blades in his hands. Upon closer inspection, those blades were part of his hands, jutting out of his nail beds. He had a torn mouth, with his lips sliced up to his ears. Out of that deathly pale, blood-smeared flesh dropped a long, twisted, forked tongue licking along his blackened lips.

His teeth resembled no human's teeth. All were jagged and pointed and far more in number than thirty-two.

He hissed as he stared around the room.

Lucy wondered wildly how he could see, given that his eyes were covered with red bandages.

"So this is where you've been hiding them, old man. We looked all over town. Gluttonous, aren't we? Keeping two for yourself while the rest of us starve!" the Reaper hissed, its voice so penetrative that Lucy could feel it inside her skull and in her bones.

"Go your own way, Reaper," Tom said, standing tall and broad between the children and the Reaper. "They are mine."

"Blood has been spilled that must be recompensed. You murdered two of ours. You know the rules. First we peel your skin, then we take your prey. I have called the others.

They are coming," the Reaper spat, thick black drool dripping from his chin.

Tom turned to look at the two and said, "If I don't make it, you know what to do. Your limning point is at the hospital. That's why I stopped you from going there. Go to the hospital. Find the Limn."

"Gut-wrenching performance by the trickster god of blood jests," the Reaper sneered.

"Yet you come after me regardless. Don't you know what I am capable of?" Tom said, and within the blink of an eye he was no longer the Other Man, the hermit traveler. He was the executioner, wielding his sword. "Come at me."

"Oh, I come not alone, but why not?" the Reaper hissed, and then lunged at breakneck speed.

Trickster God
of Blood Jests

Damien wasn't a full four feet at the age of eight, something that gave him the advantage of being quite inconspicuous while it also gave him several disadvantages. But he was a glass half-full kind of kid, as someone in his position had to be.

The benefit of being so small was that he could stand behind the sofa and not have anyone notice him. He'd perfected the art of being silent, an art that every child belonging to an abusive household has to master from a young age. He could control his breathing such that he was completely silent yet still inhaling. At the drop of a hat, he could turn around and disappear behind a wall.

He had employed these stealth tactics and many more to escape his parents whenever they were in a terrible mood, which was most of the time. There were very few moments when they were actually in parenting mode. Probably once every three months, or even rarer.

To a child who has only experienced such a reality

from the beginning, this is the norm, and he doesn't know that there are parents out there who are not as abusive, not as toxic, parents who love their children without pretense or limits. Parents who take their kids out every other weekend, if not every weekend. Parents to whom their children are not their legacy, their assets, the best thing they've made.

Damien was an asset to his parents. He just didn't know how exactly.

Until one day, he started to pick up on things that Lucy, taller by a whole foot, was not able to gather, what with her presence being so much more noticeable. Their parents shut up every time she walked into a room, and only ever addressed her when they wanted to berate her or tell her that she hadn't cleaned her room or that there were dishes that needed to be cleaned in the kitchen.

Damien, he could just crouch behind the table and his dad wouldn't notice him for hours. He'd play with his toys under the coffee table and pretend he was playing with his father, and that his father was saying things like, "That's a good boy!" Damien thought every child played with their father like this. He'd even gone so far as to convince himself that the kids in his class were big fat liars. That their parents didn't really take them to Aspen or Denver or Wisconsin Dells—that they were just pretending. Like he was pretending his father was playing army men and monster trucks with him.

One day, there was a guest at their house.

Lucy was up in her room, doing something crafty with a *5-Minute Crafts* video playing on the tablet and a bunch of threads and ribbons laid out in front of her. She also had her headphones on, which she said helped her focus with creative tasks. When Damien had asked her if he could assist her with whatever it was she was doing, she said that this wasn't the kind of thing you did with your brother. That it was a girly girl thing, and that she'd appreciate it if he went and took his toys somewhere else and left her for some moments of peace.

Damien picked up his toys and took them downstairs. Maybe he wouldn't even have to play pretendsies with his dad. Maybe the garage was a better option. Noice cancellation, after all. He'd discovered that no matter how loud he was in the garage, his parents never heard him.

He was too young to remember that once his father had tried to set up a YouTube channel for his mother, and in doing so, he'd put noise-canceling foam on the walls, hiding them with a little bit of interior design. He just knew that this was a safe space to play in a pinch.

But what was this? There was someone sitting there on the living room sofa with his parents. It must be someone important, because his parents were not in their usual states of varying inebriation. They were sober, well dressed, and had put out a whole spread for this guest.

He was a bald man, bald to the point that he didn't even have eyebrows. He was also quite young. Younger than his father. He wore a blue shirt and a black coat over it. Underneath, he was a little more casual, with jeans and sneakers. He had very oily skin, and he was constantly shifting his eyes from one end of the room to the other.

Still, Damien was sneaky enough to avoid his notice and creep into the garage. Here, it was quiet. Except—for some reason, it was not.

He looked at the door, realizing that he'd forgotten to shut it. Maybe he could play quietly. To shut the door now would mean drawing attention. And he didn't want his father beating him up in front of a guest.

As Damien laid down his toys in a neat row, he couldn't help but overhear his parents' conversation with the guest.

"I am so glad to have heard back from you. This is the hardest part of the journey, you guys. But the fact that you called us shows us that you possess the prerequisite faith to go through with this. I just want to reiterate that this is all real, and I'd be glad to go over the relevant case studies with you," he said.

"Edmund, it's...quite a lot," his mother said, "to take in. You're not asking for our cars as collateral, or even, God forbid, this house. You do realize that—"

"What I'm hearing is trad programming speaking through you. And I'm just trying to help you break past that. Consider it like *The Matrix*. I'm assuming such movie buffs as yourselves must have watched those movies. This...is the step. This is your red pill. You break free from the matrix and realize just how blind the rest are. People paying mortgages, installments, payments upon payments upon payments—rent, bills, utilities, hospital bills, insurance, premiums that get more expensive every year, subscriptions to things you don't need... Do you see it all around you?" Edmund said.

"But come on. It's batshit. Isn't it? Like, skip the whole minister talk and just level with me, man," his dad said pleadingly.

"It certainly is a leap of faith. But that's why we have case studies. Case studies that you can actually contact and confirm on your own. Think about it. If we were really a cult, why wouldn't we take your money? But that's just the thing. We don't want your money until after it's done, and even then, it's just a one-time payment of fifty thousand dollars. Let me assure you that successful candidates find fifty thousand dollars to be nothing more than peanuts in contrast to the wealth they gain." Edmund's voice was slick and quite deceptive to Damien's ears. He didn't like this guy at all. What kind of a name was Edmund, and what was he asking his parents to do?

"I mean...they're not exactly a spare kidney each. If that's what it took, we'd have done this long ago. Right?" his mother asked.

"Toby Osteen was a high-school dropout stuck in an unhappy marriage. 'Trapped' would be the word. His high-school sweetheart had gotten pregnant, and the whole affair was a Hicksville shotgun wedding. When his son was two, Toby came to us. More like found us. He had the same dreams as you. And you know us, you've been to the church several times, you know we don't coerce. We don't even preach this stuff except to those who already came upon this. Like you two did."

"To be very honest with you, Ed—" his father began.

"Edmund is fine," Edmund interrupted.

"To be very honest with you, Edmund," his father continued through gritted teeth. "We thought it was like a BDSM sex theater kind of thing. We thought the Trickster God figure was some kind of dungeon master. We didn't realize it was so literal."

"Let me get this straight. You came to Thomas Manor expecting it to be a swinging club?" Edmund snapped.

"Anything to spice up the ol' marital life," his father said. "But let me continue being honest. When I sat through the black mass, it clicked. This is how they get rich and famous over there in Hollywood, don't they? Isn't this the same principle with which politicians and rich men consolidate power and wealth?"

"For as long as there's been humanity, this has always been the way," Edmund said. "Take Toby Osteen. Last month he was on *Forbes'* Top 30 under 30 list. Got seed funding on the first try in Silicon Valley despite not knowing jack diddly squat about programming. They're saying he's going to be the Steve Jobs of decentralized computing, whatever that means. Do you want to know his net worth? It's two hundred million dollars right now. And he's only ever going to go up. Ask him if he misses his son and wife and he'll laugh at you, saying that this was the best decision he ever made."

Damien's heart sank. Just what the hell was this guy talking about?

"I presume you have the literature already?" Edmund asked.

"Yes. Yes. They made sure to give us the book. I

thought it was fiction," his father said, half-laughing. "I put it in the attic, where the kids can't read it."

"It's not. We who follow the Trickster God of Blood Jests have been blessed with visions of the Red Executioner in our shared dreams, our wildest dreams fulfilled."

"It's your wildest dream to be a fucked-up Jehovah's Witness? You gotta dream higher, bud," his father joked. His mother laughed, but Edmund didn't.

"I'd not make light of these matters if I were you," Edmund said, getting up. "Good day."

Damien heard him walk to the door. When he was gone, Damien's father shut the door and said, "Good day, you fucking nutsack."

Damien thought that his parents were about to enter the garage. He ducked underneath the workbench and hid himself behind a box. His father was the first to step in. He stepped on Damien's laid-out toys and yelped as a Lego piece wedged in his foot.

"Fucking hell! I'll tell you what I won't miss. Fucking...this! And the motherfucking mess around the house!" he said, pounding his fist on the workbench.

"Why can't we do it with someone else's kids? Why does it have to be ours?" his mother asked.

"Pretty sure the entity named Trickster God of Blood Jests needs your own blood as offering, not someone else's," his father grunted.

———

He'd hid under the workbench for half an hour, and had only come out when he was certain his parents had left. When he walked out of the garage, it was to the sight of both parents sleeping on the couch, the TV on, empty wine glasses on the coffee table.

He hadn't understood most of the conversation his parents had with the strange guest, but he'd understood one thing—there was some kind of book in the attic.

Books were a huge deal for him.

Near his house, at the end of the cul-de-sac, there was a miniature HOA-approved telephone booth that had shelves filled with secondhand books, a literary initiative by the people of the neighborhood to promote reading and book swapping. The principle was take a book, leave a book, unless you didn't have a book, in which case you could borrow a book.

Damien had borrowed all the fantasy and science fiction novels he could get his hands on from that booth, always making sure to return them. Terry Pratchett, Robert Jordan, Terry Brooks, J.R.R. Tolkien, C.S. Lewis, Brandon Sanderson, Patrick Rothfuss—he'd been introduced to the genre of fantasy thanks to that telephone booth, which was in itself a thing of fantasy.

But the drawback of not having books to leave was that he could only borrow books. There was a camera in the booth, which kept track of who did what.

And there was the added trouble that lately no one had put in a good book in there for some time, so he was real short on good literature.

The presence of a book in the house, a book that he

hadn't read, was as enticing as it could get. He checked on Lucy, saw that she was sleeping, and then immediately went to the attic. He propped himself on the window and pulled the rope down. He climbed the stairs and went into the attic, looking for the book in the mess of storage boxes and old furniture. There was a cabinet that didn't have any dust on it. Its top drawer was locked.

Damien thought like his father and mother and wondered where he might put the key. After looking around, he found that it was, in fact, right under the cabinet.

He opened the drawer and beheld the black leather book with the title *Blood Jests*. It was written by some guy named Thomas Caulk. Damien took the book to the window and opened it. There were pictures in the book. Strange pictures showing ancient rocks, strange sites, and people gathered around tall stone slabs.

"It's just a history book," Damien muttered, going through the rest of the book. He came to a halt at a page that had a very different picture than the rest.

A man dressed in black robes, wearing a hooded mask over his head, holding a tall sword. Underneath the picture it said, *Behold therefore the patron of the Bridge, the Trickster God of Blood Jests.*

It wasn't just a history book, Damien thought as he stared at the man standing in what looked like a dungeon. It was a horror book too. Maybe he'd read it after all.

"Who the hell lowered the ladder!" his father screamed from below.

Damien's heart dropped in his chest. He immediately put the book in the cabinet, locked it, and threw the key under the cabinet. When his father's head appeared from the opening, Damien was sitting by the window, playing with old, dusty, broken toys.

"Now just what the hell do you think you're doing up here?!" his father snapped. "You're cruising for a bruising, you little—"

"How come you don't ever play with me?" Damien interrupted him. "All the other dads play with their kids."

"What?!" his father snapped, his fist loosening. "What are you even doing here? How did you get the attic ladder down?"

"It was already down," Damien lied through his teeth, looking his father dead in the eyes. "I thought you'd gone up in the attic. I thought we could play here."

"Well, clearly I was not in the attic. What are you doing up here? There's rusty nails all over the place. You could get hurt. Come on down. I can play the PlayStation. You can watch."

"Can I play?" Damien asked, a little startled at how his father's usual seething rage had cooled down so quickly.

"Sure," his father said, looking over Damien's shoulder at the cabinet, then looking at Damien again. "Just come down."

As he followed his father downstairs, the lack of a beating and a scolding had disarmed him, making him forget the book momentarily. Downstairs, his father had the PlayStation open, and he was playing *Call of Duty* on it. Damien sat down beside him, watching him play the game, wondering when, if ever, his father would let him play too.

"Do you love me?" Damien asked in a very low voice, a voice that he was sure his father would never hear. But to his surprise, his father's ears picked it up.

"Huh? Of course I love you, you little hellraiser. What are you talking about?" he said distractedly, shooting enemy soldiers in the head with an AK-47.

"I just get afraid sometimes," Damien said.

"Well, that's your own damn fault for going into places where you shouldn't," his father said.

"I...I'm sorry, Dad. I'm sorry if I'm a bad kid sometimes. I don't mean to be," Damien said, his voice catching in his throat.

Andrew Bessemer put the controller down and looked at his son. His gaze met Damien's, and he could see the tears welling up in Damien's eyes. He sighed and put his hand on his son's head, bringing him in for a hug.

"You're not a bad kid. It's just...Dad and Mom, we're grownups," he said, pulling his son close. "And grownups got grownup problems. Sometimes we do things we don't really like to cope with those problems."

Damien didn't notice that his father turned back to the kitchen, where his mother was standing with a tray of cupcakes. Andrew Bessemer shook his head. Valerie glared at him. Andrew glared back and then shook his head again. Valerie finally nodded and took the cupcakes back into the kitchen.

"I wish I could help you with your grownup stuff," Damien said, burying his face in his father's jacket.

"Hey..." his father said, handing him the controller. "Your turn."

"Really?"

"Really."

Andrew Bessemer, sober for the entire day, left his son on the couch and went to the kitchen to get himself a beer.

For that one evening, everything felt normal. Damien's parents sat by either side of him, watching him play, both of them drinking a light beer, nothing else. Damien didn't even find out about the cupcakes until way later.

———

Way later being two days later.

That spell of sobriety had only lasted an afternoon. When Damien went down the following day, there were bottles of beer and a couple bottles of whiskey on the living room floor.

His parents had regressed back into their old personas, bitterly arguing with each other about something, their eyes red, the skin of their faces blotched. They were both smoking something that didn't quite smell like what they usually smoked.

Damien snuck into the kitchen. He was hungry. He'd slept all day—it being a Sunday—and hadn't had any breakfast. Now that his parents were back to their usual high/drunk selves, he knew that feeding himself would fall on his shoulders.

There was nothing in the fridge that he could eat. No takeout boxes, no leftover pizza. There was a tray covered with a lid, but he didn't know what that was. He went through the cabinets—canned food that he'd cut his hand opening. Cereal he wasn't in the mood for.

Maybe a glass of milk would suffice. He opened the fridge again, and unable to help his curiosity, he took the lid off the tray.

There were a dozen frosted cupcakes, smelling of strawberry and all the sweet goodness in the world. His mouth watered at the sight of them. He took one out and bit into it.

He then proceeded to eat two more.

He'd have eaten a fourth, but at that moment, he felt immense pain burst through his stomach, reach into his throat, and then come out in the form of vile puke spilling all over the floor.

Weakened, he fell face-first into his own sick and passed out.

AMBUSH

The Reaper's limbs were longer than he'd let on. He was swiping across the room and managing to hit Tom. Tom had several lacerations on his body from the Reaper's blade claws. The Reaper stayed clear of Tom, and therefore Tom wasn't able to hit him with his sword.

Damien stirred and woke up, rubbing his eyes and looking at the havoc around him. Aisles had collapsed like dominoes, scattering groceries everywhere. The fluorescents, the ones that had not broken in the havoc, were flickering, making the fight a dizzying spectacle.

"Let's get out of here," Lucy said once her brother sat up. He nodded wordlessly, the recent memories that had unleashed like a barrage upon him running before his eyes like a projector reel.

They crept behind the few aisles that were still left standing, peeking at the fight.

Tom had stopped trying to hit the Reaper and was

instead going toward him, taking every blow that came his way. This confused the Reaper, as it broke the fight's otherwise relentless pace.

The Reaper screeched and slashed with his claws, but Tom didn't even so much as wince as he closed the distance. He bled and winced, but finally closed the distance between himself and his foe, giving the Reaper no place to run. He was standing against the paperbacks and gift cards section of the wall, Tom's tall body brooding over him.

Tom grabbed the Reaper by the throat and squeezed.

The Reaper thrashed, slashing away at Tom's face, his neck, and his chest, but Tom tanked the hits and continued to choke the Reaper.

In another minute, the Reaper was not moving.

Tom let go. The corpse fell on the floor like a ragdoll, the tall limbs splayed, the still claws dripping with Tom's blood.

"Come!" he yelled hoarsely, unable to see where the children had hidden. "Before the rest of them find us. Come quick. I may yet be able to take you to the hospital."

"Tom," Lucy said, appearing from behind the aisle, holding Damien's hand. "You're bleeding."

"I've had worse," Tom said, wiping his face with his forearm. "And that's not what I'm afraid of. One I can handle. If it's a group, then we're doomed. I don't even want to think what happens when a Reaper horde appears. And they have been known to appear. The sun goes dark in the sky, the mist becomes solid enough to cleave through, and they walk through the streets looking for stragglers, Reapers upon Reapers. No one can fight that many."

Not wanting to hear more about the horror nor imagine it, Lucy followed Tom out of Zyn's, taking a look at it one last time. She couldn't believe it, but there was a certain nostalgia she was beginning to feel for the place. Now that she knew that leaving wasn't just a possibility but a likelihood, she felt like...

She didn't know what she felt like. Not all bad places were horrible, she wanted to say. Zyn's had been a refuge. Not even the Reaper's corpse on the floor could diminish that. She had bought groceries that had lasted the entire span of her stay here. The guy behind the counter, Nigel Clive, had been the first person to show her some warmth in here. That was more than she could say for most people back home. Where if they didn't mean business, they meant *mean* business.

She took a mental snapshot of the place before following Tom outside.

"Lucy. I gotta tell you something," Damien whispered, his voice shaking. "There's something you need to know."

"Not now, Damien. There's stuff I have to tell you too, but not until we get somewhere safe," Lucy said, gripping his hand tight.

"I don't think we're going to make it," he said, holding back a sob. "I don't think *I*—"

"Shh," Tom said, putting a hand to his lips. "Look."

They had to squint hard to see what Tom was looking at.

Several shadows jumped from the top of one building to the other. They moved fast. They were all around them, Reapers on every rooftop, snarling, their maddened gazes darting around, scouring the environment.

"I count more than..." Lucy began, but Tom shook his head.

"There's around a hundred," Tom said. "A crowd of 'em. Not yet quite a horde. I didn't anticipate them finding us so soon. Any bright ideas?" he asked, looking around. Each rooftop on Durham had several Reapers. Dressed in their black shrouds, they looked like a murder of crows come to avenge their fallen.

"Car," Damien said, pointing to the closest one. "You can drive cars. You drove us to Fun Land."

"I can," Tom said, scratching his head. "But will I be able to outrun these bastards?"

"We don't have to outrun them," Lucy said, realizing something.

"Get in," Tom said, walking over to a black Tacoma. The door opened, much to all their surprise. Tom turned the car on as the kids got in the back and strapped seat belts around them.

"Why aren't they attacking us?" Damien asked, looking out the window. There were more of them than before.

"They think they have us dead to rights," Tom

grimaced. "And they're not wrong. I don't know what the hell we're going to do."

Lucy said, "I do. Drive. Drive straight down the road and then turn to the right on Neibolt."

"Why Neibolt?" Tom asked as he did exactly as she asked.

Lucy told him and Tom listened. Behind them, the Reapers had begun their pursuit and were moving across the rooftops like swift shadows, always visible out of the corner of their eyes, but never there when they turned to look at them.

———

On the rare few days when Dad would pick them from school, the trip back home would never be just from school to home. Their father would get gas, groceries, and make a stop at the pharmacy, and so it'd take them an hour longer to get home.

Lucy and Damien didn't mind. An hour in the back seat of their dad's car, which was considerably more comfortable than the bus, was a good time, especially because their father always had music on. They didn't know that he did this so he didn't have to talk to the kids. Sometimes, he rolled down the window and smoked a cigarette.

But he always flicked the cigarette away before pulling up at the gas station on Neibolt. Once Lucy asked him why he did that.

"Because if I don't, the whole gas station just goes

floomp and then *boom*!" their dad said. "Now wouldn't that be something?"

The grotesque imagery of the gas station blowing up stuck with Lucy. It got to the point that whenever they reached the gas station, it was all she could think about. She'd scout the environment, looking for anyone with a lit match or a cigarette, her heart hammering in her throat. She'd look upon the columns and aisles of the gas station, awing at its tallness and its breadth.

"You know, this place used to be the pitstop for truckers going to Missouri, Arkansas, Kentucky, any place south. Trucks kinda have to do it to get their gas filled, their tire pressure checked, and you know, go to the bathroom, eat something," their dad once said, noticing his daughter staring around at the gas station. "But then, other newer gas stations popped up right there on the interstate with Denny's adjacent to them, and people stopped coming to this one. Bully for them."

"Huh?"

"I mean, have you ever seen a line at this station?" her father asked. He was in one of his talkative moods, and had turned the music off to talk to them. "You won't ever see a line. There's like ten aisles, all under the graceful and benevolent roof of Exxon Mobil, hallowed be their slick name. Amen. Name something more American than Exxon Mobil. I'll wait."

"Pokémon," Damien had said blankly. He hadn't even been part of the conversation. He was just looking at an anime-stickered Honda Civic that had pulled up next to them. A 2005 purple Civic with Ash Ketchum,

Brock, Misty, and Pikachu on it. The guy who got out of it was graying at the hair. Damien thought it was really strange someone so old would still be interested in Pokémon.

"Pokémon is Japanese, dum dum," his dad, who hadn't noticed the Civic, said, looking at his son's reflection in the rearview mirror. "All part of the Great Japanese Industrial Complex. You know, if it's anyone in the world that's got almost as much soft power as we do, it's the Japanese. Mario, Kirby, Zelda, Pokemon, and those are just the ones from my time. Nintendo, PlayStation, the billions of anime they produce over there tirelessly. Know what's more important than hard power?"

"I don't even know what hard power is." Lucy shrugged.

"Money, weapons, relations with other countries," her father had said. "Soft power's pop culture...influence..." He stopped saying whatever he was saying, because their turn had come.

He got out of the car and began filling it with fuel.

The reason Lucy remembered this memory clearly was because of what he did next. He turned around to look at her, a dangerous smile on his face, his Zippo between his fingers. His grin darkened and he took the top off the Zippo, his thumb on the roller.

"Dad, no!" Lucy screamed.

He threw his head back and laughed, stowing the Zippo away, clapping his hands for getting his daughter good.

But Lucy hadn't thought that he'd gotten her good.

For one moment, she had imagined the whole gas station blowing up, killing her, Damien, and their father. She was crying, eyes red.

"Oh, hey, hey. Come now. I was just—" he said, opening the car door to give her a hug, but she pushed him away, weeping.

He retracted out of the car, glaring at her angrily.

"That's how you're gonna be? Fine!" He slammed the door shut.

They didn't talk the rest of the way home, and when they reached home, Lucy didn't even have lunch. She just went up to her room, relieved that she was not dead.

————

Now they were on Neibolt, where the buildings had a lot of distance between them. As a result, the Reapers were not on the roofs, but chasing the Tacoma on the road. Several of them were fast enough to catch up to the speeding truck. They tried to slash at the tires, but Tom didn't give them a chance to do so. The drive toward the gas station was filled with bumps in the parked cars, and harsh turns to swerve clear of the vehicles parked right there in the middle of the road.

The chase was so intense and dangerous that none of the three spoke so much as a word. Damien clung to his sister and refused to look out the window. Lucy glimpsed every now and then and saw the Reapers outside the window, sneering, trying to ambush the car.

This was their only chance.

"There!" Lucy pointed to the left. Tom nodded and veered to the left. He rolled the window down and took the lamp from the passenger seat. With one fast click, he turned it on. Here, he slowed the car down just long enough that the Reapers would crowd around it.

They were everywhere—on the roof of the gas station, between the columns, atop the gas pumps, and even on top of the car, clawing away at the roof, shaking it, snarling against its windows.

Tom threw the lamp at a gas pump with brute force, fighting off the arm of a Reaper who was trying to pull him out of the vehicle.

He then put his foot on the accelerator and hurled the car through the throngs of Reapers in front of him. The car jolted as it crushed many of them under its wheels.

Lucy shot a look behind and saw that the lamp hadn't worked. It had exploded, but the explosion was so small that it had no effect.

"Any bright ideas?!" Tom yelled over the screams and howls of the Reapers. "Because the last one didn't work!"

"Gun?!" Lucy yelled.

"No gun! All out!" Tom groaned.

"Ram the car into the last gas pump!" Damien said.

"We might die!" Tom yelled, finally throwing off the Reaper who had been grappling with him. Lucy watched him roll on the ground, next to the many corpses of the Reapers that the truck had crushed, but there were far more alive and flanking them than there were dead.

"We'll die for sure otherwise!" Lucy screamed.

Tom sped the car through the gas station and aimed straight at the final gas pump. Beyond that was the exit ramp leading back onto Neibolt. He sped the Tacoma as fast as it could go.

The children braced themselves and ducked. Tom shielded his face as the car crashed against the fuel pump, uprooting it, spilling gasoline everywhere. The collision of the truck with the metal gas pump chassis produced several sparks, the gasoline catching several of them at once.

At first there was only a little fire, but then, Lucy saw her worst fear come to life before her eyes as the gasoline erupted in a brilliant blaze, the shockwave and the heatwave ripping past them. The car barely made it off the exit ramp and onto the road.

Most of the Reapers were still there at the gas station when it erupted into bright orange flames. Their dismembered bodies traveled through the air, black blood and ripped limbs falling like hellish rain.

Tom did a U-turn on the road and drove past the burning building. A few stragglers followed the truck, but the vast majority of them had turned into a congealed mass of burning bodies being rapidly consumed by the fire.

Their screams tore through the mist, the smell of their burning flesh making all three of them nauseous.

Tom sped up the car and turned right, heading back into downtown. As far as he could see, there were no more Reapers following him. Where the couple of stragglers had gone, he didn't know. Out of sight, out of mind.

"That worked!" Damien was incredulous. "Holy cow! That worked! Somehow we're still alive!"

But Tom said nothing. He drove with cautious eyes scanning the horizon. Where had the remaining few Reapers disappeared to? Had they retreated after such a staggering loss? Not likely. These were emotionless, cunning demons who didn't know the meaning of remorse or loss. If there were even four survivors, they'd find him.

But not if he got the children to the hospital first.

———

The car smelled of burnt flesh and gasoline as it pulled up to the hospital. Tom got out, eyes on the rooftops, looking for the remaining Reapers.

"Aren't those humans, those doctors and nurses?" Lucy asked warily, pointing to the doctors and nurses smoking by the entrance.

"Them?" Tom said, looking at the medical staff impatiently. "No. I remember the hospital some years ago being abandoned. But then they popped out of nowhere one day. And then their numbers started growing. I thought it was this place creating an elaborate stage for torture, but that's not who they are. Come on. Inside. Now."

Lucy and Damien, at long last, were inside the hospital. A receptionist sat at the lobby desk. There were chairs in the waiting room, some with a couple of people sitting or sleeping silently. Staccato steps on the matte floor echoed through the halls. Walls lined with pictures of flowers, people smiling, and the odd pharmaceutical advertisement for brand-name insulin, knee pain medicine, ointments for alopecia, creams for atopic dermatitis.

"Who are they?" Damien asked, looking at the doctors and nurses in scrubs, some of them coming out of rooms, others just standing there consulting amongst each other, heads close, files open in their hands.

"Apparently some years ago there was some kind of outbreak. Among those who died from the disease were also the on-call doctors and nurses. Some took to death keenly, passing over quickly. Others struggled. Some didn't even realize that they'd died and just kept on working until they realized that they were no more. Some still haven't realized it," Tom said, hand on each child's shoulder, ushering them through the hospital. He kept looking over his shoulder to see if they were being followed.

So far, no one had appeared through the doors.

Some of the staff gave Tom strange looks, seeing as how he was covered in blood and ushering two children through the hospital. Others just shook their heads and looked away.

"So they're ghosts?" Damien asked, feeling afraid.

"When the soul remains long after the body's gone, that's what they are. Now, if you want to call them ghosts, poltergeists, or anything else, that's your choice. Though, it is not a term they'd use for themselves, just as

I don't like being called a demon. They're unalive, a shadow image of the real world with real, alive doctors and nurses. This world is everything the other world is not. Where does a soul go when the body ceases giving it refuge? Well...sometimes it comes here. It's not entirely enticing or appetizing to consume them as food," Tom said.

"Ghosts are quite bland, almost like lukewarm water. It's sacrificial offerings, children whose psyches are left fractured and then their souls ripped from their bodies that are a glutton demon's dreams. And the sad fact is that at any given moment, there are millions of people across your world offering sacrifices to demonkind. With such a feast available, who would go after ghosts?" he finished, bringing them to a waiting area at the end of the first floor's hallway.

Once he was certain they were not being followed, he sat down on one of the chairs, catching his breath.

"I suppose I should tell you this before you actually see it for yourselves. But the reason you're at the hospital is because in the real world, this is where you are," he said, staring at them grievingly. "This is your limning point."

SACRIFICE

Damien hadn't wanted Lucy to go to school that day, but he was far too weak to call out for her. He'd heard his mother scolding her for not getting up on time. Damien had felt terrible that his sister got slapped and screamed at all because she was taking care of him last night, just like the night before.

———

He didn't remember when exactly he'd eaten the cupcakes, but he remembered what followed. He had puked and then fallen over unconscious. When he'd woken up, it was to find himself on the living room couch, covered in his own vomit, and something warm crawling down his legs. He could smell his own shit and piss, but that was the last thing on his mind.

In his body, it felt like hot, burning coils had constricted every muscle, every bone, and were squeezing him while also burning him. He convulsed, crying, unable to understand what was happening to him.

"He wasn't supposed to eat them," his father muttered, hand on his forehead, pacing the room.

"He *was* supposed to eat them before you..." his mother said. "Can't very well take him to the hospital, can we? They'll ask why he has slow-acting poison in his body."

Damien wailed, but not because of what his parents were saying. There was lava roiling through his stomach, traveling up his throat, and out it came. He vomited chunks of cupcakes on the sofa.

"Fucking hell!" his father yelled and kicked the sofa. "So...we do what?!"

"Go through with it!" his mother said, her eyes red, a deathly stench coming off of her. Like burning chemicals.

"She's not taken it!" Andrew Bessemer said, pointing up.

"Go through with what? Not taken what?" Lucy asked, coming down the stairs. When she saw Damien lying there on the sofa, she rushed to her brother's side. "Oh no. Oh no. What happened, Damien?"

"Stop being such a dramatic bitch. He's eaten some cupcakes that were made with expired cream. He's got food poisoning. We need to give him medicine," Valerie Bessemer said with the unaffected air of one who was watching a documentary on TV. She stood there with her arms crossed, her eyes red, biting her lips every ten seconds. She scratched her arms violently, then slapped

Lucy across the head, making her fall over on Damien's puke.

"Clean him up, you little brat! What the fuck are you waiting for?!"

"We have to take him to a hospital!" Lucy cried.

"It's just food poisoning. He'll be fine. Take him to his room and change his clothes. Then, when you're done, get some medicine from the cabinet," Valerie Bessemer said, turning her back to her children.

Andrew Bessemer stood watching the spectacle, his eyes wet. He ran his hands through his hair, then turned around to slam his fist against the wall. "Fuck!"

"It's okay, Dad. I'll look after him," Lucy said, trying to control the situation somehow.

"That's my good girl," Andrew Bessemer said, not turning to face her.

She took Damien to his room somehow, fighting the urge to puke herself. He smelled horrible, and it was her job to clean him.

He kept crying with his head against her. "It hurts, Luce. It hurts so bad. I feel like I'm dying."

"It's okay—" She didn't know what she was going to say. When she took off his pants, she saw blood streaks running down her brother's legs along with the rest of the mess. "You're going to be okay."

She cleaned him up with baby wipes, and put on new underwear and pajamas. Then she changed his shirt. He was rolling on the bed, clutching his stomach, tears running down his face.

She rushed downstairs. Her parents were standing there in the living room.

"Which medicine do I give him?!" Lucy cried.

Andrew Bessemer looked at his daughter, then nodded. He walked over to the cabinet. "Here. The pink syrup will stop him from vomiting. This one, a tablespoon, will give his stomach some rest. When you've given him these, mix this sachet in some water and give it to him. It's going to replenish his salts and fluids."

As she stood there holding the meds, she looked up at his father and almost said, *It's supposed to be you giving him these. You're his father.* But she knew that no sooner would those words be out of her mouth, her father would be triggered into giving her a rigorous beating, and then who would take care of Damien? She nodded briefly, and then raced upstairs.

Once she'd given him all the meds, she sat by his side, massaging Damien's head, running her hands through his hair.

"What happened? What happened exactly. Tell me everything," she said. She'd overheard the conversation between her parents, and her suspicion had turned into belief. Whatever she needed to do, she needed to do it secretly.

Damien told her about the guest. Though, what he said didn't make any sense to her. He told her about playing videogames with Dad. And then eating the cupcakes in the fridge.

"I...feel weak," Damien said once he'd stopped. "Will you sleep here?"

"I'll stay awake. I'll give you medicine through the night. Nothing's gonna happen to you, Damien. I'll take care of you."

"I love you, Lucy."

"I love you too, you little twerp."

———

Lucy had done that. She'd looked after him for two days, but Damien knew that he wasn't getting better. And now his sister had gone to school.

He lay there in his bed, crying, holding his stomach. He could hear them downstairs, his parents talking to each other. He'd noticed that they'd come to his room and watch from the doorway. He wished someone, anyone, would come to him and give him something for his pain. Why had he felt so hungry, and why had he eaten so foolishly? If only he'd controlled himself, he'd have been all right.

One needed energy to ruminate. Damien had run all out of his last reserves, and lay there pale, cold, and covered in sweat.

"Mom," he shouted. It came out as a whisper. Suddenly, he could feel all the atoms in the room enlarge to the size of footballs, filling up the entire house. They were invisible but suffocating, and they were making it impossible for his voice to reach his parents, who were downstairs. He could hear them.

Damien rolled over, collapsing on the floor, He crawled outside the ajar door and tried to prop himself up by holding the banister. He had to tell someone that he could not breathe, that there was fresh blood coming out of him. Lucy wasn't here. He had to tell Dad. Didn't Dad say that he loved him?

He could hear his father downstairs arguing vehemently with his mother. The house was rank with smoke rising. Damien coughed and lost his balance, falling down the stairs, bumping his head and his body on all the stairs.

"Mom! Dad!" he yelled out frantically. His vision had gone black, and now pain shot from a thousand places in his body. "Help me!"

Slow, dull, dark vision started coming back as he saw his parents walk up to him.

"Oh, Damien. Why'd you have to eat those cupcakes, bud?" his father said. "I'd almost changed my mind about what I was going to do, and then you go and eat those cupcakes. You're... Fuck. You're dying, bud."

"Dad. I'm sorry," Damien wept, reaching out for his father. To his shock, his father kicked Damien's hand away. Damien recoiled with pain, lying there on the floor.

"I guess now's the time to do it. Go fetch the book," his mother said, unable to look at Damien, who was crawling on his back, crying, whimpering, holding his hand where it felt like bones had broken.

"Why are you doing this!?" Damien cried out as his father raced up the stairs. His father's gait faltered. He nearly slipped, but he continued up the stairs. Meanwhile, his mother dragged him by his broken hand and threw him in the garage.

"Shut up! Shut up! Shut up! Just why don't you fucking shut the hell up?!" she yelled at him, rendered mad by methamphetamine and liquor. "Fucking shut up!" She punctuated her words with kicks to Damien's ribs.

His father came back, eyes blood-red, hands shaking, those shaking hands holding the very book that Damien had discovered in the attic.

"She's not here," Andrew Bessemer said.

"Her school lets out in ten. She'll be here by the time we're done with him," Valerie snapped at her husband. "No more thinking upon it, no more wasting time. I need my life to jumpstart now! Don't you?!"

"Fuck it," his father said. Only, this man and this woman were not his father and mother. Whomever they were, they meant him harm. They had poisoned the cupcakes. He could see it now, now that it was too late.

Andrew picked up the poker and handed it to his wife. He rifled through the pages and took out a note on a parchment. "Here goes. It doesn't say here we gotta do 'em both together. It's better that we kill him first, then her."

Valerie took another puff from her meth pipe and sneered hard, delivering one more kick for good measure to Damien's head. "Fucking piece of shit! Fucking get it!"

"All right, all right," Andrew said. "First, we gotta slit his skin open and make sure he bleeds. Then, I have to recite the words. We'll have to let him bleed to death. We can't fucking kill him. That's not how the ritual works. It's a blood offering."

"Get on with it!" she screamed at him.

"Please," Damien begged. He was bleeding from where Valerie had hit him, blood in his eyes, blood down his throat. He gurgled, choked, and tried to get up. There was a less than one percent chance that he could maybe outrun them if only he could get up.

It was as if Valerie was thinking the same thing, because the next moment she put her foot on his stomach and pressed. Damien yelled in pain, none of his voice going out thanks to the soundproofing.

"Okay then. Slice him. You do it. I'm not doing it," Andrew said, holding the paper up to the light.

She was waiting for the signal. She took the fire poker with the pointed end and ran it across his arm, splitting his skin open. Damien screamed and tried to hold his hand, but he was too frail and too pinned to move.

"Trickster God of Blood Jests. Here we are, jesting in blood, bloodletting, letting this blood beseech on our behalf. Beseech for wealth," Andrew Bessemer read out with a shaky voice, nodding to Valerie.

Valerie sliced open Damien's other arm. He lay there, both arms on the ground, both arms bleeding viciously, his cries deafening, his breath shallow. "Stop! Stop! Stop!" he yelled as Valerie took the poker and began digging it in his shoulder. Blood spouted from where she'd made the puncture.

"Easy. Don't have to kill him at once," Andrew said.

"Fucking do your job, don't tell me to do mine." Valerie slapped him across the shoulder.

Andrew went back to reading the words. "Beseech

for health. Beseech for glory. Beseech for fame. For influence, beseech. For long life and for good fortune. Humbly accept our offering, two souls placed on your altar, our own blood, our own flesh, now yours."

"Is that it?!" Valerie yelled, tears running down her haggard face, unkempt hair hiding her eyes. She gritted her yellowing teeth and then finally plunged the poker into Damien's stomach. "That did nothing!"

"We offered two. Let Lucy come. Then we do the rest. He can bleed out in the meantime," Andrew Bessemer said, finally looking at his son. He was unrecognizable, covered in blood, holding limply to the poker that had impaled him. "He'll take his time to die. He's a fighter."

Andrew Bessemer pulled the poker out of Damien's stomach and threw it on the ground.

Once the two adults had left the garage and gone to the living room to get even higher to wash away the weight of what they'd done, Damien turned over, his breath rattling, his body feeling light as a feather. He realized that it wasn't his body that was feeling light, but *himself*. He felt himself slipping away from his broken, bruised, bleeding body, but something was holding him back.

There, in the corner of the garage, someone had appeared.

A red-robed man with a hood over his head, holding a sword. He was exactly like the picture Damien had seen in the book.

"...blood...jests..." Damien whispered, then closed his eyes.

He heard the Trickster God walk up to him.

"Let me die," Damien begged, opening his eyes one last time.

The Trickster God put a hand on Damien's forehead, then looked at the door leading into the living room.

———

When Damien came to, it was to find himself in pain, but not as horrible as before. It was as if it was dulled on purpose, because the rest of the situation hadn't changed. He was still wheezing on the garage floor. His blood was everywhere, from his clothes to the floor, where it had started drying.

Yet he didn't die.

Not as fast as he wanted to.

His mind kept running through catalogs of memories, anything that might save him, but he could only see one thing.

That his parents had never loved him. That there had never been a point where they had treated him like a normal child. He could see who loved him, and she loved him more than all the parents in the world put together, the good ones and the bad.

She stood before him in the doorway, face aghast.

"Run," Damien said, flitting between consciousness and death frenzy. "Lucy...go..."

"What did you do to him?!" Lucy yelled as she ran up

to Damien and fell on her knees, not minding the blood. She put her hand on his neck, then on his forehead. "He's dying!"

"That's kind of the point," their father said, appearing in the doorway, bloodied fire poker in hand. Their mother stood there too, all the impatience in the world etched upon her face.

Damien wanted to morph into something—anything—to be able to stop them from hurting her. If he had the power, he'd shapeshift into a wolf or a huge knight and then slay his parents to save Lucy. He knew that Lucy could take care of him forever.

But Damien only lay there, no life in his limbs, his breath heavy and infrequent, his heart a squelching pump in his chest beating in confusion and terror.

Andrew swung the poker and hit Lucy, tearing her face open. Lucy fell down on the ground face-first with a scream. Valerie closed the door behind her and then came into the garage, stepping on her daughter's back.

"Do we gotta read that same shit again?" Valerie asked.

"No. Just split her open. Once was enough," Andrew said, handing the poker to his wife.

"But it wasn't even anything. Are you sure those are the words?!" she stammered, looking at her writhing daughter trying to break free, at her son, who lay pale and dying. It occurred to her for the briefest of moments that perhaps she had let her madness get the better of her, and that this was never supposed to happen. But in the next moment, all that regret froze in the face of her desires.

Mink. She'd wear mink and she'd wear it in circles where people wouldn't ostracize her for wearing animal fur. People who'd be rich and influential like her, far above the consequences of being canceled for their actions. She'd take private jets everywhere and eat caviar. All that rich shit that she'd never been able to do. No more economy-class flights, no more soggy-ass filet of fish sandwiches from Micky Ds.

"It's not the words that matter. It's the intent. It's the action," Andrew said. "Now hurry up!"

Valerie lifted the poker and plunged it into Lucy's back.

Lucy shrieked as the bloodied end went into her skin and ripped muscle and veins apart, spilling her blood on the floor.

"If words don't matter, let me say some shit!" Valerie snapped. "Lemme fucking..."

"Do it! Do it!" Andrew snapped back, stomping his feet on the ground in a rhythm. He had already lost it. The moment he'd seen his dying son, he'd lost it. He was operating strictly on the manic energy granted to him by the methamphetamine and a desire to see it through to the end.

"Trickster God, whoever you are. I need things, stat. Nothing fucking abstract, no 'you're as rich as you feel in your heart' bullshit loopholes. Come tomorrow, I need money. I need to be noticed. I want to move up in the world, and you're gonna make it happen. It may seem that we're fucked up people, but we don't do these blood jests lightly. We've argued with each other about it for four years! Four years, we didn't do jack shit. Now that we're doing it, you do your part, you cunt fuck!"

"Stop, please, Mom!" Lucy tried to kick her mother away. Her leg met her mother's knee. She buckled, but then quickly balanced herself. This only served to agitate her further.

She yelled, "You'll turn on me? Your own fucking mother?!"

She continued screaming in pain and frustration and anger and grief, grabbing the poker with both hands and plunging it into Lucy's body over and over and over, perforating her back. The intensity of her motion made her lose strength, but each strike reddened Lucy's torn clothes, therefore proving to be effective.

But there was a reason why Lucy wasn't moving or putting up a fight. She had her phone in her hands and had already dialed 9-1-1 while she was on her back. She'd meant to call CPS anyway. This expedited the process, even if it was too late. She hadn't said a word, but had let the violent noises in the room travel across the air and to the 9-1-1 phone operator.

At least this way, Lucy thought through the pain, at least if she and Damien were to die, they'd die after taking their parents down.

"Is she dead?" Andrew asked.

Valerie turned Lucy over and saw the phone clutched in her hands.

"Fucking whore called 9-1-1!" Valerie said, grabbing hold of the phone, letting go of the fire poker. It clattered to the ground right beside Lucy.

Lucy looked at her brother and mouthed, "I'm sorry."

Tears streaked down her temples, burning her flesh. She could feel each of the impalements her mother had made in her body, and breath was hard to draw.

"Fucking bitch!" Andrew Bessemer came forward, lifting his boot up. "You ruined everything!"

With her weak grip, she picked up the fire poker. Lucy sat up, holding one hand above her face to stop her father's kick, the other hand holding the poker up. She hadn't planned any of it. She was just trying to protect herself.

Her father slipped in the blood and lost his balance as he kicked her. He fell forward. Lucy didn't move the poker away. It went through her father's chest, clean. He fell upon her, blood spilling out of his mouth. He gasped as he realized what had happened, and then rolled over.

The poker had struck him through the heart.

"ANDREW!" Valerie yelled, throwing the phone away and falling by her husband's side.

Lucy knew that she had to finish it. She couldn't just let one parent live. She crouched on her knees and then pushed herself so that she was standing. What was something she could use? She looked around the workbench and saw, amongst several tools lying there, a hammer.

Valerie was still hunched over her husband.

Lucy grabbed the hammer, and only then saw that they were not the only ones in the garage. He stood there in the corner, witness to all this madness, a mad being in his own right, blood-garbed and red-hooded, holding a sword. He stood unmoving, his black eyes boring into Lucy.

Lucy brought the hammer up, and then with all the rage that she possessed, she brought it down screaming, hitting her mother in the back of her head.

Her mother screamed as her skull caved in, blood and brain oozing out of the hole the hammer had made in her head. She collapsed on top of her husband, lying there with the poker between them. Neither of them moved nor made a sound.

The room went silent. The red-robed man stood there like a stone statue. Lucy's strength gave out. She chose to fall beside her brother. If she were dying, this was where she wanted to die.

"Oh, Damien," she groaned, curling up beside him. Her back felt like it was on fire and yet cold and wet at the same time.

"You...saved me," Damien croaked, reaching out with his blood-soaked hand.

"I couldn't," Lucy wept, holding her brother's hand.

"They're not gonna hurt me no more," Damien said, closing his eyes.

Staying awake was a fight she didn't have in her anymore. Her eyelids were as heavy as ancient trapdoors. She coughed blood and closed her eyes, focusing on the only thing in these moments that did not give her pain: her brother's hand.

"Do you see him too?" Damien gasped. "In the corner of the room."

"Yes," Lucy wheezed. "I see him."

Sirens blared in the background. A bolt of relief shot up her body as her consciousness left her. She heard the front door being banged open. The last thing she remembered was seeing a lady cop standing there in the doorway, petrified, holding a gun in her hands.

That gun would've been real useful half an hour ago, thought Lucy, and then knew no more.

———

Pressure upon her chest. Someone pressing both hands on her.

"Pulse dropping! I need an epi stat!"

The world whirled. Lucy came to with a sharp gasp and a stern realization of pain all over her body. She stared around the strangers hunched over her in the confined space of the ambulance. On the stretcher across lay Damien, another EMT tending to him.

"They tried to kill me," Lucy said, holding the EMT's hand. "But I didn't let them."

———

She woke up again, this time to the sensation of being rushed along the corridor. She was strapped to a stretcher.

"Damien," she whispered, her throat on fire. "Damien."

"He's not far behind, sweetie," the nurse in purple

scrubs said, running a gloved hand across Lucy's shoulder. "You just hold on."

———

Another burst of consciousness, and she could feel the mask upon her face and the constant beeps and blips of machines all around. She couldn't move, but she wasn't in pain anymore, so that was good. Her mouth was swollen, a tube going in. Her eyes were bruised and puffed up. She turned her head around and saw Damien lying there on the bed beside her.

And there he stood in the corner, invisible to the doctors and the nurses in the ICU, the blood-red man.

Metanoia

"You were there," Lucy said, looking at Tom. She could remember it all now, as could Damien.

"I saw him first," Damien said, grinning in spite of himself.

"I didn't invent the whole thing, just so you know," Tom said, looking guilty. "I had nothing to do with the ritual. People have been doing it for hundreds of years. I was just the guy who was put in this place to ensure that someone was on the receiving end. You know what I mean? I was made for this purpose. If there's a life I lived before being the Trickster God, I do not know of it. All I have known is that I have this power to change things in the other world. It's not even that difficult. I touch the fabric of fate and I twist some knots and untie others. It's unnatural; even I know it. No one's really supposed to mess with fate like that, but then again, the whole ritual is unnatural. No one's supposed to kill children like that. This business kills you from the inside."

Doors slammed open and shut in the distance. Howls and the fast beats of feet on the hospital floor.

"They're here," Tom said. He promptly turned to the emergency fire axe in the wall. He broke the glass with his elbow and plucked the axe. He had a look of deep satisfaction on his face. "I've always wanted to use one of these. Well, looks like at least I get my wish."

"Tom," Lucy said, feeling afraid once more. "What's on the other side of those doors?"

They sat at the end of the hallway, in a waiting area that was no more than a wide alcove. In front of them were the ICU doors.

"Are our parents there?" Damien asked fearfully.

"They're in the hospital," Tom said, wielding the axe with both hands. "But not in the ICU. They lie in body trays in the hospital mortuary." He turned to look at Lucy with a bit of pride in his eyes. "You ought to know. You killed them."

"I...did," Lucy said, staring at the floor.

The footsteps came from the floor above.

"Blood was let. Two people died. And before anything else happens..." Tom said, staring at the windows, anticipating the Reapers. But there was commotion coming from above, as if the hospital staff were putting up a fight. "I should let you know that I consumed their dark souls. They were right there for the taking. I can mend the fabric of fate, but I cannot bring back two people from the land of the dead. By the time the ambulances had arrived, your parents had died. You killed them. And I'll say it again, their blood was let. A request stands to be made. Wish for it while I still draw breath, and I shall give you the world."

"No," Lucy said. "I don't want things that cost killing people."

"Funny," Tom said, lowering his axe as the Reapers' howls diminished. "In all my life as the broker of blood contracts, I've never heard anyone say that. So here's what I'll do for you, my child. As long as you live—and I promise that you'll live long—no one shall think of harming you. Should someone intend to do so, they shall burn until the thought is driven out of them. You will not know any more pain beyond what you've already experienced. I offer you wealth, abundance, and joy. Offspring that you will love. And the last thing that I give freely, as part of no contract but as a parting gift, you shall forget the horrors. All of them. This place. Your parents. Everything."

"I don't want to forget you!" Damien said, wrapping his arms around Tom's legs.

"You have to," Tom said, patting Damien's head. "I am part of all that is wrong with the world. I don't know what I'll do after tonight, or if I'll even survive another day in this place. There are far more Reapers out there in my world than the ones we killed. But should I live, I shall strive for something different."

"Come with us," Lucy said, tugging at Tom's hand.

At that moment, two Reapers shot through the

window by the waiting area and screeched at the kids. They had blades for hands, same as the first one.

"Go!" Tom pushed both kids through the doors. "And remember, even demons can be swayed by a little bit of light."

The doors swung shut, splashes of dark blood splattering on the windows. Tom screamed outside, his voice louder than the hisses and shrieks of the Reapers.

"Tom!" Damien yelled.

Lucy knew they were all out of time, and that Tom might not be able to buy them any more than the few seconds they had.

She grabbed Damien and ran into the room, to the two beds placed side by side with machinery on either side blinking and beeping.

She saw herself lying there, unrecognizable. She had IVs going in her body, things taped to her forehead, bandages on her bruises, and a mask on her face. Damien lay on the bed beside hers, cleaned of blood but no better than her, his skin swelling purple, his face covered in bandages, and a similar mask on his face.

A Reaper burst through the ICU door, screaming, unleashing his arms and reaching for the kids. An axe shot out of the hallway, dug into his back, and pulled him out of the ICU.

"Hurry!" Lucy gasped, seeing the shimmer of the limning point. She could see beyond this world. It was a brighter world, despite being an ICU. Warmer. The lights were on and there were doctors and nurses moving through the room, checking on the patients, consulting their charts.

"I think...Lucy..." Damien said. "I have to tell you something."

"There's no time!" she squealed as another roar came from the other side of the door.

"I remember dying," Damien said. "I don't think I can go back."

She didn't want to hear this. After everything, if her brother wasn't there with her, then there was no point going back. She grabbed his hand and stepped through the Limn.

She moved through it fine, but Damien couldn't travel through it.

He stood on the other side, in that dark world, tears running down his face.

"You have to let me go," Damien wept. "I was there, bleeding for too long. I remember dying. I'm sorry I didn't tell you sooner."

"No!" Lucy cried, and tugged Damien. "I do not believe it. You're coming with me." She pulled harder, but Damien didn't budge.

Another Reaper tore through the doors, ripping them off their hinges.

"I can't leave you behind!" Lucy screamed. "You're coming with me!"

Tom burst into the ICU and grabbed the Reaper by the head. The Reaper thrashed around, digging his claws in Tom, but Tom held on, crushing the Reaper's skull, caving it in with his fingers. He threw the lifeless corpse into the hallway.

"Help," Lucy wept, looking at Tom, who looked like he needed help as well. "He's not coming through."

Tom stood there, mouth open, no words coming. He hadn't taken another step before a Reaper showed up behind him and struck his claws into Tom's body.

Tom spat drool and phlegm and blood. The Reaper pulled his claws out and then brought them down again, plunging through Tom's heart. Tom fell to his knees, unmoving, soaked in his own blood and the blood of the Reapers he'd killed. All but one.

With Tom no longer a hurdle, the Reaper turned his attention to the two children standing on the brink of the Limn. He leaped into the air with his claws out and his mouth snarling open in a many-toothed sneer.

Lucy closed her eyes and pulled as hard as she could one last time. The Limn resisted with all its might. Damien screamed as she dug her nails into his skin. Unable to pull him any longer, she also didn't let go.

Something collided against the wall next to her, and yet Lucy, who was no stranger to pain, felt none. She opened her eyes to a strange sight. The Reaper was impaled into the wall, the fire axe going through him and wedging into the bricks. He hung there twitching, far enough that he could not reach her.

She turned to see Tom with his hand still stretched out from the axe throw. He had a grin on his face. "Told you I've always wanted to use a fire axe. These things are underrated."

"Tom!" Damien squealed. "I can't go through!"

Tom turned around and fell on his back, panting, looking at the ceiling. "I see a tunnel of light. It's strange. I spent all this time dealing long life and immortality, I never thought to grant that wish for myself."

"Help us," Lucy cried. "Or we're stuck here forever."

"Not that bad of a barter, if you think about it," Tom wheezed. "Stay here long enough, survive as you did, and you might become one of the many demons that call this place home."

"I don't want to call this place home," Damien said. "Please."

"I think I'm done for, kid," Tom said. "I see the light growing bright. I think I'm done. So this is what death feels like. Heartburn and a hangover."

Lucy grabbed hold of Damien's shoulders and made him look at her.

"What do you remember?!" she snapped.

"I remember dying," Damien said.

"No, you don't!" she said.

"But I do."

"No, you don't."

"No, I don't."

"Good."

She pulled him by the shoulders through the Limn once more.

Two more Reapers came into the ICU, stepping over Tom, approaching the kids. They wielded fire in their hands. One of them looked at Tom, licking the Trickster God's dead face.

"You didn't die," Lucy said.

"I didn't die," Damien said, reaching forward and hugging his sister.

The Reapers hurled their fire at the children, at the beds, at the curtains, setting fire to the room. For good measure, one of the Reapers sent a flaming ball hurtling at Tom's body.

Fire took hold of Tom's body, catching on his blood-soaked clothes, burning away his beard, rending his flesh red. Sparks rose into the air. Fire took the ICU ward by storm. Flames from one wall to the other.

And in the middle of the flames stood the Reapers, looking at the Limn, craning their necks around to see where the kids had gone.

The fire spread from the ICU to the hallway, using all the furniture and the oxygen cylinders as fuel. Explosions shot out of each of the windows as the fire consumed the first floor and then traveled upward.

The ghosts stood there like grim shadows against the violent light, watching the place they called home go up in flames.

As if to remedy this catastrophe, it began raining in Pinebrook once more. The rain drove the mist away, and tended to the gas station fire on Neibolt and the hospital fire downtown.

When all was quiet once more, the last of the rebellious flames doused by the downpour, Pinebrook became still. Moonlight beamed through the night sky, stars shining into the black canopy above, a solemn reminder to those who lived here that there was a world out there beyond the curtains of fog.

Epilogue

Nurses Patricia and Tracy were not supposed to sit on the chairs meant for visitors, but it was the graveyard shift, and visitor hours were over some six hours ago. Besides, no one ever visited the kids lying comatose in the ICU.

The only flowers and cards that were there were customary ones sent by the state government, Child Protective Services, and Pinebrook people who had heard everything about the atrocity and had sent their love and wishes.

The ICU was no place for such things, but the nurses took their time removing them every day in the hopes that should either child wake up, it'd be to the display of warmth and affection, and not the grim, clinical reality of the ICU. When the cards had stopped coming after a week had passed, the two nurses recycled them, pretending to throw them away every night, and then putting them back up.

Today, Tracy had brought the flowers. Tomorrow, it'd be Patricia's job.

They wore purple scrubs and Nike shoes with fortified soles. You did not want a needle accidentally falling on your foot and giving you a dose of epinephrine when you didn't need it. Nothing better than hardened jogging shoes to give you that protection. Also, it was easy on the heels.

Both of them were at the end of a double shift, running strictly on coffee and nicotine tablets, a habit an older nurse by the name of Meg had put them on, insisting upon the nicotine even if they didn't smoke.

"Who messed with the thermostat?" Patricia asked, looking around, tugging at her neckline. The room felt abundantly hot and humid.

"Dunno," Tracy, the younger of the two, said as she walked up to the thermostat control and looked at it. "No one changed it. It's the same. Who do you think would be stupid enough to get sued to oblivion changing the ICU's temperature?"

"Meg. Meg don't care," Patricia said. "If her psoriasis acts up, she's sure to turn any room's temperature up. I swear, it's like she's got some kind of guardian demon who protects her from lawsuits. She's practically Neo dodging them all."

"Too soon," Tracy said, shaking her head.

"The demon thing? You really think that's real? I think their parents were messed up people who'd watched one too many horror movies and thought 'em real," Patricia said, swiping on her phone casually.

"Doesn't matter if they're real or not. If people believe in them, people do fucked up shit. That makes God real in my eyes. As does it, Satan, demon, hell. A thing doesn't have to exist in order to be real," Tracy said, coming back to the chair.

"There's that philosophy minor speaking," Patricia chuckled. "I mean, who the fuck does that? You think Socrates had scrubs on at night, administering injections to Greek patients?"

"It's more embarrassing than that," Tracy said, turning red.

But she forgot what she was saying. She was sure she'd seen the girl's hand twitch. But that could be just one of the many things comatose patients did.

"Spill. We're not going anywhere," Patricia said, putting her phone down. She looked at the boy, whose bandages she'd changed just an hour ago. There weren't other patients in the ICU. Most people went to Urbana-Champaign. The hospitals there were better, and it was just forty minutes away. Then she looked at the girl. Both their cardiac monitors showed the same thing they'd been showing for the past few days. Steady heartbeats sometimes faltering into arrythmia.

"I was dumb. I thought psychology and philosophy were the same thing," Tracy said.

"Who let you become a nurse?" Patricia chuckled, slapping Tracy's shoulder playfully.

"Same dumbasses that let you become one," Tracy laughed.

Patricia opened her mouth, thinking up of a good retort.

But then the monitor chirped. A staccato flutter unlike the rhythm that they'd memorized over the course of the last week. Then a long, warning tone.

Both women froze, staring first at each other incredulously, then at the children.

"Did you—"

The girl's fingers moved again. Not a reflex this time. A slow, deliberate curl. Her pulse spiked on the screen, climbing in jagged green peaks.

Tracy was on her feet first. "Lucy?" she said, voice tightening. "Lucy, can you hear me?"

The girl's eyelids trembled. It was subtle. A quiver under bruised skin. Then a faint crease between her brows, as if she were irritated by the light.

"Oh my God," Patricia gasped.

The boy's monitor followed, a sudden acceleration that set off a soft alarm. Damien's chest rose deeper than it had in days. His throat worked around the tube. A low, raw sound escaped him.

"Okay. Okay," Patricia snapped into motion. Her training replaced the shock she was experiencing. "I'm paging Dr. Keller."

She hit the call button on the wall and spoke into it, voice steady but pitched higher than usual. "ICU. Possible return of consciousness in both pediatric patients. We need attending, respiratory, now."

Tracy was already at Lucy's side, checking pupil

response with a penlight. "Lucy, stay with me. You're in Pinebrook General. You're safe. You're going to be okay."

Lucy's eyes opened just enough for the whites to show. They darted, unfocused, panicked. The heart monitor screamed higher.

"It's okay," Tracy said quickly, adjusting the oxygen flow. "You're okay. Don't try to move."

Damien gagged against the tube. Patricia was there instantly. "Easy, easy," she murmured, assessing. "We may need to extubate. He's initiating breaths on his own."

Footsteps pounded down the hall. The doors burst open. Dr. Keller, a balding man with deeply tanned skin, came in the room, surprise dawning upon his face, pulling on gloves, respiratory therapy behind him with a cart.

"What've we got?"

"Spontaneous eye opening. Purposeful movement. Tachycardia," Patricia reported. "They're waking up."

Dr. Keller stared at the monitors, then at the children, as if recalibrating reality.

"I'll be damned," he muttered. "All right. Let's get to work."

Their hands moved with efficiency, checking tubes, adjusting the settings. Dr. Keller gave the orders that the nurses followed immediately.

In the chaos, Lucy's gaze found Damien across the narrow space between their beds.

For a second, everything in the room seemed to dim. Her fingers twitched toward him. Damien's eyes, bloodshot and dazed, shifted sideways.

He saw her.

And through cracked lips, around plastic and tape and the sterile brightness of the ICU, he tried to speak.

"Lucy."